"Raw, honest, and original. Nussbaum does an excellent job describing and developing the characters in her fictional story . . . It's impossible not to connect to each and every one of them . . . Her multi-faceted, detailed description of a life unknown to most of us is riveting and keeps you turning the pages in anticipation of what will happen next . . . I would definitely recommend this novel as a fascinating read and a work of art."
—*Now You Know*

"A heartbreaking story of cruelty and hardship, but also a hopeful tale of resilience, love and friendship. *Good Kings Bad Kings* will make readers stop and reconsider—or perhaps consider for the first time—what it means to be disabled and why we fear those who are different from us."
—*Shelf Awareness*
(Kerry McHugh, blogger at *Entomology of a Bookworm*)

"Remarkably funny—a humanist feat. The characters are lively, ingenious, and, importantly, interesting—spiritually intact as people, not just sketches of this or that disability."
—*Chicago Reader*

"Not only shines a light on a segment of society often ignored, in art as well as life, but also is a really great read."
—*The Washington Post*

"Filled with hope and humor rather than gloom and doom . . . The author's skill and insight make each of these people real and understandable . . . A much needed look into the often neglected area of caregiving for disabled adolescents."

—BookReporter.com

"Well-meaning, well-written and well-plotted, with qualified justice for some of the bad guys and hope for a few of the oppressed: A most appropriate winner of the 2012 PEN/Bellwether Prize for Socially Engaged Fiction."

—*Kirkus Reviews*

"A stirring debut from a determined writer and activist."

—*Publishers Weekly*

"Susan Nussbaum's debut novel is eye-opening, devastating and laugh-out-loud funny." —*Newcity Lit*

Good Kings Bad Kings

Good Kings
Bad Kings

a novel by

SUSAN NUSSBAUM

ALGONQUIN BOOKS OF CHAPEL HILL   2013

Published by
Algonquin Books of Chapel Hill
Post Office Box 2225
Chapel Hill, North Carolina 27515-2225

a division of
Workman Publishing
225 Varick Street
New York, New York 10014

First paperback edition, Algonquin Books of Chapel Hill, November 2013.
Originally published by Algonquin Books of Chapel Hill in 2013.
Printed in the United States of America.
Published simultaneously in Canada by Thomas Allen & Son Limited.
Design by Anne Winslow.

This is a work of fiction. While, as in all fiction, the literary perceptions and insights are based on experience, all names, characters, places, and incidents either are products of the author's imagination or are used fictitiously.

LIBRARY OF CONGRESS CATALOGING-IN-PUBLICATION DATA
Nussbaum, Susan.
  Good kings bad kings : a novel / by Susan Nussbaum.
    pages cm
  ISBN 978-1-61620-263-7 (HC)
  1. Children with disabilities—Institutional care—Fiction.
  2. Institutional care—Employees—Fiction.   I. Title.
  PS3614.U874G66 2013
  813'.6—dc23   2013001350

  ISBN 978-1-61620-325-2 (PB)

10 9 8 7 6 5 4 3 2 1
First Paperback Edition

For Taina

Yessenia Lopez

My *tía* Nene said three is the magic number and when three things happen to you that are so, so bad and you feel like the whole wide world is just throwing up on your new shoes, don't worry. Your bad luck is about to change.

And I am sitting inside a room that smells like a urinal toilet at a place called the Illinois Learning something something. It's only my second day here and would you believe these people already got me in the punishing room? So this is three.

My name is Yessenia Lopez, and before they stuck my butt in this place I went to Herbert Hoover High School in Chicago, Illinois. I went there on account of I am physically challenged, and they send the people which have challenges to Hoover. They send people with physical challenges, but also retarded challenges, people been in accidents like brain accidents, or they're blind or what have you. I do not know why they send us all to the same place but that's the way it's always been and that's the way it looks like it will always be because I am in tenth grade and I been in cripple this or cripple that my whole sweet, succulent Puerto Rican life.

My last day at Hoover was the beginning of all hell breaking loose. I was going down the hallway like usual minding my own sweet business when Mary Molina comes straight up at me and real, real close she says—

No. I cannot even say the words to tell this story. That's how bad those words was that that bitch said to me. But I looked in that horsey-looking face and said, "You trifling *desgraciada sinvergüenza*. You want to confront with me? You gonna pay the consequences."

That wasn't the first bad name she called me but it was gonna be the last.

Tía Nene told me if anybody talk down on me or talk down on the people of Puerto Rico or get up in my face like they think they better than me, I need to kick that two-faceded person's ass. I told Tía Nene before she died—okay, not really before she died, it could have been I told her after she died when she was already up in heaven with the Lord Jesus—that I would always remember her and always remember everything she taught me. I told her in my mind before I left for school on that very day that I hope she knows I always want to make her proud. Then I imagined Tía Nene kissed me on the top of my head and said, "You do what you gots to do and have a good day, *chica.*"

My mother gave me to my *tía* Nene on the day I was born into the world. My *tía* was more my mother than my real mother ever was. I even look like my *tía* because I gots big eyes and long, wavy hair and my real mother gots tight, curly hair and little, beady eyes. And my skin is more darker like my *tía*'s—not dark dark but just dark—and I am more curvaceous even at my young age, just like Tía Nene. I called my *tía* my mother and she called me her daughter and that's that.

After school was over I went outside to where all the buses was at, waiting to load us up and drive us home. The fumes coming out the buses looked like big white clouds because it was cold. You could see the breaths coming out the mouth of all those pupils just like Indians sending smoke signals. Everybody was all bundled up in coats and hoods and it was hard to see who was who but I knew to look in the little yard next to where the buses line up. That's where she always goes. That's where I saw her.

First thing I did was wheel right up on her, pull my footrest up offa my chair, and grab onto that hair to hold her steady and whack her acrost the head, and then I pushed her right offa her chair. But I'm still holding her mop in my fist, so when she went down I had a big clump of that ugly-ass hair in my hand and she was screaming her Mexican butt off. Then I hop down offa *my* chair and sit right on top of her and pin her down to the ground. By now I can feel a bunch of pupils around me, everybody shouting, trying to get close, trying to see what's happening, and all of them yelling, "Fight! Fight!" and she's trying to push me off and hit back but she couldn't land more than a scratch on my face. But that was all I needed 'cause when I wiped blood offa my cheek I felt everything rise up in me and I lifted my footrest high up in the air and I gave her a *thwack*! Then blood starts trickling down from her mouth and the cheering goes higher and I raise up the footrest again *thwack* and again *thwack*! Then Veronique, my best friend from fourth-period hygiene, busts through the crowd and starts yelling, "Yes-sie! Yes-sie!" till it sounded like every challenged person in all of Hoover was shouting my name and I gripped my footrest real tight and felt my arm raising up high in the air—and then a security guard grabbed my wrist hard and yanked the footrest out my hand and drug me up on my chair and pushed me inside to Mrs. Maloney's office.

I looked down at myself and I had blood all on my pink overalls which I was wearing that day and under my nails. I felt my cheek 'cause it stang from her putting her claws on me.

Mrs. Maloney kep' asking me why did I do it, why did I do it, you know? And I told her the truth. I got no need to lie. I said, "Because she called me a Puerto Rican bitch."

I'm not sure if getting three months at Juvie for aggravating assault counts as the number two bad thing that happened or the number three bad thing. I'm pretty sure Juvie was number two.

The number one bad thing was when my *tía* passed into the next life. So it could be the number two bad thing was going to live at St. Francis Home for Young Women where they sent me after my *tía* died. St. Francis was a pain but it was okay. It was a whole lot better than living in a foster family with a bunch of people who could be freaks and rapers. So I'm gonna have to say, Juvie was *def*initely the number two bad thing. And this place, the one I'm in at this very moment? This Illinois Center for Cripple whatever, is three. This is where I got put after I got out of Juvie.

And I'm sitting here in this urine punishment room because that pimple-headed heifer Benedicta, my quote roommate, stole one of my teddy bears out my collection I won playing body-parts bingo, so I chopped up her blanket. Or I started to until some bald dude interrupted. It's not like she was in the bed at the time.

I only been here two days but I already hate it. Even worse than Juvie. But I can't talk no more now 'cause I see cigarette smoke all outside the window of this punishing room, so it must be that bat Candy come to get me. Candy's a houseparent. That's what they call them here. After she sucks that thing to the nub she'll open the door. That's what the boy from on my floor said when they was pushing my chair to the elevator. I guess he's been in this room hisself a time or two.

Okay, I got a question. If three is the magic number, then do you get three *good* things after you finish with the three bad? Or just one good thing and then three bad things again? 'Cause if that's how they work it, then it is not fair. Or what if another thing happen that's bad? That's four bad things in a row, so that can't happen, right? I wish I knew to ask Tía Nene for more details at the time.

I wish I knew to ask Tía Nene a whole lot of things.

Joanne Madsen

The ad was posted by the Illinois Learning and Life Skills Center, or ILLC. I was immediately captured by the awkward acronym. ILLC is a state-run nursing facility for adolescent youth through age twenty-one. It's just like a regular nursing home, but instead of locking up old people they lock up young people. They were looking for a data-entry clerk. Not really my thing, but then again I don't really have a thing. Data entry sounded like the kind of job that would satisfy my lack of ambition. No one really thinks about the data-entry clerk. Do they? Data entry allows one to soar beneath the radar and avoid the usual workplace Sturm und Drang. Not that I wouldn't work hard. I always work hard. When I'm working.

Of course the longer you are unemployed, the more they want to know at job interviews why you were unemployed for so long. And though my family has never seemed to progress beyond the denial stage as regards my quadriplegia, there is such a thing as job discrimination. People will see me coming through the door, wheelchair awhir, and momentarily freeze. Then they will marshal their resources and nervously reach out to shake my gimpy hand and smile enthusiastically while they mentally feed my résumé to the shredder. My family said I am my own worst enemy and I have to be more assertive and perhaps I should go back to school for something I can do. They also said I blamed others for my disability. What does that even mean? Do they think we're living in a made-for-TV movie?

I'm rich. Not mad rich but I am a multi-thousandaire. I'm like Rockefeller compared to 99 percent of the rest of the disabled people on earth. There are poor people and then there are poor disabled people. One of those things sucks, but both together suck stratospherically.

I was hit by a bus a long time ago. The No. 8 Halsted. But the CTA paid me generously to apologize for hitting me, which is why I enjoy my lavish lifestyle of jetting off to exotic locales whenever I feel like it. And I do feel like it from time to time, but frankly, what with the inspections of one's privates for explosive devices, the prospect of a broken power wheelchair in areas where local crips travel by wheelbarrow, and the ever-present dread of traveler's diarrhea with no wheelchair-accessible bathroom for miles, traveling is no vacation. Let me say only that the world, Earth, is not a hospitable place for crips.

My job is way far away. South by southwest. Back of the Yards neighborhood, so called because it's next to the old Chicago stockyards. Hog butcher of the world. I'm a North Sider, so I could take the bus to the Red Line but I'd have to take two more buses after that. The No. 8 Halsted Street is a straight shot. So here I am. The air is humid with irony.

My duties are mostly typing. There must have been dozens of far more appropriate applicants. People who type with all ten fingers, for example. But for the first—and I feel certain only—time I think I got a job be*cause* of my disability. It's well known in crip circles that the best place for a crip to get a job is a place that's swarming with other crips. So I applied, emphasizing my computer skills, which are pretty good, and how important it is for disabled youth to see disabled adults in the workplace. Places like this love the idea of role models. There was no haggling over the miserable pay either, as money is no object for me. No salary could possibly be too low. They could pay me in rat turds and I'd happily put them in my wallet. What I needed more than money was human interaction.

Recently, over the past five years or so, my world had been shrinking, slowly but quite surely. At first I'd take little "breaks"—just not leave my apartment for a day. But my breaks started creeping up to, say, five or six days in my apartment with no outside contact. Not including my personal assistants and the Thai Palace delivery guy. I didn't have cabin fever. I certainly was not agoraphobic. I just behaved as if I was.

Sometimes I imagine there is an entire subpopulation of people who live out their lives in nine hundred square feet of space. The TV plays, the *pad woon sen* is delivered and consumed, the sun comes up and goes down. One day our subculture will be discovered by Ryan Seacrest and one by one we'll be sniffed out by German shepherds and burst in upon by lights and cameras and forced to attend a mixer. With each other.

Then one night I caught a glimpse of myself in the bathroom mirror and stopped. I realized that I'd been in self-imposed solitary at that point for nine days or possibly ten or eleven. I asked myself if I was prepared to look back at my life when I was old and know I had wasted it. I determined at that moment to rouse myself out of my complacency. And here I am on the Halsted, on my way to work. And that's the inspirational true story of how I overcame my disability and became a contributing member of society.

My first week I learned that people refer to ILLC as "ill-see." Emphasis on "ill." The Illinois Learning and Life Skills Center may not sound like the name of a nursing home, but that's how they work it. Naming these places is all about misdirection. ILLC might sound like a fun after-school program with arts and crafts and barbecues but it's just a place they put disabled kids that struggling parents and the state don't know what to do with. Inside, it smells, sounds, and looks like your standard-issue nursing home. Same old wolf but in a lamb outfit.

I've worked there only a week. Taken on the whole—eighty young institutionalized crips—the situation is pretty depressing. But somebody's got to do data entry for almost no money, so why not me? The kids here are called patients. The woman who runs the place goes by the supersquishy name Mrs. Phoebe. She calls the kids her children or her angels. Ick.

I'm about as messed up physically as any of the kids, but I don't have any mental disabilities. Most of them here have both. For instance, in addition to spina bifida or cerebral palsy, they have some kind of intellectual disability or maybe a few learning disabilities. A few have psychiatric disabilities. Some of the kids were taken out of abusive homes and they're traumatized by that. The biggest difference between the kids and me is that I'm a whole lot luckier. I mean, I just work here.

Most of the kids are chair users, but they have manual chairs. Quite a few are too gimpy for manual chairs and should have power chairs so they could get around on their own, but it's against the rules. That's unofficial. The official practice is that everyone who needs a power chair gets one. But just the other day I asked why this one girl, Mia, didn't have a power chair, and Mrs. Phoebe said Mia wasn't ready for a power chair. But I'm looking at her, she's planted in this one spot all by herself, can't move an inch on her own, can't talk to the other kids, has to wait for a staff person or one of the kids who can walk to notice her so she can get a push. Mia looks about as ready for a power chair as anyone I've ever seen.

After I got hit by the No. 8, I went through a rehab process and they finally gave me my first wheelchair. It was manual. No matter how hard I tried I couldn't do more than push myself a few feet on a smooth surface. Carpet was like quicksand. People had to push me everywhere. I'd end up staring at a fern or getting my feet smashed into a wall or being held hostage in the middle of someone else's conversation. I could see where I wanted to go but was powerless to make it happen.

Maybe because no one is paying attention to Mia, she's captured mine. She seems a bit tired and a little wary. She's a pretty girl, Mexican, with a thick black mane tied into a high, messy ponytail.

The good news about Mia is she has a boyfriend named Teddy. He's this skinny, pale blond kid who wears a suit—I mean a real suit with a jacket and everything—every day. And a tie. The suit is always wrinkly and food-stained and one pant leg is usually scrunched up higher than the other, but he is dead serious about wearing this suit every single day. Sometimes he'll take his jacket off and then you can see his little plastic fireman's badge on his shirt. I love this kid. He wears glasses with lenses so thick they make his eyes look like planets. Teddy is a nonstop questioner—he talks a lot and he's really outgoing and friendly and totally unruly, so he annoys the adults but makes the other kids want to be his friend.

Unlike Mia he has a power chair, so he's constantly moving. Sometimes he attaches Mia's chair to his with a piece of bungee cord and they roll around together.

I have my own little office with a desk and a too-tall file cabinet. There's a window but I think it actually sucks light out. It's an unwindow. It's placed at the very top of the room, right next to the ceiling, and the glass is opaque. I have a computer and plastic trays filled with handwritten files that I'm supposed to enter into the computer. I can only type with two of my fingers, one on each hand, but I'm used to it and I'm pretty speedy. I have some other duties too, all tasks I have no interest in doing, but I don't mind. Dissatisfaction with my work makes me feel more employed.

After I enter the files in the database, I'm supposed to keep them updated, so I'm beginning to know a little about the kids I see in the halls. I know Teddy has an intellectual disability as well as a physical disability. His IQ is 74 but that's hard to believe. He's so smart. Mia is a ward of the state and has lived here since she was eleven years old. She was sexually abused by her father and has cigarette burns on her arms and back. All this I type into the computer.

Some of the things people write in the files are subjective nonsense. A certain kid "acts like a baby" or "is evil." I do not type it in. Poetic license. I have to put in IQ scores because the first page of every kid's database info includes a place for IQ, right up there with name and age. I hate doing it. It's just that I've been here only a week.

I never get home before 7:00 p.m. First thing I do is wash up really thoroughly and then sit in front of the fridge eating whatever I see. If I have wine I'll pour myself a glass, but I don't have wine because I haven't had time to pick any up. I've forgotten how much energy it takes to actually do something all day without liberal napping throughout. So I drink a lot of water, tilt back, and look around me and think how much I love my apartment and my CD collection and the trees just outside the window and my wok and my futon couch, even though I can't sit in it because I can't transfer by myself. When you spend your day in a noisy, stinky nursing home filled with people who have no choice but to be there, you become more appreciative of your eclectic dish and coffee-mug collection and your wall of oak bookshelves including two entire rows of classic science fiction and a whole shelf that slides out just for your *Oxford English Dictionary*. It's all in the luck of the toss between living in a cozy apartment with a view and living in an institution where someone's asking you about your bowel movements and you have to go to bed at seven o'clock every night no matter what.

No one works at nursing homes unless they're scraping the underneath of the bottom of the barrel. The kid thing makes it easier though. People think there's nothing more horrifying and depressing than a disabled child, but even when kids are all messed up and spazzed out and needy as hell there's still a ton of good energy coming off them. They're so funny and surprising and they are who they are.

It may not be everyone's idea of a dream job. To severely understate. But when I wake up in the morning I have a destination. If someone should happen to ask what I do, which of course no one ever does, but my point is, I have an answer. I work in a nursing home.

Ricky Hernandez

When I get to Mrs. Schmidt's classroom, I see right away it's Pierre again. He's up outta his chair and he's waving his arms and doing his little jumpy thing. He's screaming, "Gimme my Baby Ruth! Gimme my Baby Ruth!" The other kids are just sitting there and Mrs. Schmidt looks at me real exasperated, like will I help her, so I say, "I have to wait for Louie," because you're supposed to have two people if you're going to grab a kid up, but Mrs. Schmidt is freaking and she says, "I don't care! He's out of control!" so I go over to Pierre to see can I get close enough to grab him. It ain't a problem though. He knows me from the two other times I had to tackle him. Soon as he sees me walking over it's like the air goes out of him and he quiets down. He practically offers me his arm. I say, "Come on with me, Pierre. Let's go."

First time this happened I had to put him into a basket hold. Imagine I'm behind you holding your arms like you're hugging yourself—that's a basket hold. It's the position your arms would be in if you were in a straitjacket, but you're being hugged, so it's more calming. I like the hold because sometimes a kid will relax into it. Not all the time though. Some of them just get madder when you put the basket hold on them. But with the arms like that they can't hurt themself.

Next thing is I have to take him to the time-out room. As we're leaving, Mrs. Schmidt calls to me, "He was eating his crayons! Don't feed him!" Real nice. Calling the kid out in front of the world.

On the way to the time-out room I try talking to him, but he's not going for it. I say, "So how you doing today?" and he says, "Fuck you." This kind of thing is not unusual. I just think of it like, you know, that's the disability talking. Pierre has the ADHD. He's real hyper and he just can't settle in, he can't concentrate. I know he's got some other stuff too. He's got that thing that the veterans get. Post-dramatic stress. Believe it or not with a young kid, but some of these kids been through some hairy shit already. It'll make you sick to hear it. I don't know what happened to Pierre but I remember the day he came here he looked pretty beat up and he must have had thirty, forty stitches in a bald patch on his head. Sometimes if you look at him from a certain angle, his face looks like he's got the weight of the world on him. Kid is fourteen. I look over at him now and he says, "What you staring at?" I caught a glimpse of that blue crayon caught in his teeth. His teeth are real white. White like how kids' teeth are because they haven't turned all yellow from all the coffee and what have you.

"I ain't staring. Just looking," I say.

My *tía* Briselda lived with us growing up. My mom's sister. She was retarded which now they're supposed to say "intellectually disabled" but nobody here uses it much. We got a lot of kids here who are intellectually, you know, retarded. Man, she was stubborn. My uncle had this whole song about her, about a bullfrog because a bullfrog is stubborn or has a reputation for that. She was a hard case, Tía B., but we had a lot of fun with her. You know, we didn't know any better. She died way back.

By now, we should know better how to treat them. Here they use the time-out room as a punishment. They have some other ways to punish the kids, but judging from the times they call me to come and hijack one of them from a class or whatever, the time-out room is a favorite. It's basically legal, I'm pretty sure, except right now, since it's supposed to be me and another person taking a kid out, not just me alone. The kids hate time-out and I don't blame them. It's embarrassing, the teacher calling them out in front of the peer group like that, and the time-out room itself is no picnic. It's got a smell you can't get rid of, which I know because I tried. The walls are carpeted and all the smell has settled in that. I brought in carpet cleaner, Glade, whatever I could think of, but none of it worked. The Glade was bad because of the chemicals—the kids can be allergic and then instead of a pissed-off kid you got a pissed-off kid with a asthma attack or whatever. Hives sometimes.

So the room stinks. There's no window you can open either, so. But what do you do when a kid is causing a big disturbance or whaling on another kid or what have you? You gotta do something, right? Removing the kid, I mean, there are worse things. I come from a family, real hands on, you know? Let your fists do the talking. I don't know, you know? Is that bad? I mean, my parents loved us and they did what they knew to do. My mom, she'd ask you to do something once, and you don't do it and she asks again—"Take the laundry to the Laundromat," or whatever—and meantime you're still reading the back of the cereal box, I'll tell you what happens. She whacks you on the head. Sometimes she'd just take ahold of whatever she could grab onto, a hunk of hair or an ear, and drag your ass in whatever direction she needed you to go. And you'd go. You would definitely go. My dad the same thing. He must've ten, twenty times told my brother Angelo, "Stop hanging around with those gangbangers." He called them "sod oh mon biches," like "sons of bitches," because of the accent. He told Angelo, "You gonna get busted, you gonna end up in jail," but Angelo wouldn't stop. One night my dad unscrews all the lightbulbs downstairs. When Angelo comes in and it's late, of course, because he's been with the bangers, he tries to turn on a light. Nothing. My dad comes out of the dark swinging a two-by-four and beats the living crap outta my brother. My dad felt like talking didn't work no more. I ain't saying that would be my way. But that was them. They were old school.

One time I was babysitting my nephews and we were at a table drinking some juice and the little one, about four—Junior, we call him—was a little excited. Jumping up and down and laughing and he spills his juice. All over the place and I start yelling at him. Really yelling and I look at his face and his lip is quivering a little and his eyes are beginning to drip and he looks like he might crumple up into a little ball. Oh, man. Little César Junior. I remember thinking how I wasn't never going to do that again. Hurt a kid or yell at a kid like that. Why teach a kid to be afraid? I ever have a kid or kids, I guess that's a way I might act different from my parents.

Pierre says, "Can I have something to eat now?"

"I'm sorry, but I can't give you anything now, buddy. Soon, okay?" It's good to keep a little dialogue going with Pierre and get his mind off his problems. "So what kind of computer games do you like? You ever use those computers they got around here?" Now that we're at the time-out room is the time he might try to bolt, so I tighten my grip a little on his elbow.

"I want some pizza."

"Pizza fan, huh? What's your favorite kind?"

"Pepperoni."

"Get out. That's my favorite! You like onions?"

I'm like six feet, 190 pounds. I'm the tallest person in my

family. For a Puerto Rican I'm like a giant. But if he's resisting me, even a skin-and-bones kid like Pierre wears me out. He's not big—for fourteen he's a little guy. So he's little but when he's mad he's a handful. He has the mental problems but he also has a physical thing going on. Something with the legs, maybe rickets. We have about eighty kids here, all kinda mental, physical, whatever. They're actually very cool kids.

The main thing I do is drive the bus. I load up a bunch of kids in wheelchairs and take them to school, little field trips, or to church or what have you. When I ain't driving, they call me when a kid gets out of line. I'm a bus driver/cop. Somebody's gotta do it, I guess. No, but I like it here okay.

Pierre goes into the time-out room no problem. He's still talking about pizza and he's looking twitchy. Once I get him in the room, I can sit down and watch him through the window that looks right into the room, make sure he's okay. He starts pounding on the door but it's carpeted so he can't hurt himself. That's okay, Pierre, pound until you wear yourself out. That's what we're here for.

With Pierre—he's skinny as hell, so if he's hungry, why not give the kid some food? But that's what they do to a kid who's really acting out sometimes. They'll make him skip a meal or they'll do a "delayed meal" deal.

Pierre sometimes'll take some food out of the kitchen, crazy stuff like a pack of frozen hot dog buns. I caught him with a Salisbury steak once, which was a pretty big mess. He's such a little guy, I don't know. The rickets, if that's what it is, comes from not getting enough food when you're growing, which is how come I think it's rickets. Like I'm Dr. Hernandez now. But his legs are all bent and he's got a pretty big limping problem and that's the way rickets look. I'm just guessing, it ain't like I'm all up to speed on this shit. But you know, his main problem is the mental, not the physical.

He sits down in the corner, staring up at the ceiling. He acts like he has a gun and he's shooting at something or other. I don't know why Pierre gets so mad. You'd need to be a lot smarter than me to figure that out.

My opinion is, it's possible to know too much. I like to take each kid at face value. I don't want to memorize someone's file or chart or whatever they got and think I know them by that. That's bullshit. If I get to read your chart, then you should get to read mine. That's how I feel.

After another fifteen I'll tell Mrs. Schmidt how good he did so he can go for lunch. Feed his inner beast. Some of the houseparents want to leave a kid in there for longer but they're doing it for themself. Not for the kid. The adult just wants to hang out in the basement and talk to whoever passes by, you know, take a nice long break. And that's not right. Do your job, man.

Pierre throws up then and I can see from out here there's blue crayon in it. I'll be the guy to clean that up later. That's all right. I seen way worse than a little recycled crayon.

When the kids start coming down for their lunch period, I

see Mrs. Schmidt and I say how I was just about to let Pierre go, how he's all calm. She's says, "Well, he's supposed to get a delayed lunch, but okay. He can eat." I say, "Yeah, he's really hungry," and she says how he's got to learn not to act up in class.

Yeah, don't be hungry. Have some crayon.

Michelle Volkmann

I just left Oscar Mayer Children's Hospital Parents' Resource Fair, where I was hoping to recruit one or two possibilities for one of our client's facilities. It was a waste of time but you never know. Once, I recruited two children from there, but that was over a year ago. I get paid for beds filled, so after I left Oscar Mayer's at about seven thirty I headed over to a homeless shelter I know that's not too far away. If I don't get a hit within half an hour, I don't care, I am going home.

I'm on the success track. Those are not my words. That's what Tim, my boss, said. I'm a recruiter for Whitney-Palm Health Solutions. If you're in this field you've most likely heard of us. All our contracts are basically skilled-nursing facilities but they're all different. What I mean is, we have some of what you might think of when you think of a nursing facility, like "oh, nursing home" kinds of places, but we also have some places for kids. I recruit for the Illinois Learning and Life Skills Center. I love that place. It used to be that places like ILLC were state-run, but the state made a mess of it and now they pay our company—which, unlike the state, knows how to run a business—to do everything. It takes business acumen to run a nursing facility. If Illinois knew anything about making money, there wouldn't be so many potholes in the streets.

I love Whitney-Palm and the VP there is my boss, Tim, who is gorgeous and of course his wife looks like a runway model. He is so on my side and appreciates my work and he tells me, "Michelle, if you have a problem of any kind or you're not happy here, you can come straight to me because we want to keep you happy."

Honestly? I can really see myself being in charge of a big business like Whitney-Palm someday. They're definitely grooming me for management because they are paying for me to take a class that's being taught by an important businesswoman who is totally respected in the field. Her name is Helen Fairweather. She's very well known.

Every time I recruit a new person for a Whitney-Palm facility, I get $300. So that explains why I'm still out here at eight o'clock in the stupid night looking for parking at this homeless shelter.

But the work I do is important because I'm getting people off the streets and into warm beds with three meals a day and medical care. Do you have any idea how many people are out there without medical? Or dental? Seriously. My mom has this constant coughing thing because she smokes, but she says she has no idea what she'd do if she didn't have her job with insurance even though it's not the greatest insurance. She manages an Aldi in Valparaiso, Indiana, which is a supercheap grocery store. She really likes it there but work is about the only thing she likes in her life. I told her how she could get free psychiatrist appointments or at least lower-priced ones with her insurance but of course she refuses to see one because she's crazy. No, I'm kidding. Oh my God, parking.

The shelter is ladies only and is actually in a church, but this area is creepy at night. It's dark for one thing. My entire family basically refuses to come visit me because they all lived in Valpo or the UP for their whole lives and they think Chicago is full of criminals. In Valpo the fanciest restaurant is an Outback Steakhouse. I am so serious.

They were showing *Finding Nemo* at the shelter. You're homeless and watching a movie about this homeless fish. But it's a Catholic place, so maybe it's the only thing they could find that was G rated. The ladies already had dinner. The good thing about recruiting at shelters is that if someone is desperate enough to need to be in a place like this, they are open to suggestions. You'd think it'd be easier to recruit the ones who've been out in the streets for a long time, but no. Uh-uh. It's actually the ones that have just landed here. The new ones are more—they're like, "Ahhh! Get me out of here!"

So while they're watching *Finding Nemo* I look around to see who might be good to talk to. That's how I recruit. I just keep talking to people until I find someone who is interested in hearing about Whitney-Palm's lifestyle alternatives.

I'm standing at the door when I see this woman who is kind of fiftyish and she has a big cut over her eye with stitches in it, so I think she looks promising. I go over to her because we have a nursing facility in Darien that we just signed, but the woman sees me coming and says, "I ain't interested," real gruffly. Well, fine, excuse me for living, but just then I realize I tried recruiting the same woman last week at a different shelter.

Then I see this black girl get up and walk out. She has a really noticeable limp and she rocks from side to side when she walks. She might not be handicapped enough for ILLC but you never know. She looked like about fifteen or fourteen, which is perfect.

I follow her out and she sits down on a bench in the hall. I introduce myself and ask her if I could sit down. First thing I notice is she has her hands in her lap and one of them is all in a fist and twisty looking, like definitely abnormal, but the other hand is normal. Maybe her foot is twisted too and that's why she limps. She says her name is Cheri. "Cheri Smith. With the accent on the second part. The 'ri.' Not 'cherry,' but 'Che*ri*.'"

I'm thinking, "Okay, whatever." She has this way of talking that's like jerky. I don't mean like "you're a jerk" but like her speech came out stiff sounding. I ask her if she's had dinner and she says she has. I ask her if she liked the movie and she says yes. Then she asks me if I have a Kotex. She says, "My cycle just come on."

I go, "Oh, I don't have any. But maybe they have some here. I'll go ask, okay?"

So we walk over to one of the nuns or whatever to get Kotex and thank God they have it because these places, believe it or not, don't always have stuff like that. Nobody thinks about things like Kotex or tampons because they just don't. Like the only homeless people in the world are guys. But the shelters need pads and tampons to be donated too. I think I'll bring it up at Whitney-Palm tomorrow and get people to start a fund. You can really make a difference with something as simple as a sanitary napkin.

So I walk with Cheri to the bathroom and I'm waiting out in the hallway and I have no idea what she's doing in there but whatever it is must take forever. I mean, how long can it take to change a Kotex? Maybe she's like rinsing off a little. When I was sitting next to her she really had a bad smell. Nothing personal. It's just a side effect of being homeless.

When we sit back down I ask her how she came to be here and she says her parents kicked her out.

"Oh no, I'm really sorry. When did that happen?"

"Two days ago."

So I go, "What happened? Do you mind me asking?"

She says, "I met a guy at T-Mobile and we got to talking and he followed me home and when we went up to my room he took his thing out of his pants and I got scared. I got really, really scared and I told him he would have to leave my house."

The thing about this job is people will tell you anything.

So I go, "Oh no. Did he leave?"

"No."

"What did you do?"

"I kept telling him that I didn't appreciate him pulling his thing out and it was disgusting and it made me sick."

"So then what happened?"

"He left. And I just felt so scared, you know? I felt really nervous and agitated and when my mom came home I told her what happened and she got mad and said she and my dad couldn't take it no more and for me to get out the house."

Honestly? Cheri is not all there. I'm like—she brings a total stranger home and first thing he does is whip out his penis and then she tells her mother? She's really sweet like I said but—weird, you know? Still her mother shouldn't have just kicked her out. Not that I know all the details, but still.

She loves my hair. She asked if it was a weave but it's not. I have long, silky hair like a Chinese person.

I ask her if she has a disability and she says, "I have schizophrenia." Oh my God! Just like that. I could've asked this girl anything and she'd just answer. I *meant* what made her hand all knotted up—I had no idea she had a mental issue. She didn't seem schizophrenic. Not that I know all these schizophrenic people, but you get this image in your head of someone who's really out of control.

So I tell her about this place I know with other kids who are handicapped and how she would have her own room and be safe and go to school and never have to be in a homeless shelter. I ask her if she is on Medicaid and if she wants me to call her parents and talk to them about that place so Cheri can go there. Cheri is underage, only fifteen, so her parents have to sign her in. So she gives me their number and I give her my business card. Now I just have to hope the parents are onboard. Finding a potential patient is only the first step.

I walk her over to the sleeping area, which is I swear to God a bunch of pews. Not even cots. That's where people have to sleep, on these hard wooden pews. I'm not sure if Cheri totally understands everything I say but when I see those pew beds I know that I am helping her. I can't imagine being fifteen years old and being homeless plus schizophrenic plus her one twisted hand and whatever was going on with her feet. At least ILLC has beds. It has everything. Lots of kids her age and everything. I did exaggerate a little about having her own room. But sometimes that does happen, especially for kids who have mental issues, I think.

I'm already spending the $300 in my head. I'm getting two new tires for my mom's car, and for me I might get a winter coat at Old Navy or pay part of my Visa, depending on what the tires cost. Homeless shelters can be really profitable. I mean, I'm kidding, but it's true.

Yessenia Lopez

They sure as hell better give me some other room than this one. I am fifteen years old! What am I doing up in here with these stinky children can't even take their ass to the bathroom? That there should be a crime.

If this is what it means to be award of the state, you can have your award, I don't want it. I can take my own booty to the bathroom.

Benedicta—but I call her Shamu the Whale—was all crying and acting like she didn't even know she stole one of my teddy bears. Then Beverly just happens to find it in Shamu's drawer under some clothes. It all happened just like I said and nobody said nothing about sending her wrongful, trifling self to the time-out room. That's what they call the punishing room here. I just call it the Toilet.

When I was in Juvie for aggravating assault on Mary Molina? They had a room like that. The guards called it administrating segregation but the convicts called it the Hole. I never got put in the Hole though. The Hole scared the crap outta me.

My first night at Juvie I met some of the other criminal elements at dinner. I sat next to Yoyo, short for Yolanda. Yoyo was busted for dealing crack. Her teeth fell all out her mouth so she could only eat soft stuff and she always covered her mouth when she ate her food so you couldn't see the food falling out of it. She had two babies and she was so, so, so skinny. She said she started out by dealing but started up using it too and that was when she got caught. Her charge was possession of a control substance.

I met another girl, Erica. She was a lesbian. I'm use to it on account of my *tía* Cha Cha who is the mother of my cousin Carmen is a lesbian and she used to bring her girlfriend or husband or whatever you want to call it to Tía Nene's place on Christmas. You can usually tell who is a lesbian because if it walks like a duck, quacks like a duck, and dress like a duck, hey—it's a *duck,* you know what I'm saying? There were other girls there 'cause of theft, and some for being in gangs and hating and assaulting on each other. But there was one girl who had just come out the Hole that very night. Her name was Maricela. She was real quiet and she didn't look too good. You could see she was cute but she seemed like she was having a hard time to figure out should she use a fork or a spoon, you know? Anytime anybody said hi to her she flinched like it hurt her just to hear that. Maybe she was a badass before, but you sure wouldn't know it no more. I thanked the Lord Jesus Christ that I had my *tía* Nene as long as I did because when I saw some of those girls up in Juvie, I had to wonder where in hell they mamas was at, you know?

When I went to bed that night I said a prayer to the Holy Virgin herself and I told her that I was gonna be good and I would not cause no trouble and I would keep to myself and go to all the appointments they make you to go to. Once I make a decision, I stick to it.

Now I am stuck in this new hellhole. In the daytime I'm back at Herbert Hoover with alla its drama. In school we're learning about Hamlet. Okay, do he like Ophelia or not? Did they get their freak on before the story starts? 'Cause that girl is depress about something.

Some of the other people here go to Hoover too. I go on the bus with like fifteen or twenty other of the teenage people they gots on my floor. The bus driver is name Ricky and he's Puerto Rican like me and that boy kills me. He is hilarious. And he's hot, okay? The boy is a tall Puerto Rican which if you ain't one of my peoples you just don't know how hot that is.

There is a few people here who don't go to Hoover because they already graduated. They have classes in life skills what suppose to make them ready for the badass world when they get old enough.

Some of these children definitely do stink. Especially the

younger ones, but not only them. I'll just be minding my business and somebody'll go by me, pass by like it ain't no big deal,
and all of a sudden ka*pow*! I'll be hit in the face with the smell
of raw freaking shit! Somebody clean these children up, *please*!

I got one friend here. Her name is Cheri. She got put here
right after me. We was both in the bathroom and I said, "Hey,
don't you go to Hoover?" and she said, "I sure do," and I said,
"You ever have Miss Coleman?" and she said, "I love Miss
Coleman," and I said, "Miss Coleman is my favorite teacher!"
so we got bonded right offa the bat. I said, "This place is
jacked up but at least they gots mirrors in the bathroom," and
we both laughed so, so hard 'cause at Hoover they didn't keep
no mirrors in the bathroom, or at Juvie. That's because they
afraid us children will break them up and stab each other or
the teachers or ourselves. They afraid of their own children.

Once you laugh with a person? That person is your friend.
You can't help it. And for me and Cheri we neither of us had
laughed since we got put at ILLC, so we are friends for real.

I told Cheri about my *tía* and being award of the state and
moving to the St. Francis Home for Young Women and then
to Juvie. And by the time I got my sentence chopped off to
three months they didn't have no more beds at St. Francis and
here I am. Cheri told me how she was a vagrant and how a female with pretty hair tricked her and now she cries every night
'cause she misses her mama and daddy real bad and prays to
the Baby Jesus to make them come take her home. But they
said for her to stay put here, maybe this place do something

with her. They wash up their hands of their own child. I feel bad for her. I really do. Cheri even got the pretty-hair lady's business card. She says one day she's gonna call that lady up and tell her off for shutting her up in this pit.

Sometimes when I'm lying in my bed and Shamu is sleeping, I try to clear up my mind, but Tía Nene keeps coming into it and I try not to think of her but it's like the pink elephant. You see one in a room, you just gots to think about it.

They made me see a counselor at Juvie name Ms. Flowers. She said I could call her Patricia. She said she read my record from Family Services, and she seen I've had lost people, such as my *tía,* but also my mother and father. I told her the only one I lost was my *tía* Nene. Those other two are still alive and kicking, far as I know. I told her I never even seen my father, so I don't feel like I lost a thing and he's just the sperm donor if you ask me. I told her my mother was *tech*nically my mother? But my *tía* Nene raised me and made me the woman I am today. She asked me do I ever talk to my mother since Tía died and I said sometimes. I don't hate her but I don't like her either, I said. I told her *again* how Tía Nene is my real mother. So don't get me a foster mother or a adopting mother 'cause that will never happen. I will die first. Patricia said she respect my feelings and it wasn't up to her to put me with a foster nobody. Then she wanted me to talk about Tía Nene again.

I told her. *I do not want to talk about Tía Nene.* She just wants me to cry. Then she goes, "I admire how good you done handling that difficult situation." She goes, "I don't think too many people could do as good as you." So I go, "If I'm doing so good, then why I'm a convict?" We both laughed at that. And then I did talk about my mother being a crackhead and how my *tía* took over raising me and taking care of me and being with me in the hospital when I had to go there because of my disability making me sick and the time my mother came to visit me and I caught her in the bathroom smoking crack out of a car antenna. And then my time was up.

One time even before Tía Nene was sick I heard her talking to Tía Carmen and telling her, "When I die, who's going to take care of Yessenia? Who going to do that when I'm gone?" and that made me feel mad because even Tía Nene never seen me for myself. Even she thought somebody always gots to take care of me. But I can take care of myself. I don't give a damn what nobody thinks.

I don't.

Teddy Dobbs

I got a plan to run away. I'm gonna go right before they're set to ship me out of here. I been figuring it out but there's still a few details that need a little work. I know how I'm gonna sneak out, that's easy, but I'm not sure where I'm gonna stay at. The plan has to be perfect so I don't end up in a place even worse than this place.

I saw this guy once when my dad was driving me back here last Christmas and he was a wheelchair guy in the middle of Pulaski with no pants on. Just sitting there in his chair. It was winter too. It was cold. Cars zipping all around him. And all he had on was a old pajama top. He didn't have no pants on even. I asked my dad if we could give him some money, so my dad stopped the car and gave the guy ten bucks. My dad said the guy would probably use it to buy booze. I always think about that guy when I think about running away. I'm pretty sure that couldn't never be me though. Another problem I have when I think about running away is every time I really get going on my plan my head goes off someplace else. It's like I know I got to figure this out and I'm telling myself to think on it and next thing I know I'm thinking about what it's like when Mia touches me or that time my dad took me to see the Cubs.

You get a allowance. Every month Mrs. Phoebe and them give you thirty dollars. It ain't like it's their money. My dad said it's my money because Mrs. Phoebe and them take it outta my SSI check and then they keep the rest. Thirty dollars might sound like a lot but it don't go so far for a whole month. Bernard spends alla his on smokes. One pack at a time because if you buy a whole carton it'll just get stole. We're not allowed to smoke but me and my buddy Bernard got a lot of little nooks and crannies we know about. We're like the Keebler Elves 'cause we got nooks and crannies. There's a place down the hall from the physical therapy room where they got this big old swimming pool that nobody's used for like a lot of years. It had a electric thingamajig to lift the kids in and out of the water but it got broke and nobody ever fixed it. But I got the key from when Mr. Wehle left his key ring by the sink in the boys' bathroom and we keep it hid at where Bernard tapes it under his bed in our room. So when we need a little privacy we go in there. I wish I could smoke but I can't hold a cigarette. Bernard holds 'em for me sometimes. There ain't even any windows, so nobody's gonna look in and bother us. You know what else we like to do? We jerk off. We sit at the edge of the pool which ain't got no water in it and try to land it inside the pool. It's awesome.

Mr. Wehle got fired anyway. Not 'cause of the keys but 'cause Shawn Hooks ran away when Mr. Wehle was supposed to be watching and Shawn didn't get back for almost a week. He went to his old neighborhood and did drugs.

I'm starting to save my allowance up. It's part of my plan for running away. I saved last month's allowance for a week and I was gonna give it to my dad for safety but then Louie stole it. I know it was Louie 'cause he's a asshole and I had it the night he worked and next morning it was gone. I had it under my seat cushion and he was the one who plugged my wheelchair into the charger after I was in bed. It don't do no good to complain. They just say, "I didn't do it! I didn't do it!" and you can't prove it they did.

When I'm on the loose I'm gonna get a place to live and a aide. I'm gonna go to bed as late as I want. I'll eat dinner when I want. I'll have beer. I'll take the bus wherever I feel like it.

One thing I'm wondering is if Mia would be real mad if I hired a hooker so I could try doing sex. I wouldn't love the hooker. If I was doing it to get good at sex so I'd know all about it when I'm doing it with Mia—maybe she wouldn't mind that. I wonder how much do a decent hooker cost?

I'll be twenty-two in six months. Can you believe I'm twenty-one years old and never been laid? I been having a boner nonstop since I was ten. Ask anyone and they'll tell you. But my birthday is Bye Teddy Day for me. The day I turn twenty-two they want to ship me off to a old people's home. They're gonna stick me with the grandmas and grandpas.

So that's why I got to run and the sooner the better. I ain't doing it all half-ass like Shawn and other kids who run away from here. I'm getting out and I ain't coming back.

Oh no, it's Nurse Donna.

She says, "You're not allowed to loiter here in everybody's way."

So I says, "Ain't nobody around here, so how am I in the way?"

"Teddy, I am telling you to move."

"Why can't I sit here? I ain't hurting you."

"You are hurting me because I need a clear pathway here and you're in the way."

"That ain't fair."

"Do I have to call a houseparent to physically remove you?"

I couldn't think of nothing to say back to her when she said that.

"All right," Nurse Donna says, "I'm calling a houseparent."

I go to the elevator to get away from her and decide to ride up to two and see what Mia's doing. Mia's my hot Mexican mama.

When I got put here I was fifteen and Mia was thirteen. Mia was the hottest girl here and still is. But we didn't get to be boyfriend and girlfriend until I made her fall in love with me. I'm charming. I know how to dress, is one thing. I wear a suit every day. And a tie. I got a black suit and a brown suit. One day I wear the black and one day I wear the brown and at the end of a couple weeks one of the houseparents puts them in the washer and then I start over again.

"Hey, my hot little Mexican mama! It's your lover boy!"

"Teddy!"

"Can I get a little kiss?"

"Jus' a leetle one." That's how she talks. She has a Spanish accent.

"Hey, is your hair different?"

"Do you like it?" Mia says.

"It's pretty."

"Demetria wrap it in a circle. See? And she putting a scarf around my neck but not right now. She gonna put it after eberybody finish school, you know? And she putting makeup all over my face. Oh my goodness, I so exciting!"

"You don't need no makeup. You're just gonna look more prettier but that's okay I guess. Can I kiss you again?"

"Okay, jus' a leetle one."

Toya grabs Mia's chair and yanks her away. She's one of the houseparents. That's how it is here.

Toya says, "Teddy, will you get away from that girl. She's got physical therapy now." Then she grabs Mia away. Mia don't have no say about it.

"We was having physical therapy right here!"

Then Toya says how I'm a piece of work. She says, "Leave this poor girl be. And your suit needs washing."

"No, it don't. You can't wash these kinda clothes too much. It ain't good for them."

"Well, you smell. Something needs washing."

"Bye, Teddy!" Mia says. "I see you at dinner!"

Mia's been living here since she was eleven. She has CP, which stands for cerebral palsy. She's got a pretty big Spanish accent. I didn't get every word at first, but now I understand everything the first time she says it. She needs a electric wheelchair but she only has a crappy manual one. For a while she didn't even have the manual chair and they made her lie in her bed all day. Then finally they got her this chair she's in now. One of the footrests is broken and the seat's too big and too wide. She fell out once. And ever since that time, they strap her into it, and she thinks it makes her look like a baby. I don't think it makes her look like a baby. I don't even notice it. But that's women. They worry about how they look.

And she can't see too good. She can't barely see the board and she has to hold a paper up practically to her face.

I don't care about any of that. She's my hot Mexican mama and I love her and she loves me.

My dad got my electric chair from his insurance. My dad is cool. He comes to see me here. When I was born I had a tumor in my back. The doctor took it out but I can't walk now or move my arms all the way 'cause of the tumor. It's a good thing they took my tumor out 'cause I might've died.

Nobody comes to see Mia, so when my dad comes to see me he brings her stuff. One time he brought her a sweater and one time he brought her a blanket. Mia got took away from her family. She talks about them like how she misses them and they miss her but they never came here once since she was eleven years old. She says they can't visit 'cause something I forget what. She has scars on her arms from before. I knew this guy once, Eric Morales, he was my friend in seventh grade and he had scars the same as Mia's scars and his scars was from cigarettes. Like cigarettes getting put out on him. I called him the Human Ashtray one time in front of my dad and my dad got real mad at me. I didn't know it was a mean thing to say. I asked Mia about her arm scars once. We wasn't even boyfriend and girlfriend yet. She said she didn't remember but I'm pretty sure it was cigarettes.

They told my dad I'm retarded. They told him first at regular school and then when I moved in here. My dad said that's just a word they use that means I got a different way of learning stuff. That's the way I think of it because I sure don't feel retarded. My friend Ryan's retarded and I asked him if he feels retarded and he said no. So I guess I am but I don't notice it. And I look normal except for not walking and my arms not working perfect. From the tumor.

Most people here don't get too many visitors. Some of them

got took away from their parents like Mia. Some of them got moms. Bernard has a mom and brothers and sisters who come to pick him up and take him home the whole weekend sometimes. His dad's in jail. I ain't seen my mom but one time in the seven whole years I been here. I don't give a shit. I wouldn't've met Mia if I never came here.

Ricky Hernandez

There's one of those heavy rains going on, typical nutsoid Chicago weather. But the rain is coming off the buildings in sheets and it looks like midnight out there even though it's only, uh, six o'clock. I'm done for the day but I think about that new secretary in a wheelchair and how she's gonna get home in all this. Because I've seen her out at that bus stop sometimes. So I knock on her door and I ask her does she need a ride. She's in the middle of putting her coat on anyway. I want to ask her does she need help with that, but who knows, you know, maybe she could take that the wrong way. She's doing pretty good putting it on for herself. Takes her a while but gives me a chance to look. I've seen her around but more from at a distance. She's good looking. She's got long bangs that she hasta keep sticking behind her ears, and skin without a mark on it.

Real smooth. But anyway, she's like, "You sure it wouldn't be an inconvenience?" and I say I wouldn't ask you if it was. She says, "I was so worried about getting soaked. My chair would squeak for a week." Then we go outside and I tell her to wait under the awning till I pull the bus around. Which I do, and I'm locking her chair down inside the bus and I look up at her because I'm down on my knees with the tie-downs and she gives me a big smile. Nice. Then off we go.

She lives north, up by Ashland and Wellington. I say, "How are you liking it here at the center?" She says she's real happy to have a job. She says how long have I been working there and I tell her a year. She says, "Oh," and do I like it. I say, "Yeah, this is the best job I ever had. I like helping people. I like being a part of the solution." She doesn't say anything, so I go, "I used to drive a cab. What a racket that is. Those owners got you in a stranglehold. You want to make a dime, you better be able to work round that clock, 'cause they got you by the balls till you pay them the rent for the car plus you pay the gas, or something goes wrong with the car, that's coming outta your pocket. You know, you think, 'Oh, here's a good way to pick up some cash,' right? You know? I'll be a cabbie, right?" What a load a crap that is. Who do these guys think they are? Sorry for the language."

She says, "No problem. I'm comfortable with profanity." That struck me as hilarious the way she says that: "I'm comfortable with profanity."

"Don't get me wrong," I say. "I didn't hate the job. I'm a

people person. I enjoyed hearing the fare's opinions, except for the real idiots."

She says, "How can you tell a real idiot?" So I say, "I give up. How?" She says, "No, I mean, I'm asking. What did a person act like when they were being—"

"Oh yeah, yeah, no, no, I got you. Well, besides me," I say, "let's see. You know, the people who get into the cab and they're coming all over themselves because why? Because they got a cabbie who ain't Arab or whatever. This is what gets me. They go on their little 'towel head' or whatever rant, and all the time they're talking to a Puerto Rican. It's the only time I ever knew being a Rican made me so lucky. But okay, I did pick up a lotta nice folks too. All kinds. I had lawyers, doctors, *actors,* like once I picked up Regis Philbin. Real nice guy. I picked up deaf people who were speaking sign language to each other. People in chairs. I just couldn't make a living at it." When I'm nervous I talk too much.

She says, "Yeah, it's one of those jobs where you have a weird intimacy with a total stranger until you drop them off and never see them again."

"Yeah, that's it. It's like *Taxicab Confessions.* You hit it on the head. You ever see that show?"

She's gotta be, I don't know, late thirties? Kinda baggy clothes, like she's embarrassed of her body. A lotta women think that baggy fashion looks good on them. Most men, if you're like me, you want to see the outline, and you don't get that with baggy clothes.

I like to see the body. I like to see the curves. I don't care what it is, you know? Big ass? I like that. Women are so embarrassed about their asses. Especially white women. They don't want you to see the meat. I knew this girl, she'd be backing away from the bed just so I didn't think she had a fat ass. I told her, "Come on! I wanna see."

I've been attracted to many different women, like, there's no pattern to it that I can tell. My ex, for example, did not have big tits, but the rest of her body was unbelievable. Slim waist and big ass. She was hot.

I say, "It's good for the kids to have you around. They all want your wheelchair."

"I know. So few of them have power chairs. What's up with that?"

"Yeah, I don't know, I never really thought about it. But you're right."

"Maybe they're afraid that if all the kids had power wheelchairs and could move on their own, ILLC would turn into a giant crip demolition derby."

"Oh, man. That would be so cool." We laughed at that, which was a little icebreaker.

She says, "No, I'm serious though. The reason Mrs. Phoebe won't give out power chairs is because power chairs would give the kids more autonomy. Keeping them immobile makes it easier on the staff."

"Yeah. I can see that. I just never heard it put like that."

She doesn't wear heavy makeup or perfume. I agree with

her there. Hold all that makeup because it just looks fake anyway. I had a girlfriend once and I'd say to her, "Hey, you don't need all that. You look good." She was addicted to the stuff, I mean, she couldn't pass a lipstick in a window on the street but she had to stop and check it out. Every time I walked into her bathroom she had more crap in there. That was the only girl I ever really fought with. I mean physically fought with. Not over the makeup but other issues. She was jealous. And I wasn't even doing anything, but she'd get mad—really like screaming, calling names, if my cell rang and it was a female name and she didn't know who it was. One day she hauled off and hit me, and I hit her back. Hey, I was seeing stars offa that smack, so I gave it back to her. Not hard, you know, I know I'm stronger. It was more reflex, you know? And I picked up my jacket and walked out her door. And I remember this—I'm walking out the door, and I'm thinking, "That's it. I will never see this person again."

A big lightning strikes just then over the lake and the rain really comes down.

She says, "Wow, the water looks like it's boiling," and I say, "Yeah, the rain hitting it kinda makes it look like that."

She says, "I never would've made it home in all this. My chair would be drowned, you know? I'd be a wreck. It's not too much out of your way, I hope."

"No, it's fine. I like driving."

"Where do you live?"

"Me?" I say. "I live southwest. Not too far from the center."

"Oh no. You'll have to turn around and double back. This is cra—"

"Don't worry about it. It's no big deal."

"You're really saving me."

"It's my pleasure. I don't mind."

By the time we pull up to her place, things have slacked off. Pouring down buckets one minute, a little sprinkle the next. I go to take the tie-downs off her chair. I'm hoping she'll give me one of those smiles again. I ask her, "You like the neighborhood here?"

"Yeah. I like the trees and it's quiet for a neighborhood in the middle of the city. There are some nice restaurants. A lot of ethnic—variety . . ."

"Like what do they have?"

"Thai, Peruvian, Ethiopian."

"All in the same neighborhood? My neighborhood has one thing and that's the Krispy Kreme. But I'll have to try that Ethiopian. What is that—like what? I'll walk you to your door," I say.

"No, you don't have to."

"I have an umbrella I keep in here. Come on."

"Well, okay," she says. "It's spicy. And hot. Ethiopian food. Sort of in the neighborhood of Indian tastewise. India's not too far from Africa, so . . . well, actually it is kind of far. Across this big sea, so I guess that was . . . not a good theory about the food."

We're standing at the entrance to the building and I'm like

shaking her hand—not really shaking 'cause her hand doesn't have much of a grip. But she stuck it out there for me to shake, so hey. She's fine with it, so I'm fine with it. I look at her little hand in my big paw and then I look back at her face and she's staring at me. I get a little rush, you know?

She says, "So they let you drive home in the company car. Not too shabby."

"Yeah, well, not exactly. I'm gonna drop it off back there at ILLC. I'm the guy with the black Neon in the parking lot. I'm the peon with the Neon."

"You have to stop back there too? Oh no, the least I could do is keep you company on your drive back."

"Yeah," I say. "Come on, hop back in." Then we had another little chuckle. "Nah, I'm fine. I got a Metallica jam in the bus. I'll see you tomorrow."

Tomorrow. Nice.

Jimmie Kendrick

You couldn't tell by looking at me I was homeless. I mean, I was clean, okay? And I carried my stuff in my duffel bag, slung over my shoulder. It's not like I was dragging a loaded shopping cart. Linda let me come in every few mornings to shower and wash out my clothes, and then I was out in the streets again. She had to be out of there early to get to work. Linda's a girl I met back when I first got to New York. There wasn't anything between us. Nothing romantic. She was just a good person. Sometimes I'd get a meal there too. An egg or a piece of toast. I didn't wanna ask her, but if she offered, hey. I mean, Linda had her own problems. She had two kids back in North Carolina and she was trying to work her way back to them and she was basically on a shoestring her own self. Her place was—you wouldn't believe how small a place people would pay money for there. Her place was like two closets put together. I wouldn't even ask her could I leave my duffel bag there because I felt guilty taking up even that little space. The shower in her place was like—you didn't want to bring the soap in*to* the shower with you. You couldn't barely bend an arm up to wash your hair.

Linda gave me a dollar once or twice, but I would never ask her. If she wanted to give it I wouldn't turn it down, but I would never ask. Usually I bought a bag of Doritos. You can make a bag of Doritos last—whew, I mean, I could make that little bag last me through the day. Another thing I'd do is you can buy those little bags of cookies two for a dollar. A small pack of Louis Rich turkey hot dogs—also a dollar.

I wouldn't panhandle. You know what I'd do? I'd find money. You can actually find a quarter here or there, even a dollar. Keep your glance downward. I also found subway passes on the ground. They'd drop out of folk's pockets and I'd pick them up, see if they had any money left on them. But like I say, to look at me, you wouldn't know. But I was. Dead, freaking homeless.

I stayed on the train most nights. It was crazy. It was just . . . bad. I mean, I'm a big woman. I'm big, I've always been big, and by big I mean I'm tall, I got a lot of muscle on me, I got weight—or I *had* weight—but I know how to handle myself. I know how to carry myself and I know how to defend myself. But I don't ever have to defend myself because nobody wants to start anything up with me.

So I don't fear for my safety. But I do sometimes fear for other people's safety. Like I'm not afraid of getting shot, just other people getting shot. My mom used to say, "Oh yeah, you think nothing is going to happen to you because 'I'm Jimmie Kendrick.'" But I don't know. I just feel that way.

I protected a young tranny once when she was about to get a beat-down. Just stepped in and took the blow, gave the guy a couple headbangs and that was that. I don't think I was more than fourteen at the time. It's just instinct, you know? I see a man beating a woman, I just feel prepared to deal with whatever might happen. Bar fights—I broke up so many of them, you just don't know. I broke up a fight in the middle of a conversation I was having once. Two men. Reached over and *poom poom*! Went right back to the conversation. That's been me for as long as I can remember.

But the things you see when you're on the streets. I mean, I was in this little fast-food kind of place, not one of the big chains, but a mom-and-pop dealie. We're deep in the hood now. Like you can get a dog and some fries for sixty-nine cents. Okay. Guy comes in, goes over to the guy at the counter. There's this Plexiglas partition, right? Like you see at the movie theater where you slide your money under the cutout and they slide you back your ticket. Anyway, this guy, he goes up to the counter, he says, "He didn't get his salad."

I'm thinking, "Hmm, they don't have any salad." This is not the kind of place you go if you want a salad. So the guy behind the counter goes away, comes back in a hot second, slides—I kid you not—a brown paper bag under the cutout, and the other guy leaves.

And these are not black people! Just for the record. They're Puerto Rican.

But it's not over. A few minutes later, the same guy comes *back* in, goes to the counter guy, says, "He said you forgot his sauce." I'm like, "What the hell?" So an*oth*er brown bag comes sliding through the cutout—this one must have that special sauce in it. Guy takes the bag and slides a fifty back to the counter guy. Who pockets the cash.

That's just the free-enterprising spirit in the hood. Salad sauce. I'm pretty sure Paul Newman doesn't have a line of that.

So how did I get to that point, you might be asking yourself. I know because I asked myself that same question. Well, okay. Here's the deal. I always could sing. I don't know. I just—I mean, I can *sing*, you know? I got a set of pipes on me. I don't mean to brag or sound full of myself, but—it's just something I can do. What can I tell you? It's just a gift. I believe the gift is from God, but you can believe what you want. And that's what took me there to New York City.

I had met a woman after a gig one night, here in Chicago. I sing with a band here. All-lesbian band. Anyway, this woman's name was Daphne. She said she was a record producer, she wanted to rep me, she believed she could really, like, introduce me to some important people. She said I could live with her as long as I needed. She had a place in Brooklyn. She was a stud herself, so I knew it wasn't a sexual thing, and I asked around and she checked out.

So I packed my things and I moved out to New York. I found my way to Brooklyn and moved in with Daphne. The deal was, she was going to finish up her current project, soon as that was done she'd book the studio time and we'd make a CD. Meantime, I would do some clubs, get introduced around, that kind of thing.

Daphne put me up but she didn't feed me. Problem was, when I had pulled up stakes in Chicago, I had, like, nothing. I had been working pretty much to pay the rent and the bills at that time. It wasn't like I had money piled up in the bank. I had enough for my plane ticket and, like, maybe a week? Two weeks? I figured, Daphne's hooked up, she's going to get me enough gigs in clubs or whatever to get me through. Yeah, right. The gigs I did get were, like, every couple months. I got no work singing backup for other artists, which she said she was going to set up. All I had in my pocket after the first month was my keys and my ID. And a dead cell phone. So the lack-of-food issue started up way before the homeless issue.

If you're thinking I'm an idiot by now, you're not thinking anything I didn't think to myself a hundred—no, a million times. But I swear I thought this woman was for real. I had lots of people approach me before her, same deal, "Hey, I want to rep you, I can really help you, take my card, I'm going to hook you up," and all of that, all the time. And I knew to be on my guard. I was taking my time, taking my time, until the right thing, the right offer. And I thought she was it.

I finally packed up my duffel bag and left Daphne's place. I doubt she even noticed. And that was the beginning of my life in the streets for real. I tried every way I could think of to raise the cash to get back home, but I couldn't get any work. I passed a store window one day and saw this thin, beat-down-looking woman staring out at me and realized—she was me. And by that time I looked homeless. I sure did.

My sister, Jackie, flew me back to Chicago. Sometimes I wake up and for a few seconds I think I'm still in New York. I swear I can feel the rumbling of the subway train in my body. I have to tell myself "I'm home" a couple times, just for my heart to slow down.

But wow. I missed my band, I missed my church, my friends, my *fam*ily. And Joanne, who is somewhere between the last two. Joanne is framily.

I never called Joanne from New York. I couldn't. I had too much pride. Or not enough or *whatever* it is, but I was just in survival mode then. I was, like, totally inside myself. I don't think I said more than thirty words out loud for the whole two months I was homeless.

When I see her, she's racing down the hallway to meet me. I met up with her at this place she's working now, a nursing home for disabled kids. A few blocks from where I grew up, in Englewood. We just hugged and kept on hugging. She looks great. She just looks really—she was a sight for sore eyes, okay? I am so serious.

We walked over to a little bar I know not too far from her job. I'm still getting over that Joanne—my Joanne—*has* a job.

We were sipping our drinks and talking about—just everything, and she says, "Are you working?" and I tell her, "Only thing I could find was picking up cable boxes for Comcast. I had to drive my own car—well, my nephew's Ford—and the gas cost more than what Comcast was paying me. So it was cake for them but I had to quit."

And right then and there Joanne says she could probably get me a job working at the same place she was working at. She said, "If you don't mind doing that kind of work." Please. It wasn't like I hadn't done that kind of work before. Doing personal care for people. I did it for Joanne. That's how we met in the first place. I said, "Hey, bring it on. When can I start?"

It took about a week. They had to do a background check, which took a long minute, and I already had my CNA—certified nurse's assistant—and there was a training they did which was ridiculous, but hey, whatever. I would've leapt through a flaming hula hoop if I needed to.

I've been staying with two of my nieces and their five kids and we're squeezed in pretty tight. But now I can find something affordable in the hood. I'll probably need a fridge and a stove, but I can get those dirt cheap in the hood too. They'll overcharge you on delivery—that's where the fix goes in—but if I can find a nice place with a landlord who'll cover some of that, I'll be cool. I'll need a mattress from somewhere, and a plate and whatever, but that's no biggie. I cannot even imagine what it'll feel like to be in my own place again. Alone. Quiet. I already know what I'm going to do the first night. I'm going to light a candle, lay back on my mattress, and relax. Just feel the peace. Breathe in and breathe out. Think about . . . nothing at all.

Ricky Hernandez

Yeah, so I was strolling through the place looking for Candy who's one of the houseparents, to drop off her paycheck because it was by mistake put in my envelope. I'm on my way back from a buddy a mine's anyway, I was picking up some weights of his he was trying to unload because he's getting his floor sanded—long story—so it's no big deal for me to stop and drop the check, is what I'm saying. Candy works nights, so it's a little weird because I'm not usually in the place late like that. It was midnight. So I go on up to two and one of the guys who works up there on the boys' side, you know, he's a houseparent, guy named Jerry, skinny as hell, he's a little bored and does that thing people do when they want you to stop and talk. They pin you down, you know? You know, they talk nonstop, never really ending a sentence so you got no choice but to stand there. I'm okay with that because these night gigs can get pretty lonely and when everyone around you is in bed asleep, you might find yourself nodding off along with them. So I let the guy go on, just let him free-associate for a while. Sometimes I'm listening, listening, blabbety-blab, you know, and sometimes I drift away. He mostly goes on about the money, how shitty it is, how hard he's got to work, and all of that. Then he's off on this thing about women, and who he's fucking or who he wants to fuck, or what he likes, or whatever. I'm like, okay. Hey, I like talking about sex as much as the next guy. And you know when you're with another guy you're gonna say some things you wouldn't want to say around a woman. That's just the way it is. I prefer talking about sex with a woman, personally. Because just talking about it—like you're just having a conversation—that's a turn-on. That's all foreplay, and anytime that happens is good. I don't care if it don't lead nowhere, it's still good. But talking to guys about sex—totally different thing. Guys are raw. One time—I was nineteen—I'm fast asleep over at a buddy's house and I open my eyes and there's a hooker, you know, giving me a blow job. My buddy's standing there laughing. I'm sure as hell not going to stop her—hey, I'm not going to stop any woman from giving me a blow job. Plus it was my birthday present, so whatever. But what I was going to say is, I don't have this "all females are hookers" mentality, whereas some guys are, you know, they're definitely not cool in that area. This Jerry guy, who I'm now noticing has some real aggressive breath on him, is all "cunt" and "slit" and "bustdown" and I'm starting to, you know, to edge away from him, looking to make my getaway, and I say, "Okay, uh-huh, yeah, see you when I see you"—but the guy won't shut up, so finally I say, "Look, man, I gotta be on my way," and I start walking and he's *still* talking and half the way down the hall I can hear him talking about some girl and she's this and that and how he likes to fuck her or whatever but, like, it was raw. It was raw. I'm torn between stopping and telling him he shouldn't be talking trash with kids around who might hear you, and just getting the fuck away. Then he breaks off from what he's saying and says, "See you later. I gotta bird."

Creep, you know?

I was thinking I oughta tell Joanne about this Jerry character. I remember I was thinking that. But we got off on this tangent like we sometimes do. I guess I told her like the dummy I am about that hooker/blow job experience I had way back when. She says, "So you would never turn down a blow job?" and I say, "No guy is gonna turn down a derb." She says "A derb? Are you kidding me?" I say, "Yeah, a derb, a blow job. Same deal." So she says, "So even someone who is being paid to have sex with you—you're fine with that." And I'm like, "Why not? She's getting paid good money." She says, "So even if this woman's pimp forces her to either suck your dick or get the crap beat out of her, that's okay with you? Because women love sucking off strange men's cocks, so it's worth it for her?" So I say, "You don't know she had a pimp." Then she says, "What about the women and girls and boys who get kidnapped off the streets of Ukraine or Mexico or the Philippines and forced into sex slavery? You would be just fine if a slave gave you a blow job?" So I say, "I'm not hiring anyone to give me a blow job! It was this thing that happened when I was nineteen!" She says, "But you said you could never stop anyone from giving you a blow job. Excuse me, a 'derb.'" I say, "When did I say that?" She says, "You *said* you'd never stop anyone from giving you a blow job." I say, "I'm just saying I like blow jobs." So now instead of this conversation going in the direction I hoped, she gets into this thing about women and children being forced into sex slavery. She shakes her head and says, "You'd let Hitler give you a blow job?" So I say, "Yeah, I'd love Hitler to give me a BJ. Why not?" And then I could see her turn her head down and try not to laugh and she says, "It would be fun for you to look down and see that little mustache going up and down, up and down, huh?" And I say, "Ooh, you're getting me hot," and she looked at me and rolled her eyes, and she is damn cute when she does that. Maybe she'd kill me for saying this, but that whole conversation? It was a turn-on for me.

Only thing is, I never told her about Jerry the sex fiend. It's probably no big deal. Guys like that are all talk for the most part. You might not pick him out for Houseparent of the Year, but you know. Can't fire a guy for talking, right? He's got the right not to remain silent.

Mía Oviedo

The firs' time he come I was sleeping. He pull open my eyes and I don't know what is happening. I say, "What you doing?" I wan' to say, "Stop doing it," but he put something in my mouth. He put something like a towel in there real hard and hold his han' over my mouth and the thing he put in there, in my mouth, it push in my throat and I can't breathe. I make a noise and he tell me something real bad, real . . . bad in my ear real close so nobody hear. I know something bad going to happen. He talking to me and I don't understan' what he say because he talking so fas' in my ear and I don't want to know what he say and I so scare you can't belief it. He smell bad. He smell like, he smell like, something bad, something—it make me sick. It make me sick! Help! I can't breathe! I know what he want to do! "Please no, no," I say. "I don't want to—don't, don't, I don' want—stop it, *no lo hagas, déjame. ¡Déjame! ¡Me estás lastimando! Déjame, por favor, por favor. No más, no más.*"

He stop it then. He looking at the door. His hand still on my mouth. He whisper at me. He mad at me.

I no tell. I say, "*No le voy ha decir a nadie, sí, sí, no le voy ha decir a nadie.* I not going to tell. I not going to tell nobody."

And then Jerry let go of me and he go away.

When I cry I trying not to make no noise. But I still very scare and I keep awake after that. I keep awake all night and when it not so much dark no more I close my eyes but it don't matter because he inside my eyes.

Jimmie, she is new, come to help me to get dress in the morning an' she see I throw up in my bed but she not mad. She is very nice. She say am I sick and I say to her I not sick, I ate a bad thing, and she saying do you feeling better and I say I feeling better. She wash me and she say, "You got your period? There's a little blood here," and I not sure what to say. I say, "I don't know." Jimmie say, "Do you want me to put a pad on you?" I say, "Yeah, okay." Jimmie say, "Didn't you just have your period?" and I say, "I don't think," and Jimmie say, "Is only a few spots but maybe you wanna stop by the infirmary, okay?" I say, "Yeah, okay."

I pray alla the time that he don't come back. I don't tell nobody what he do so he won't be mad. When I am in the bed and it get dark I see him there, he watching from the closet. He sitting on the top. On the top of the closet. Like he be sitting on the top and at firs' you don't see him so good because is so dark but then you see him like a big bird holding on with his claws and he watching. Oh my goodness, I so scare then. I want to scream when I see the big bird but I don't want to make no noise. I not sleeping till the sun come in and make the big bird go away.

Las' night he come back. I hear shoes walking outside the door and I so scare that he coming and nobody hear him. Not Fantasia, not Candy, not nobody. Candy the houseparent don't hear him and no one hearing him but me. Fantasia in the bed nex' to me. She sleep too hard. Nothing waking her up.

He sneak in my room and put his han' over my mouth. He say I better not to say nothing or he put something big in my mouth and he laugh. He say am I gonna be a good girl and I say yeah, yeah, I a good girl but I don't say it, I jus' nodding. He take away his hand then and I don't say nothing. I a good girl.

He whisper a lot of things. I pray for God to take me, please, God, I want to die. He put his face close and he say, "I gonna eff you. You want me to eff you," and all bad things like that and he putting his tongue in my mouth. No, no, *no lo hagas, no lo hagas,* and he put his hand on my—you know, and my legs. I want him to stop. I screaming and screaming but again his hand on my mouth very strong on my mouth and I can't breathe and I can't do nothing. He do the bad thing to me. Oh, *me estás lastimando, no Papi, no más. ¡No más! ¡Por favor no más!* He say don't tell. *¡No le voy ha decir a nadie!* He say no-body gonna belief me. They never belief me. He say, "Snitches get stitches." Snitches get stitches.

He say, "I like it when you call me Papi."

Today I don't feel so good. My coochie hurt real bad. I never telling. I swear God.

Teddy wan' to eat breakfast at my table. I don't wanna eat nothing and I don't wanna talk and I want for Teddy to stop. He laughing all the time like something so funny. Like he know about me. Like he know. Teddy just laugh and laugh with his friends. I ask for Toya please I gotta go to the bathroom please and she take me. I keep my head down so nobody see my face. I thinking, "Why he say I call him Papi?"

Joanne Madsen

Mrs. Phoebe says we get audited every year and the services the kids receive have to be in the database. There's also the possibility of a surprise inspection by the state although she says that's very unlikely because ILLC is so well managed. My immediate task is to enter everything on record starting from now and working backward to 2000. That's over ten years of three- or four-inch-thick files per criplet.

The paperwork in the files is often illegibly handwritten, in pencil sometimes, has stains of unknown origin, or never made sense in the first place. Some forms were used for a few years and discontinued. Others were invented along the way. There's no consistency to how they're filled out—some people write three paragraphs and some write three words. Besides histories, the forms are supposed to record the health care the kids receive, the amount of medical supplies each kid uses, doctor appointments, counseling sessions, release-of-information forms, hospital stays, number of recreation hours spent, transportation provided. Number of pickles eaten, amount of air breathed, blinks per hour. I'm in the belly of the beast.

Mrs. Phoebe says they are changing over to a better system where the houseparents will input data onto computers themselves. She says all this will happen in about six months, but they have to get up to date. I ask who will train the staff in the use of the database and she says, "I thought you would do that." I'm a dead man.

After a few hours of typing in all this minutiae my neck starts aching and my eyes get blurry whenever I look away from the computer screen. My pupils have dilated to the exact circumference needed to stare at black letters on a white screen. Looking down a hallway or at someone's face is actually painful.

I have to tilt. My wheelchair has a miraculous tilt mechanism. I press a button and it tilts back. You can tilt back so far you're actually looking at the ceiling. You can't imagine the practical applications this has. Besides the obvious, which is comfort. Take the dentist, for instance. It's bad enough to have to go to the dentist, but imagine having to ask him to help lift you out of your wheelchair and into the dentist chair. I mean, really. Inevitably one of your shoes falls off during the process and your clothes get all smashed up and then you get two or

three hygienists in there apologizing way more than is neces-
sary. Now all I have to do is tilt and cringe.

After days and weeks of nothing but forms and numbers,
you'll start to notice how certain forms you wouldn't expect to
see all that often seem to pop up quite a bit. And some forms
you'd predict you'd see all the time you rarely see at all. For
example, out of approximately eighty kids, how many times
do they end up in the hospital in a seven-month period? Not
just the ER but full admission. A few? Ten? Try thirty-two full
admissions in a seven-month period. Those are documented
instances of the ILLC doctor on call—Dr. Caviolini—
referring a child for a hospital stay. About nine infections and
eight pressure sores. Sixteen trips for what appear to be several
CTs or MRIs and various other tests per kid. One girl died
from MRSA, that superbug the hospitals are freaked about
because it's almost antibiotic resistant. That's a lot—a *lot* of
serious health problems. I haven't been in an emergency room
or admitted to a hospital in years. And I am really disabled.
Really disabled. In theory, at least, they're supposed to keep
these kids healthy.

At about five thirty I go down the hall to the accessible
bathroom that I share with the girls. None of the staff bath-
rooms have accessible stalls, of course. At ILLC, all crips are
children, including me, apparently. Mrs. Phoebe even pats me
on the head from time to time. I've tried to object, but it happens really fast, like a drive-by patting.

Most of the kids are in the cafeteria at the moment, so I

have the bathroom more or less to myself. There's a girl about ten years old who has just finished spraying her hair with what smells like bug repellent and is now leaving.

"Hi, Cleo, bye, Cleo," I call to her.

"Bye, Jane," she says. Most of them don't know my name yet. But they're getting closer.

Ricky drives me home about twice a week. He comes by my office at six o'clock. Sometimes we go to Mr. Beef and sit in the ILLC bus eating and talking. Tonight we're on our way to a place called La Fonda in Pilsen.

I'm taking a few swallows of beer when he says, "Want to come to my nephew's birthday party?"

It takes all my self-control to refrain from a spit-take. I'm unprepared for the family thing to rear its ugly head so soon. I'm 90 percent sure the invitation means no more or less than any of Ricky's questions—his conversation is relatively free of subtext. In any case, there's no way I'm going. Where there's a birthday party, there is family, and you never know how someone's family is going to react. To the disability.

"I'm sure it won't be accessible," I say. "People's houses never are. You know."

He says, "It's at Chuck E. Cheese."

I say, "You want me to go to Chuck E. Cheese?"

"Yeah, why not?" he says, with a mouth full of tortilla chips.

"You can't even hear yourself scream in there. There'll be five hundred preadolescents amped on high-fructose corn syrup. I'm not even exaggerating."

"And?" he says.

"Thank you. I'm really glad to be invited," I lie, "but it's not a good idea. For me to go."

He shrugs and says, "Okay."

I was hoping he'd ask why it wasn't a good idea, but being a person who relies heavily on subtext, I didn't say so. The guacamole arrives to change the subject.

"I have a question," I say. "How many of the kids at ILLC would you guess were admitted to St. Theresa's during a seven-month period in 2011? I'm only up to mid-July."

"Don't know," he says. "How many? Can you pass the green salsa?"

"Admitted. Not just the emergency room."

"Ten percent?" he says.

"Well, I didn't do a percent thing," I say. "I just added up the number. Out of eighty-one kids. That's how many kids we have now, not then. Then it was eighty. How many?"

"Hold up. I'm lost."

"Thirty-two out of roughly eighty kids were admitted to St. Theresa's in a seven-month period."

"Really?" he says. He pours the salsa over the guacamole. "Sounds like a lot. You think that's a lot?"

"Yes, I do," I say. "That's almost half the kids. In about half a year. That's a lot, right?"

"They're always sick. They're always coughing or sneezing all over the place. ILLC is like one of those—what do you call 'em?"

"What? I don't know."

"No, where there's viruses and flu—one of those—and they do tests and swab the germs on it. Come on, one of those—"

"Petri dishes?"

"Petri dishes. It's like that. The place is crawling with bugs."

"Okay, but they get referred to the hospital for tests. Specific tests for X-rays and scans and MRIs."

"A lot of the kids have these shunts," he says, drawing an imaginary picture on his head with his finger. "Shunts in their heads. Like if they have spina bifida or cerebral palsy they wind up with shunts a lot of times. It's like they get fluid building up in their heads and the shunt drains the fluid off. To somewhere, and you can't see the tube. It's not obvious, it's, you know, little, you'd have to look for it." He gives up on the illustration. "They get sick all the time from those. All the time. They get headaches—migraines—and throw up and the nurse calls the EMTs. Or sometimes they get sick from bedsores and they run some high fevers from those, so that's another reason. It sounds like a big number but for these kids it could be normal."

The waitress comes with our dinners and says, "Can I get you anything else?" She says it to Ricky, but I figure it was meant for both of us, so I ask for more napkins.

"Why do they get all those bedsores?" I say.

"From not moving around as much, right?"

The waitress returns with a few napkins and presents them to Ricky. I have the power to become invisible in some restaurants. I just never know which restaurants. Or how to turn the power off.

I say, "But isn't that something they're supposed to do at a place like ILLC? Make sure they move around more? Help them change positions when they're in bed? Take care of their skin?"

I don't really know why I'm pushing this. The thing about shunts makes sense and a lot of crips get sores. Even non-nursing-home crips. But it's a guaranteed side effect of nursing-home living. They might as well put it in the bylaws. I eat a bite of enchilada and drink a little more beer although I can already feel that my face is warm. This whole "nephew's birth-day" thing has put me off my feed.

"I bet ILLC uses the cheapest mattresses on the market," I say. "It's like they want them to get sick."

"What," he says, "you think there's a conspiracy to make them get bedsores?"

"Why not? How else can you explain it?" I can hear myself and I sound angry. I look up at him to see if he's getting angry too. He's smiling at me. Oh. "I'm just—ignore me," I say. "I'm delusional from looking at forms all day."

"I remember this one time though," he says, reaching over to brush some fuzz off my sweater. "The doctor—what's his name?—Spaghetti, Rotini . . ."

"I am not guessing," I say.

"Ravioli," he says.

"Dr. Ravioli," I say.

"Right," he says.

"You mean Dr. Caviolini?"

"Ravioli is easier to remember."

"True," I say.

"Yeah, so Dr. Ravioli sent one of the kids, Michael Jackson—"

"Yeah, I know Michael Jackson," I say. "Not the 'Billie Jean' Michael Jackson—"

"Right, right, the spina bifida Michael Jackson."

"Right."

"So he was fine, right? Totally cool. Great little guy. Out of the blue, Ravioli sends him to the hospital for a week. I drove him over there. Michael's like, 'Why am I going to the hospital?'"

"Why was he?"

"I don't know. When I pick him up the next week, I ask Michael is he feeling better. He says he wasn't sick, he just had some X-rays."

"What hospital?"

"St. Theresa."

"What's that place like?"

"It's empty," he says. "You walk around even a little and it looks like a ghost hospital. They closed up one whole floor. Not enough patients."

"Wow. How do they stay open?"

"I don't know."

"Well. It must've been something. With Michael Jackson. ILLC being a petri dish," I say.

"Ya think? The kids' rooms smell like moldy diapers. And the houseparents don't always clean up after they leave a mess. Some of 'em are cool—Beverly, Toya, Victor—but some of them, I don't think they really give a shit. What do they make? Ten or twelve an hour? So you know . . . it is what it is."

"I wash my hands about sixty times a day now. I'm thinking of buying a Tyvek suit."

"Sexy," he says.

"That's why I'm buying it."

"About time," he says.

"What?" I say.

The waitress comes by and asks Ricky if everything is okay. I realize that not only am I invisible, but she's flirting with him. It's a double-invisibility whammy. That's one of the reasons I do not want to be all involved with anyone. Why do I care about a random very attractive waitress flirting with him? Or anyone flirting with him? I don't care is the answer. He can ask the waitress to go to Chuck E. Cheese.

"What's up?" he says.

"All that data entry was so boring I made up a big mystery to keep myself amused."

"It's good that you question things. I like that about you."

"Thanks. But I don't know what I'm talking about."

"Yes, you do."

"No. I don't know much about the kids. I don't really know

how the money part works. I never paid attention to how Medicaid works. And why are some hospitals full and some empty? I'm just new. At the job."

"No, I hear you."

I eat as much enchilada as I can. Ricky's fajitas are long gone, so I offer him the rest of my dinner and he digs in. For the first time I notice that his face is crooked. He has droopy eyelids with a fat fringe of black lashes and a white scar that runs through his left eyebrow. His hair is black, almost blue, like the way they draw the hair on men in romance comic books. He isn't standard-issue handsome, but he is sexy. I can feel my heart speed up a little just looking at him. Or maybe I'm having a heart attack from the refried beans.

He says, "Can you imagine how those kids would flip out if they served this for dinner over there? Or if they got to eat here? Just go out and eat like this? Something like this—this is a dream for them. My family never went out to dinner. I never ate at a real restaurant until I was like eighteen or nineteen. Not that we were all deprived. We weren't hungry. Not seriously. We ate, but you know, we weren't always sure what we were eating."

"What do you mean?"

"Did I ever tell you about the pig snout?"

"No, that hasn't come up."

"It was actually pretty good. And I go to get some more, right? My mom put it in a stew kind of deal. So I'm trying to spoon up some of the good stuff and I look in the spoon—the ladle—and I notice something in there looks a whole lot like a nose and it's got hairs sticking out of the nostrils."

"Okay, no. You don't want your food to actually look like the animal if at all possible. I could never eat animal crackers for that reason. I thought you were going to tell me something really bad, like—"

"Like we ate cat food or dirt?"

"Exactly," I say. "Or bats."

"Oh, fuck."

"I like you," I say.

"I like you."

"I'm—thank you. You always make me feel better. I—I love being with you."

"I love being with you," he says. Then he looks in my eyes, but I could only look back for a couple of seconds.

"My pupils are different sizes," I say. "You think I should worry about that?"

"Let me see," he says.

I look up at his face again and he smiles and I smile back, but then I look away. I don't flirt. But then I look up at him again.

Yessenia Lopez

Tía Nene would've been proud of me that it took three aides to pull me off Benedicta a.k.a. Shamu. It took Beverly, Jimmie, and Louie. That Louie looks like a cop. I'm not sayin' he *is* a cop? But he got the look.

Benedicta's a freak. Even her lies are lies. She was all crying and acting like Little Miss Who Me when the whole time she had stole my black nail polish that my friend Cheri gave me and what she purchased with money from her own allowance. Benedicta said she just happened to have that same nail polish. Do you believe she had put some of that polish on her nails already? The girl's just not right in the head. Like I told Cheri, if you took my nail polish and you already knew I was a ex-convict and a menace to the society and you knew I had my eye peeled on you anyway? I mean, would you keep stealing from me? Cheri said no, she definitely would not.

And Beverly told Jimmie how this isn't the first time and how me and Benedicta been pushing buttons on each other before, but I think I finally got lucky 'cause that Jimmie?—she a lesbian—Jimmie goes, "Okay, if they don't get along, maybe one of them can move out of this room, move to a different room." Hello! That's what I been saying since the day I got here.

Benedicta perked up at that. She's a wrongful, lying bitch but she knows her only hope is for me to be in a different room. So even though Jimmie is only a aide? She tells me to start packing up my belongings. Beverly is like, "Can you do that?" to Jimmie, and Jimmie is like, "We'll find out." And she laughs and Beverly is all cool, like she's not mad that Jimmie just did that and she likes Jimmie. Maybe Beverly is a lesbian her own self.

I'm gonna be very honest with you now. When Jimmie did that, you could see that that woman was a Person to Know. I hope they don't fire her.

We got permission to move me to my new room from Anissa who is the supervisor in charge of all the aides, a.k.a. houseparents. And while I'm on the subject they better forget about that "houseparent" crap right now. I only got one parent in this life and she's passed, so I don't wanna hear it.

Anissa is a Muslin Indian and she wears a scarf on her head

so you can't see her hair but even with her scarf that woman is hot. I bet the males always trying to get over with her. Today's her last day though, so that's the end of her. I told her, "Anissa, girl, just give me your castaways, that's all I ask."

My new room is the exact same shape of room as my last room but instead of Shamu I gots Cheri, so her and me is both real happy. I repo'd whatever Benedicta stole offa me which wasn't much since I don't barely own nothing. Just what my caseworker got me from the place I lived at before Juvie and before here which was my clothes, my teddy bears—one polar bear and two brown ones—and my crucifix with Jesus on it. I said a prayer to my *tía* Nene who watches over me and loves me very much. I know she's in heaven and is having fun all the time and not worrying about paying her debt on her credit cards.

Cheri's last name is Smith. Me and her is still getting along real good. But she scares me sometimes. One night she started in screaming and woke me up and woke up her own self. I asked her what the hell was her problem and you know what she said? She said there was somebody in her dream saying mean things to her. So I told her, "Cheri, if you got somebody saying mean things to you, you gotta tell them meaner things back." I can see I gots a lot to teach the child.

They got the most stupidest rules in here that I ever heard of. First one is, you got to pass a test to get on the elevator by yourself. Eccuse me? I think I know how to take a elevator!

What I'm suppose to do? *Fly* down the stairs? Did somebody not notice I am challenged? But they still made me take their stupid test and now I can take the elevator all by my little crippled self.

Next thing you gots to do is you're not allowed outside the damn building alone without passing another one of their bullshit tests. By "outside the building," they don't mean plain old outside either. They mean outside like "stay on the grass in front of the door." That's what they're talking about. They think you're too stupid to even walk out the door on your own. I was raised in the city. I grew up in the Puerto Rican ghetto. I think I know how to walk outside a damn door. Anyway, I passed that lame-ass test too.

I know they gots some children here, real children who are below being teenagers yet. But even they know how to walk out a stupid door. There might could be a few children and even teenage ones that couldn't do a elevator by theyself. They too challenged. So I say then help those peoples and leave us others alone with your dumb-ass rules!

Awright. You ready for rule three? You're not allowed alone on a bus—a regular bus that I been taking by myself since I was a *child*—without a houseparent. This is almost worse than Juvie. At least at Juvie you were sup*pose* to be punished. And would you believe that they won't even let me *take* that test till I been locked up in this snake pit for three entire months? Jesus Christ my Lord and Savior, please look down on my sorry ass and give me some serious mercy *please.* I'm so serious.

Me and Cheri only got one more month in purgatory though. Once we pass that test? We're going shopping. If it weren't for Cheri who feels the same way I feel about everything, I don't know what I'd do.

Ricky Hernandez

Pierre's back in the time-out room today. Mrs. Schmidt said he told her he had a stomachache and he kept making whistling noises. I wasn't sure if she meant his stomach was making whistling noises or if the two things were separate. I say to her maybe he could be sick. "You want I should take him to the nurse?" She says, "No, take him to time-out and then come back." I say, "I can't put him in there and leave him alone," and she says to just do what she tells me. She says he just wants attention. The fuck? I'm not going to leave him in there and no one's watching. This Mrs. Schmidt is a piece of work. She's always saying negative stuff about a kid right in front of him and everybody. So I take Pierre out in the hall.

"Hey, let's go to the nurse and make sure you're okay."

"No way!" he says, and he kicks the wall. Kicks it as hard as a kid with rickets can kick a wall. But he's yelling, "No!" and freaking out in general.

"You don't wanna see the nurse?" I say. "You don't have to." We start walking to the time-out room.

"When I was in school," I say, "I had a teacher like Mrs. Schmidt. She was a bad apple, you know? Always talking down to me. But you know what? When I got older I realized she don't matter. She's a blip on the radar, you know what I'm saying? I met lots of other people, teachers too, who treated me real good, respectfully, you know?"

He's not really listening. He's off in Pierreville. When we pass the infirmary and he sees he really don't have to see the nurse he calms down a little and when we get downstairs he walks right into the time-out room, just like he was home. Then he does a few kid-style karate chops to the wall and yells, "Fucker!" at it. I say, "Pierre, if you feel sick you let me know." But then he sits down in a corner and settles his legs so he's comfortable and stares at the ceiling. His body's in action the whole time though. Fiddling his fingers and squirming around nonstop.

I told Joanne about Pierre. What I know about him, which ain't much. She knows who he is and some stuff from his file, so I thought she might like to get to know the little guy. Maybe she might have an idea or two of how to help him. The thing is, Pierre reminds me of my nephew Pucho. They both have that "If somebody tells me to go right, I'm going left" personality. I don't care what is the issue—they both hafta make everything harder than it has to be. I always think of Pucho when I see Pierre.

So Pucho was picked up for possession last week. He runs with a gang, you know? Latin Kings. A real bunch of knuckleheads.

You can't talk to him about it. You say, "You're gonna wind up in jail," he just says, "So?" And online he's got pictures of him all "I'm the man" and wearing his colors and holding a spliff. On Facebook. For the world to see. I talked to his mother, my sister, and she's thrown in the towel. She's like, "What do you want me to do?" I'm like, "Tear the computer out the wall." You know? There is no reason for this crap to happen. I grew up in a tough neighborhood, I had peer pressure, so what? You never saw me joining a gang.

Pucho is smart, he's, you know, talented, his teacher said he has artistic talent, he has good potential. Give him a pencil, a pen, he can draw whatever you say to draw. He sees a woman or an animal and it comes out on paper—exact. But he'll add a little something of his own to give it a twist. He drew a complete comic book once.

I went to visit him a few days ago. Juvie is definitely prison, but it's more like prison lite. I've seen the inside of a couple real prisons, visiting my uncle Ramón at Stateville and when my brother did a year over at Twenty-Sixth and California, a.k.a. County. You get frisked three times before going in, but hey, no problem. I didn't have to go through what my brother did before he got led into the visitor area—cavity search, the whole bit. This is all to humiliate the person—to let him know who has the power. Because they're watching through the whole visit anyway.

I asked him one time, "Hey, are you sure you want me to come back, because I know what you go through," and he said, "Yeah, man, come back." That's intense, you know? Man is so hungry for human contact from the outside he'll go through that humiliation. You know what the inmates call the cavity search? They call it "the wave."

The visitor area is a long hallway, separated lengthwise by real thick glass. The whole place smells like ass. They got these little metal stools screwed down into the floor for you to sit, and for each place to sit, there's a hole in the glass. One hole covered with a—like a metal filter, and you put your mouth up next to that hole and yell through it to the person you're there to visit. Then you shove your ear next to it when you want to hear the inmate, your loved one or what have you. Now this hole is the last place in the world you'd wanna put any part of your body. Every non-toothbrush-using, herpes-covered mouth in the city's been up in that thing. And everybody is screaming because you can't hear anything. There's babies crying, mothers screaming at their kids, pissed-off jealous girlfriends all up in a guy's face through these little holes. The wall under the glass is covered with gang graffiti and there's all sorta nonsense carved right into it. Right next to where I sat one time, I don't know why I remember, someone wrote, "Tip Top is a cunt." Real nice.

But Juvie is no picnic. Those kids are definitely in jail. After you—the visitor—get frisked and go through the thing, the metal detector, you can go sit down at a table and they bring in your loved one and you can play cards and stuff. They do this thing: They got three or four chairs at a table and the backs are numbered. The inmate has to sit in chair number one. At every table, they gotta sit in the number one chair. It's either a one or an *I*. Maybe an *I* for *inmate*. I don't know. But they always have to sit in that chair, and they can't get up at all. They can't stand even. But you can hang with them for an hour, and it's not bad.

When they bring Pucho out, I hug him and I can see he's fighting down some emotion. Tough guy. I wanna go into my "scared straight" routine, but I'm thinking about keeping it loose, letting him talk.

So we sit, and Pucho says, "I thought you were gonna write me off," and I say, "No, I'm not ever gonna do that. But you know, I'm mad at you because I see you throwing away your life."

And he tells me what happened, which basically amounts to yes, there were some drugs in the car, but he didn't know it was there because it was his buddy's car, and it was reefer.

I'm like, "It was just weed?" But I know it wasn't. My sister already told me. He was busted with speed and quaaludes and maybe some X—whatever. He goes on about some dude who has it in for him and he is the victim here and—at this point I can't listen to no more and I say, "Yeah, and you're guilty."

I told Joanne about Pucho. She said, "I think the day will come when prisons will be recognized for what they are and they'll be abolished. They'll keep some of them around as museums, to remind people of the level of barbarity we're capable of. I'm serious. It has to end. It has to."

Uh, Earth to Joanne? Hello? Joanne can be a little nuts sometimes.

She reads books about prisons. I was over at her place one time and I see this thing she cut out from a—like a magazine. Her favorite magazine called the *Plumed Serpent*. It's an article about what the effect is on a person to be in solitary confinement, and that a lot of people in prison have disabilities. It had a section about locking kids up in solitary too. She said even a short time can really fry up a person's brains. She said the time-out room was a kind of solitary confinement. I never thought of that. Which to me is a shock since she grew up a little sheltered and I grew up the opposite. When I was a kid, I thought everybody had somebody in jail. Family, friends, you know. Neighbors. Or getting out of jail, or who'd served time already or whatever. It wasn't until I got a little older that I figured out not everybody had that. That there were all these people out there, mostly white people, who didn't have family doing time.

We ain't made it yet, made love, you know. I don't know what the deal is exactly about why she's holding back. She said she needs to take her time. She's worried I might not like her body. Can you believe that? That's like 75 percent of the women I ever been with. Women are always afraid some guy ain't gonna like their body. Somewhere along the line, a lot of women got some crazy ideas about themselves not being good enough or sexy enough. I know why Joanne feels that way is because of her being in a chair and all that. And I can see why. I mean, *I* can't see why, personally, but when we're walking around, it's true: People look. They do. Maybe they're looking because they think she's hot, maybe they think she's a freak, I don't know and I don't care. I like the whole package. It don't matter to me. When the chemistry's there, it's there.

I'm thinking about all this while looking through that little window watching Pierre asleep in the time-out room. Never went back to see what else Mrs. Schmidt wanted. It's illegal. Leaving a kid in time-out alone is illegal. They all do it here, but it don't make it right.

I don't want to wake him but I can hear kids begin to go into the cafeteria and I don't want him to miss lunch. I wait awhile longer, then I go in there and call his name real soft because I don't want to touch him when he's not expecting it. I did that with him once and he jumped real hard. Maybe someone used to smack him awake in his past. So he comes to and I ask him how he feels and he says, "Can I have lunch?" and I'm like, "Sure, of course, man," and I offer him to take my hand and he does and I walk him over by the cafeteria and send him on his way. That was the first time I ever touched Pierre, not counting the times I was tackling him.

Michelle Volkmann

Tim and his anorexic wife just got back from their cruise all over the Caribbean and he brought everyone in the office coconuts filled with rum mixed with a chocolate-coconut-flavored stuff which is delicious, plus we all got Visa cards with a hundred dollars on them. He is—oh my God—so generous.

He showed us pictures of him and Gail in their stateroom on their balcony with the most incredible food on a buffet. One picture is this big ice-sculpture fountain and Tim told us that instead of water coming out of the fountain it was vodka.

Tim had this long meeting with Dr. "Call Me Roman" Caviolini today. He is always saying to all the girls here, "Call me Roman, call me Roman." Which none of us do. He is such a freak. One time a girl here actually did go out with him and he took her to a man's barbershop at night and it was closed but he had a key and she had sex with him on one of those chairs you sit in when you're getting your hair cut. Dr. Caviolini is not exactly attractive. He's like fifty and that's okay, fine, but he has a potbelly and a mole on his eyelid.

Dr. Caviolini is the doctor for a bunch of the nursing facilities that have contracts with Whitney-Palm. He and Tim have regular meetings about patient welfare and problems at different facilities and that kind of thing. That's another reason I respect Tim is a lot of people at the executive level are only interested in keeping Medicaid and Medicare off their backs and making money. Not that Tim doesn't want to make money. People have a right to earn a good living. This is America, et cetera. But just the fact that Tim takes time to meet with a doctor who works in our facilities is something I truly am impressed by.

After the meeting was over, most of the staff got to have lunch with Tim and Dr. Caviolini and Tim had ordered in this amazing lunch for everybody. He does this every couple of months if there's a special visitor to the office or just for no reason. Today there was a buffet of Greek food with hot gyros and those spinach and cheese pies which I could eat forever and tons of baba ghanoush and a big pan of amazing roasted veggies and that garlic-dill yogurt dip and two dessert trays of custard tarts and baklava. A lot of times Tim gives us his tickets to these galas that the different drug companies do. Like banquets and receptions for doctors and hospitals and nursing-home operators. The food is delicious and sometimes you get these goody bags with Godiva chocolates or fancy soap. The perks here are so good partly because of Tim's philosophy of running a business and keeping the employees happy and motivated.

Dr. Caviolini thinks he's hilarious. He's always telling stupid jokes and he told us he went to high school with some guy in the Mafia. No one believes him. And he's always saying stuff to me which I guess is supposed to be funny like, "When are you getting married? The first or the second?" and I say, "I don't know," and he says, "The first chance you get," and then he bursts out laughing like it's so hilarious. I have no idea what he's talking about. And it pisses me off that he talks about the Mafia because Chicago has a bad reputation and I think people really believe there's still a Mafia here. One of the girls who works here saw a reality show about Chicago Mafia wives. I'm not really a TV person. My parents spent every spare second screaming at each other when I was growing up and they would turn the TV up superloud so I couldn't hear them as much which of course was so not helpful. I don't know why they stayed together as long as they did, but it didn't really help that they got divorced because they just kept screaming at each other every time my dad brought me home from the weekend or if they were on the phone. I have a TV because my mom wanted a new one, so she gave me her old one when I moved here, but I barely ever watch it. When I turn it on it makes me think of them fighting. Maybe its good that it happened though, because now whenever I'm in a stressful situation I'm good at just making my mind go away. Really. It's like nothing bothers me.

After Dr. Caviolini left we all got new assignments and Tim increased my recruiting responsibilities. I have no idea how I'm going to recruit more people than I already am but he also gave me a list of new sites. Some of the sites are on the South Side which that's fine but I really do not know my way around there very well. I told Tim I was uncomfortable thinking about getting lost, so he said the company would pay for a navigation system. And he said if I showed higher recruitment numbers he would increase my bonus from $300 to $350 per bed filled *or* he would buy me a new Smart car if I filled ten beds in three weeks. Which would be amazing except it would also be a miracle because there's no way I could ever fill that many beds in three weeks or six weeks. He said he wasn't telling anyone but me, but the company was expanding and buying a couple new facilities and there were exciting things happening that he couldn't tell me now but it might affect me in a good way.

I would really love a Smart car. The only reason I still have my grandma's gigantic Pontiac with two hundred million miles on it is because she gave it to me when I lived in Merrillville. Where I haven't lived since I got my associate's degree. Then I got this job with Whitney-Palm which is practically all driving. My tires are totally shot and I probably need new brakes and the window won't even open on the driver side which is fine most times but last summer I thought I was going to puke from the heat. I cannot even imagine how fabulous it would be to park a Smart car after having to park this boat in the city of Chicago which I'm sorry but it's like musical chairs because there are twice as many cars as spaces available.

So here I am at Oscar Mayer Children's Hospital at another parent's night at seven thirty at night recruiting my butt off. There's not much of a turnout, only about six parents and the rest are Oscar Mayer staff or other people kind of like me, people who aren't from here but have products or services the parents might want for their kids who are patients. It's a really nice place actually. They have all these toys for the kids and giant pillows that I guess the other children, the brothers and sisters of the handicapped kids, can jump on while the parents are at these educational nights. It's sad because the parents all look really tired. They don't ask many questions, so I don't know what they're getting out of this. They're probably pretty poor because it's a charity hospital. Some of them don't even speak English.

After this I'm going to a shelter for women on Cottage Grove which is on the new list. I'll basically be lucky if I'm home by ten o'clock. Sometimes I feel like all I do is work, go to sleep, wake up, and work.

Jimmie Kendrick

Yessenia has a picture taped to her shelf of a young woman standing behind a little girl with crutches. They're standing on the sidewalk, snow piled up all around. With all those greystones it has to be Chicago. Logan Square maybe. The young woman is leaning over the girl with her arms around her like, you know, like she is showing the girl how to wave at the camera. The two of them are laughing. That look on little Yessie's face was making *me* smile too.

"This your mom?"

Yessie says, "Yeah. My *tía* Nene. She was my mom though."

I had passed her room earlier and I slowed up when I saw her sitting there and she called out my name and asked me did I want to come in.

"You guys look like two peas in a pod," I say. "She's pretty. You look a lot like her."

Yessie didn't say anything back, so I looked at her and she was just smiling and nodding.

I say, "How old were you in this picture?" I wanted to ask her where her mom, or her auntie or whatever, like, where was she? Because it kind of didn't seem like Yessie had anyone.

She says, "I guess I was about three. She didn't get sick till I was ten. She didn't get really sick till I was thirteen."

"Can I ask you—"

"She died. Last year. She had cancer."

"Oh," I said. "I'm really sorry to hear that. You guys must've been—I mean, you can see from this one picture how close you were. For real though, I'm sorry for your loss."

She shrugged. "Yeah, right. Whatever."

I say, "I lost my mom to cancer too. I was older than you though, about twenty-two at the time."

She looks at her lap then and rubs her legs back and forth with her fists. She says, "I'm sorry."

I say, "Hey, you ain't got nothing to be sorry for. Not a thing." I close the door. "*Noth*ing to be sorry for."

She says, "What kinda cancer?"

"Did my mom have? Breast."

"Mine too." Her face started to crumple up.

I put my hand on her shoulder.

She started to cry. I stood there for a minute and patted

her shoulder. I mean, I didn't want to rush her. I was trying to think what I could say next that might help. Even though I know there's nothing really.

"I know it might not feel like it," I say, "but you're going to be okay. It's crazy but the pain you feel kind of changes into something else. I'm not saying you'll stop missing her. You'll always, always miss her. But you'll miss her in a way that doesn't hurt. If that makes any sense."

She says, "How long until the pain changes?"

"Well, you're on the right track with what you're doing now. Talking about her, keeping her picture close, crying out some of that pain. You're doing just what you need to be doing. Time takes care of the rest."

"How long did it take you?"

"Wow. I don't remember exactly," I say, "but I wanna say maybe two years."

"Two *years*?"

"Well, okay, I mean, it's not like you can put a date to it. It's different for different people."

"It could be *lon*ger than two years?"

"No, no," I say. "Two years is probably at the most. But it's different for everyone. One day you wake up and you just don't feel as sad."

"Two years," Yessie says.

"At most."

"Sometimes I miss her so bad I feel like I'm just gonna blow up or—I don't know."

"Hey, losing your mom—uh-uh. That's the hardest thing I ever had happen to me," I say. "So if you ever feel like you need to talk, or even if—if anything, I'm there."

"Like friends, right?"

"Yeah. And I'll tell you about my mom too, because there's times I really want to tell someone about her but I don't know who to tell."

"Jimmie?"

"What?" I say.

"I hope you don't think I'm crazy but I felt like the first time we met when you was pulling me offa Benedicta? I felt like, 'She and me is gonna be friends.' I really did."

"Well, I pretty much felt that way too," I say. "So I guess that's how it's gonna be."

Joanne Madsen

Ricky stops by my office every day after he drops the high school kids off. Usually he closes the door and we immediately start making out like we're giving simultaneous resuscitation. But I still see him touch other people—other women. I guess he's just a person who touches. Women flirt with him a lot. He is fairly adorable. I guess I'm a little anxious about that.

Ricky's comfortable with people in general, but I stay hands off until I get written permission. I never know if I'm reading people's signals correctly. I might assume someone is interested in me and come to find out they're just pondering how I go to the bathroom.

I wasn't always so cautious. I had a relationship once that started out really well, but as things went on, the guy turned mean. I didn't see the signs. Famous last words. The guy—his name was Dennis—started to be really critical of me. Critical of everything after a while—my lack of social skills—and I am just shy, or low key maybe, but he convinced me my behavior was equivalent to projectile vomiting at anyone I was introduced to. He also criticized the way I pronounced words, my taste in music, my clothes, and, to add insult to injury, my body. The guy was an infection. And I let it go on for over a year. By the time Dennis broke up with me—I didn't even have the spine to break up with him—he had pretty well strip-mined my self-confidence. But that came back in time, in little ways at first. I started listening to jazz again, which he never liked. I started using the toothpaste I like instead of his crappy Pepsodent. I started eating tomatoes again because he hated tomatoes. He didn't even want the taste of tomato on my lips. But I also stayed away from men. I stayed away from everyone, really. Until now.

Since I work through my lunch hour, I always take a break later in the day to wander around the halls when the kids are between classes. Some of the kids are nineteen or twenty, so they're mostly out of school, but ILLC runs a couple of classes each day billed as Independent Living Skills classes, which are supposed to prepare them for when they age out of here and which I genuinely hope are not as bogus as they appear to be. The kids are supposed to learn about money—how to make a budget, how to pay bills, all that stuff—but they're learning from workbooks. These are kids who have never had more than a few dollars in their pocket in their whole lives. They've never owned a checkbook, purchased anything more expensive than a Mr. Frosty, they don't have the first clue about banks or monthly statements or buying groceries. Mrs. Phoebe won't even let the kids take the bus alone because she says it's a liability issue. Everything is a liability issue. Ricky said that most of the kids here have never even crossed a street by themselves. Eighteen- and nineteen-year-olds. Kids like this are trained to stay helpless. So they have to stay institutionalized. There's no other way to explain it.

My friend Zora is an activist. She's the one who got me my first subscription to the *Plumed Serpent*. She tried getting me to go to protests about the institutionalization of crips. The thing is, large groups are my bête noire. I finally attended one protest with her a long time ago and it was horrible. The police went crazy. They treated the crips almost as violently as they treat noncrips. There were even a few broken wheelchairs left in the street after they dragged the protesters, including Zora, off to jail. Zora and I lost touch after that. I think she was disappointed in me for leading an empty and meaningless life and enabling my meaninglessness with the settlement money from the Chicago Transit Authority. It's just as well. If she knew I was working in a nursing home for juveniles, she'd hate me.

Sometimes I time my break so I'm there when Mia and her boyfriend, Teddy, get out of class. Teddy showed me how I can attach a bungee cord between one of my handlebars and Mia's armrest and pull her around that way. If you show these kids the slightest bit of attention, they'll become your best friend. They're like sunflowers and you're the sun. But she's not in class today. Maybe she's not feeling well. I can't find Teddy either, which is too bad because I wanted to tell him about my idea.

Teddy will be twenty-two in a few months and he'll be transferred out of ILLC because when you're twenty-two, the state views you as an official adult. But he doesn't have much say about where they send him. It will probably be another nursing home, but not for juveniles. He's this great kid, really funny, always getting into trouble, and a lot of the kids here look up to him. He doesn't have that institutionalized mentality. But he has a significant disability and, from what I can see, no support and no skills that would enable him to survive on his own. He'd be fine with a little help, but how will he hire assistants and pay them or even fire them if he has to? They do a pathetic job of teaching them here. I met Teddy's dad once, and he was great but he didn't seem like the kind of guy who could take on the bureaucracy. Then I was leafing through the *Trib* a few weeks ago and there was an article about nursing-home abuse in a string of places on the north side of the city and in a few suburbs. There was a quote from a lawyer who works at the Center for Disability Justice, a place I'd never heard of. I called and left a message and about a week later Elaine Brown called me back. She said she'd send me some information. I got the info yesterday, so I wanted to show it to Teddy. Maybe he'll want to go over there and meet with a lawyer. Maybe there's a way he won't have to go to another nursing home.

But Mia—I'm not so sure what will happen to Mia when she ages out. She showed me her workbook a while ago. She's basically blind in one eye and needs large print, but her workbook is in regular-size print. So I asked her if she told her teacher and she said no. I said, "Why not?" and she said, "It's okay." So I said, "What if someone said to you, 'Mia, you can't go to school anymore. No more school for you.' Would that be okay?" She said, "I don't know."

It's like she's trying to make herself invisible.

Not that invisibility is hard to achieve when you're a crip. We're minor characters in someone else's story.

ILLC is a state facility, but because the government has been regularly contracting out chunks of its publicly owned programs to the private sector, the state made a deal with a private company to run ILLC's day-to-day operations. So it's not really state-run because now a private company, Whitney-Palm Health Solutions Inc., takes care of everything. Whitney-Palm is supposed to turn ILLC into a well-oiled model of efficiency, and because Whitney-Palm is profit-driven, they're doing everything they can to keep the overhead low. They must be getting paid a nice chunk of change for taking over. The vice president will be at the board meeting tonight. Whitney-Palm only won the contract about a year ago, so I guess I'm getting in on the exciting ground floor of the new and improved state-of-the-art ILLC.

At five thirty I take my yellow legal pad and go to the conference room, tong myself some triscuits and a few cheese cubes, and spear a couple microwaved mini—egg rolls. One of the egg rolls rolls off my paper plate and under the table, but I pretend not to notice and pull into my place for the board meeting.

The board members trickle in. None of them have disabilities or are parents of kids with disabilities, and there's only one person of color, a middle-aged Hispanic man who owns a public relations company.

I don't actually participate in meetings. It's my job to take notes, strictly fly-on-the-wall stuff. Tim McGraw from Whitney-Palm is there, with another Whitney-Palm person named Michelle. She's a patient recruiter. Sounds ominous. She looks like she's in her latish twenties. She wears clear nail polish on long nails, and high, high heels with one of those female versions of a business suit. Pretty hair.

The meeting begins. Whenever anyone refers to disability, they use the word "handicapped." Or sometimes they'll say "handicapped or disabled" together. As if they personally prefer using "handicapped," but they realize there are some new-fangled notions out there about saying "disability," so they're covering their bases. I'm a little stunned the ILLC board is still struggling with this one. It confirms my every instinct that these are some of the very last people I would consider for a body that makes decisions about "handicapped or disabled" kids.

I myself prefer "crip," or variations on "crip," strictly for personal use. Some crips think using "crip" should be retired for good, because it reveals a deep lack of self-esteem, besides sending the wrong message to the noncrip majority. I disagree. I still find "disabled" pejorative. Why not take back the king of all pejoratives, "cripple," and re-empower it by giving it the crip imprimatur? All I'm saying.

Mrs. Phoebe barely says anything at first, just adds a few details. It's weird to see her be so deferential. Tim introduces Michelle Volkmann and explains that she is a valued Whitney-Palm staff member and here to observe. He announces a few things that need to be approved budgetwise, and one by one the board approves his proposals.

Then Tim asks Mrs. Phoebe for her report. Mrs. Phoebe announces that there has been a new lawsuit for wrongful death brought against ILLC by the parent of a ten-year-old boy who was an ILLC resident between 2010 and 2011. She adds that another suit from 2003 and two suits from 2005 have been settled. She reports that ILLC has been staph-free for an entire three-month period. ILLC is at full capacity, or every bed filled, thanks in part to the efforts of Michelle Volkmann. Everyone claps and Michelle thanks them. Mrs. Phoebe ends with a report of a generous private donation to ILLC from the president of St. Theresa's Hospital.

The report sounds disturbing to me, at the very least, yet the board members nod with concentrated expressions, except during the part about the donation, which meets with great approval. I decide to compartmentalize this and get back to it later.

There are a few board members with questions but the whole meeting is over in ninety minutes. No one notices the egg roll under the table.

Teddy Dobbs

Me and Bernard was just standing around by the cart where they keep the cleaning stuff. We was, you know, like standing around. Except we can't stand. Ha. There wasn't nothing going on, as usual. They was gonna make us go to bed in a while. Bernard took the bottle of soapy stuff the janitor keeps on the cart. I took some straws 'cause you can't never get one of those when you need one. I would've took more but I can't close my hand good. Then we left the cart and roamed. That's what I call it when me and Bernard are just walking around with no place to go. Like how cell phones roam. We're just like cell phones.

At night there ain't nothing going on here. Bernard was supposed to go home today for a couple days 'cause he ain't been in a while but none of his brothers or sisters was gonna be there to carry him up the stairs. They live on the third floor. That's another reason we was roaming 'cause we was both in bad moods.

"I'm gonna write to the TV show where they get the guy who gets bullied and the guy who *is* the bully, you know? And say I'm like handicapped and a wheelchair person, right? And tell them all about Louie and they'll get one of those fighters, you know? And he'll beat the crap outta Louie and I'll get ten thousand dollars. You wanna do it with me? I'll give you half."

Bernard said, "What show?"

"The show on TV that has the bully and the guy getting bullied. You gotta see that show. You never seen it?"

Bernard said, "No. You get ten thousand dollars?"

"Where you got ten thousand dollars at?" Yessie and Cheri was in the elevator right as me and Bernard was passing by the elevator. So we went in.

I says, "A TV show."

Yessie goes, "They gots shows where you can win a million dollars. Why'd I go on a show and get me ten thousand dollars when I can get me a million dollars?"

Cheri goes, "I wanna go on *The Price Is Right*."

Bernard goes, "Where y'all going?"

Yessie said, "Nowhere. Where you going?"

I go, "We don't know yet. Wanna come?"

Yessie goes, "Hell yes. We're bored as dirt."

Cheri laughed at that. Cheri laughs a lot. She doesn't talk much. Sometimes she falls asleep. You could be making noise or one time I saw her at dinner with her head on the table. I guess she gets pretty tired.

I go, "Just keep pushing different elevator buttons for a while."

Bernard says, "We gotta bottle of this soap stuff. We might do something with it."

Yessie goes, "Let's ruin something."

Bernard says, "That's what we was thinking."

Sometimes when we get real bored we like to mess things up a little. Mrs. Phoebe got real mad one time when me and Bernard found some superglue and glued the phone receivers to the phones.

I go, "What should we do?"

Cheri goes, "Pour some soap in the pop machine?"

I go, "Yeah, but I like the pop machine."

Everybody said yeah. And we didn't wanna wreck the TV neither.

Bernard said, "Let's sneak in the staff bathroom and squirt soap all around."

Yessie goes, "I'm in."

Bernard goes, "We need a lookout. You wanna be the lookout?"

Cheri goes, "I'll be the lookout."

Bernard goes, "If an adult comes along you have to give us a heads-up. And you gotta talk them out of coming in."

Cheri says, "Okay."

We got out on the ground floor and the first person we see is Joanne. Me and Bernard go, "Hey, Joanne."

Joanne goes, "Hey. What's the word, hummingbirds?"

I says, "How come you're still here?" and she says, "Just finishing up."

I says, "This is Yessie and Cheri."

Joanne says "Hi, Yessie and Cheri. Where are you all off to?"

Cheri goes, "Nowhere."

Joanne says, "Okay, well, have fun. See you later, alligators."

I go, "Bye, Joanne!" When she was gone I said, "I feel bad messing up Joanne's bathroom," and Bernard says, "She can't go in them toilets anyway 'cause they ain't assessable. Joanne's got to go over by the pop-machine bathroom," so I felt okay after that. Yessie says, "You mean she works here?" and Bernard says, "Joanne's cool," and I says, "She's nice," and Cheri says, "Why she in a wheelchair?" and none of us knew.

The staff bathroom ain't too big. Just the two stalls. Cheri's standing outside keeping watch, but me and Bernard and Yessie is all in wheelchairs and my chair is a electric chair, so it's pretty big, so when one of us needs to move we all gotta move to get rearranged.

Yessie goes, "I got a idea. Long as we're here, wanna plug up the toilets? You ever tried that?"

I go, "Last time we was in here we got caught, so we didn't get a chance to do nothing."

Yessie says, "Okay, the best way to do this? Is Teddy, you unroll the toilet paper, and Bernard, you start putting it in the toilet. I'm gonna see can I find extra rolls in one of these cabinets." Then she hiked herself up off her chair and onto the sink-table thing.

I go, "We could start squirting the soap on all the toilet paper too and when they try to flush it'll get all bubbly."

She goes, "Oh Jesus Christ my Lord and Savior, look what I found."

Yessie opened a cabinet and there's about a ton a toilet paper rolls in there. Then we hear Cheri in the hall saying kinda loud, "Hi, Ms. Phoebe," and us three freeze up. Mrs. Phoebe goes, "Hello, Cheri, how are you?" and Cheri says, "I'm fine," and then she laughs and we hear Mrs. Phoebe's shoes walking past.

Then me and Bernard keep on stuffing the toilets fuller and fuller. Bernard shoved a whole roll of it in there.

Yessie squirted soap on the mirror. "Hey, did Old Skinhead really use to be a prison guard?"

Yessie calls Louie "Old Skinhead."

I says, "Yeah, and he has a Taser."

Bernard says, "He *says* he got a Taser."

I says, "You think your dad got tasered ever? In the penitentiary?"

Yessie says, "Your dad's in the penitentiary? My dad's in the penitentiary too! Least that's what I heard. I don't even know my father's name."

Bernard says, "My dad's at Sumter Correctional in Florida."

I says, "Louie told Jason Remke he tasered a guy's balls."

Then we heard Cheri in the hall. "I don't know. I think I hurt my ankle. Can you help me go to the nurse?"

Yessie and Bernard got real still. Soon as we heard Cheri go off we sneaked out. Bernard says, "Cheri's good at that," and Yessie says, "I didn't realize she was so talented," and I says, "Yeah. She's a real good lookout."

We went to the infirmary and got Cheri 'cause she told the nurse she was feeling better. She has a limp anyways but she limped harder for a while just to be safe.

When we was back at the elevator talking about how awesome it was gonna be when Mrs. Phoebe went in that bathroom and tried to flush one of the toilets, I remembered how I didn't think about Mia one time in a whole hour. I wish I could tell Mia how I ain't thinking about her. I don't want to talk about what she did to me. Bernard said I must've done something wrong but I didn't do nothing.

The thing about what Mia did is she didn't even tell me why. I'm going around thinking everything's okay and alla sudden she don't want to be with me. Maybe she thinks she's too good for me. She hurt my feelings and I ain't never gonna be her friend or fiancé no more.

Cheri said, "That was the best time I had since I got here."

Bernard said, "You can be our lookout anytime. Dang, girl. You was good."

Yessie says, "Teddy, I knew you was a badass. That suit's just to throw them off."

I go, "Yeah, I guess I'm a badass."

Yessie says, "Well. It was fun hanging out with you two."

We was at Yessie and Cheri's room. Cheri said, "We could sit at your table for dinner tomorrow."

Me and Bernard said that'd be awesome and then everybody said bye.

Late in the night, I can't make my mind stop thinking. Even if Mia begs me to be her fiancé again, it's too late for her. She'll be real sorry but I won't care. She'll see when I get a new girlfriend and look real happy. I wonder do she have a new boyfriend?

Jimmie Kendrick

I got permission to take Yessie on a little field trip last night. We didn't go exactly where we told them we were going. I said we were going to a Valentine's Day party at Navy Pier. We did go to a Valentine's Day party, but it was at a hall on the West Side where a group of lesbians I know throw a party every year. There are usually three or four hundred lesbians there, and I'd be singing.

I think Yessie is too cool for school. She's my girl. She'd been on me about when could she come hear me and my band. I told her what the scene was gonna be too—like, just women. All types of women, who are all types of lesbians. Now Yessie acts like the world is her yo-yo, okay? But the truth is she's just a kid. You know. She's seen a whole lot of hood life in her young years but not too much of the gay scene, so I was a little nervous.

I came to pick her up at ILLC at about seven and she was waiting in the lobby, all made up and wearing a tight, sleeveless, low-cut top she bought at the Dollar Store. It couldn't have been more than twenty-five degrees outside and do you know that girl was not wearing a coat? I had to get out of the car and go into the building and say, "Yessie, where's your coat at?" She looks at me all innocent. "I don't need a coat. I'm warm enough."

"Oh, really?" I said.

"I don't need me a coat! I'm a warm-blooded person! It runs in my family. We don't none of us ever wear coats because we gots a very high, high ability to stay warm. I'll be uncomfortable all night with a coat."

"Uh-huh. Well, you're gonna have to be uncomfortable because you're not leaving this place without a coat."

When she did finally go back to her room and get the coat, we went back and forth a time or two about her putting the coat *on,* but she finally did.

I folded up Yessie's wheelchair and stashed it in the trunk and we took off. I said, "So how you doing?" and Yessie says, "Do you know this is the first time since before I was a convict that I been out in the night going someplace other than the hospital? Girl, I am *ready.*"

"Wow. That's crazy," I said.

"Can I ask you a question?" she said.

"Course you can."

"When you're not working, do you always dress like a man, or is that your costume for singing in? 'Cause I haven't never seen you out of your uniform."

Now you might be thinking these are the questions I wanted her *not* to ask, you know? But I wanted her to ask. That's another thing about Yessie I like, is that she asks questions. So I answered her. "Well, I always wear men's clothes, but I only wear a suit and tie when I'm singing at something more formal. Like I might not wear a suit if I had a gig in a bar. But I might. It depends how I feel."

"Oh," she said.

"Just 'cause I feel more comfortable dressing like a man doesn't mean I want to be a man or act like a man. You see what I'm saying?"

"I think so. Just 'cause I like to dress like a hoochie don't mean I wanna be a hoochie."

"Yeah, okay, something like that, I guess. Yeah." The girl cracks me up.

"Can I jus' say one thing though? You look good in that suit, Jimmie girl. For a female you make a fine-looking male."

"Thank you. You know who got me this suit?"

"Who?"

"Joanne."

"Who's that?"

"You know Joanne. Joanne! Who works at ILLC? She's in a wheelchair?"

"Oh, *hell* no! She your girlfriend?"

"No, no, no. Joanne's a friend."

"I guess so if she's buying you suits."

"She got me this for my birthday because she knew I didn't have anything to perform in."

"She a lesbian too?" Yessie said.

"Nope."

"Oh."

"You know people who are straight can be friends with lesbians and vice versa. Just like you and me are friends."

"I guess if you like her, I might like her too."

"I think so," I said.

"You got any ciggies?"

"No, I don't got any ciggies! What you want cigarettes for?"

"I like one every now and then. That's all. I'm not a addict."

"Well, I'm glad to hear that."

It started to flurry a little bit, so I turned on the wipers. When I went through the process of getting permission to take Yessie out tonight, I realized I didn't have my story, you know, what I was going to say, okay? I put in the written permission and next thing I know, Beverly's asking why don't we take a whole group of the kids together? She thinks we're going to the pier, right? And I like Beverly, Beverly's cool. And under other circumstances, like, if I was telling the truth, I would've said, "Great, let's—let's go." I hate lying. I don't like myself when I'm doing it, and it's like, once you've told the lie, you have to—to make sure you don't get tangled up in it. I was ready to tell the one lie about where we were going, but then when Beverly asked can she go too I had to improvise and—that's just, once you start improvising, anything could come out. You know what I'm saying? But I think I managed to keep Beverly off the scent.

Yessie said, "So there won't be no eligible men there tonight?"

"Uh, not the kind you're lookin' for."

"Oh, that's nasty. You're horrible."

"Like I said, just women."

"I know. It's just a shame how I'm looking so hot and won't be no males there to fall in love with me. Ain't I looking fierce?"

"You definitely are."

"It is a crime to look this fine."

"You are too much," I said.

"Uh-uh, but for real, Jimmie. I look okay?"

"Yeah, you do. You look really great."

This is the first big gig I've had since coming back from New York. Maybe I should've been nervous but I don't get nervous. Not before a gig. Singing has always come naturally to me and going onstage—it's hard to explain—I mean, it's different onstage than in church, okay? It's weird because in church, I do get nervous sometimes. It's like, being onstage with the band is for *my* glory. But in church it's for God's glory. Whole other thing. But I knew I was gonna give it tonight, I was gonna really open up. Making our way to the dance hall after parking the car with little Yessie keeping me laughing, I felt about as good as I've felt in a very long time.

When we went inside, it was like walking into another world. Everyone dressed up, the DJ working the playlist at top volume, twinkly colored lights all over, and oh my goodness, the women. Women everywhere. Femmes, studs, men trans-women and vice versa, women you didn't know what they were, and a few drag queens to liven things up. All colors, sizes, and combinations. I looked at Yessie to check how she was doing and she looked a little, I'm not sure, I think she looked kind of—worried. I said, "You okay?" and she said, "Uh-huh."

Before we got to move too far into the lobby, this older black woman who was one of the party organizers grabbed my arm and said, "Jimmie?" We followed her to the backstage area, weaving our way through a whole mess of people dancing or standing around talking and drinking. I was trying to clear the way for Yessie's chair, steering women out the way with a hand on their lower backs. It was too loud to ask anyone to move.

Our first set didn't start until eight thirty, so we sat down and Yessie had some pop and I squeezed a couple drops of Singer's Throat onto my tongue. The rest of the band had just finished the sound check and they were getting their last few minutes of chill time in before we went out.

"Did your mama know you was a lesbian?" Yessie says.

"Yeah. I told her when I was about fourteen but I think she

knew before that. She still made me wear dresses to church though."

"You in a dress? I don't think so."

"I know. But my mom was cool with it. After a while. I mean, it wasn't her first choice. But she got past it."

Yessie got escorted back out to the main hall so she could watch the show, and me and the band hung just offstage while we got introduced. I looked out at the crowd and that place was packed. I can't even say how many people were out there cheering and clapping. We always open with "I'm Every Woman." Always. Then we mix it up with some Pattie LaBelle, or Gladys Knight, some Chaka Khan—I sing everybody. I love Anita Baker—"Givin' You the Best That I Got," "Sweet Love." I saw Yessie dancing with three other women at once, young black hip-hoppie lezzies. Yessie was as good a dancer in her chair as everyone else was on their feet, showing off her salsa moves. When I sang "Midnight Train to Georgia," Yessie was right up front, looking up at me with a big smile on her face, so I said, "Hey, everybody! I wanna give a shout out to my very good friend Yessie," and Yessie screamed and the whole crowd laughed and clapped. "That's Yessie! That's my girl!"

"Go, Jimmie!" Yessie shouted up to the stage, and then the crowd went nuts and I sang "You Are My Friend."

Backstage I mopped the sweat off my face, sipped on a bottle of cool water, and stood in front of the fan. There were a gang of people backstage already and I tried to make it over to

Yessie, but oh my goodness, if you could see the women coming up and crowding around, I mean it was crazy. Then I hear
Yessie's voice over the crowd and she's yelling my name and
telling people to move out the way and they actually do. The
crowd just parts for her. I bent down and gave her a big hug
and introduced her to everybody even though I didn't know
who all of them were.

The band had a break for an hour, so we went on out to the
main hall. It was like stepping into the Wayback Machine—so
many people I knew from back in the day. Meanwhile I'm
getting hit on by more women than I know what to do with. I
must've been full-out propositioned like fifteen, sixteen times?
Two of 'em were couples. Do you know I can't remember
the name of one of those women? I'm pretty sure there was a
LaTanya or a Tawanda in there somewhere.

When we were driving back to the center Yessie said,
"Jimmie, you better get yourself some female repellent spray."

"Aw, come on now. Did you have a good time?"

"I had the best time I ever had in my life! I had *so,* so, so
much fun."

"You're not traumatized?"

"I'm not turning into a lesbian if that's what you mean."

Getting to know her is—I feel I understand her, you know?
My mom is dead and her mom is dead. Yessie is—basically
she's on her own. She's got a lot of relatives but nobody close.
And her family is so much like mine. She has crackheads and
crack hustlers in her family, and I have crackheads and crack

hustlers. We both have family in prison. My oldest brother, Richard, is in prison the rest of his natural life.

It was late, so I decided I better walk her up to her room in case she ran into a houseparent questioning where she'd been. The clock was still running on my lie. We got off on two and by then I was pushing her chair because she was dragging. She's got used to a seven or eight o'clock bedtime at this place.

We didn't run into any houseparents. I know Candy is on tonight and Adrian and Victor. And Jerry. Yeah, it's Friday. I am not trying to run into Candy. I helped Yessie get into bed and get comfortable, hung up a few of her things because I know she likes everything neat and tidy. Most of the time she picks out her clothes for the next day before she goes to bed, but tonight the girl was asleep before her head hit the pillow.

Walking back to the elevator I heard a couple of the girls talking in their room, so I dropped by to say good night. They were all like, "Jimmie! Jimmie! You on tonight?" It was Demetria and Krystal. Demetria was half-asleep sucking on her thumb—she's sixteen years old—and Krystal was wide awake. I put an extra blanket on Demetria's bed and gave them both a pat on the head. When Krystal turned over I saw that the bald patch she'd made from pulling out her hair was getting bigger. I'm gonna have to start giving her a comb-over.

I settled the girls down and headed out. During the day you can't hear yourself think, but when they're all asleep you could hear a rat pissing on cotton. That's how I knew I was coming up on Candy. I heard her flick her lighter on. When I turned the corner to the elevator, there she was, leaning back against the wall and sucking in on her ciggie, cheeks all pulled in and one eye squinted against the smoke.

"Hey, Candy. You might wanna think about putting that thing out. We got children on oxygen here, remember?" She looks at me and, I swear to God, aims a stream of smoke right at my face. "Right back atcha," I said, and I stepped on the elevator.

Oh, Candy, Candy. She's a whole *sack* of bitches.

Michelle Volkmann

This woman is just sitting there glaring at me. I'm not looking at her but I know that's what she's doing. I guess I'm supposed to feel sorry for her but oh my God, she is a total bitch. I've been here all morning going through her precious files which by the way are a major mess but I am doing it because it's my job. Like I'm sure I really love just sitting here and going through files all day.

This is not the greatest week for me. I am so embarrassed. I have no idea how, but I got gonorrhea. And I use condoms! I don't understand it. Maybe the condom broke or his disgusting gonorrhea sperm got out somehow and now I have to get tested for HIV in another six months because what if the asshole I slept with had that too? I texted him. He claims he had no idea. The nurse-practitioner told me it's possible he didn't because men don't always get symptoms and then she gives me this lecture about my sex life. *So* not her business. Thank God the drug rep from Pfizer was at our office and he gave me a bunch of free Xanax samples. He has no idea about the gonorrhea, of course. And of course he comes on to me but he's married and I'm really not attracted to him.

So I'm on very powerful antibiotics for the next two weeks. I told my best friend Ariel in Valpo and Ariel said I shouldn't be so down on myself because gonorrhea is just a virus you catch like if you catch a cold or the flu and why are people so ashamed of catching one thing so much more than some other thing? I said because you don't catch the flu from having sex and then I realized that yes, you actually can catch the flu from having sex like if a person sneezes on you, so I felt better.

Plus my mom called to tell me my dad is getting married again. So she's real upset, she was crying, and the person my dad is marrying is young and my dad is fifty-five. I told my mom, "Why are you so upset when you're always saying what a jerk he is?" and she says, "I'm not upset for myself, Michelle, I'm upset for you." So I say, "But I'm not upset," and my mom goes, "You will be when your father dies and all the money he was going to leave to you is going to his bimbo instead." I said, "Mom, I really don't care and I have to go right now, I have work," and she says, "Will you be going to the wedding?" and I say, "I really don't know this second, okay?" But I know I'll go to the wedding. I just don't want my mom to be upset.

She's been divorced from him for thirteen years and she still sits home waiting for him to call. I said, "Mom, I'll come to Valpo this weekend and we can go shopping." She said, "Don't do me any favors," and I said, "I'm not doing you a favor. I just miss you." Which is bizarrely the truth. Then we hung up.

Today Tim gave me a break from recruiting, so I'm at the Illinois Learning and Life Skills Center all day and probably tomorrow and maybe Thursday which is good because I can just work and not think about my mom or the gonorrhea. I'm supposed to gather all the information about what they spend money on here so Tim can see where costs could be cut or scaled back. Even though it's boring, it's also interesting in a way because I am learning so much. So far I hate to say it but it doesn't look like there are very many places to cut back. I know I'll find waste because Tim said this place is basically hemorrhaging money. But the person they have here who does all their data entry is breathing down my neck. All morning she's been like "Blah blah blah blah blah!" She started out nice. She wanted to hear more about Whitney-Palm where I work and do I like my job and the usual conversational things people say. And I am a people person by nature, so normally I really like meeting new people. I complimented her on her work too, just to put her at ease so she wouldn't think I was judging her. Which I am judging her in a way because her data is basically a mess and a whole bunch of information is not even in the computer. Also, she's not very computer-minded or savvy because I saw her cell phone on her desk and it was really old. I also complimented her on how great it was that she had this typing job even though she could only use two fingers. She looks at me like blank faced—just staring at me—and then she says, "Thanks." I guess I was supposed to feel all "I'm this horrible person" because I mentioned her handicap or disability or whatever. So she hates my guts now. Like I give a shit with all the Xanax.

Then she starts asking me about what a patient-recruitment person does, which is mostly what my job consists of. So I say to her, "Well, I go to different places where there are most likely to be people who need help with shelter and medical, and I tell them about Whitney-Palm's lifestyle alternatives and if they're interested I help them arrange to go to live in one of our variety of options." So she says, "*Lifestyle* alternatives?" like I'm a total idiot with my tongue dragging on the floor. So I go, "Yes. Why, is that bad?" And she goes, "I never thought of a nursing home as an actual 'alternative.' No one would ever choose to live in one."

This is *not* what I'm in the mood to talk about right now, so I just say, "Well, everyone has their opinion."

Then she didn't say anything. She just sat there.

I say, "Well, what do you want to do? Throw all these children out in the street?"

"No. But I can think of better alternatives. Would you want to live in a nursing home?"

I say, "If I needed one, but I don't."

She says, "Well, you're lucky you don't need one—yet. But I don't want to take you away from your work."

"Oh, don't worry," I say. "You won't."

Tim said to go through the database for numbers of everything—especially the number of empty beds and how long they stayed empty, and number of beds per aide. So like if there's ten filled beds, how many aides do they need? Also, the amount of supplies the aides go through on average per bed. Also, how many employees and what do they do? Such as nurses, doctors, counselors, physical therapists, kitchen staff, administrative assistants, or security guards. Not teachers because they get paid by Chicago Public Schools. The director of ILLC gave me an organizational chart, but it's out of date like everything is out of date here. You can see why the state needed Whitney-Palm to take over. Tim thinks it's inefficient and could be saving lots of money. He's a genius at streamlining places and in the long run it makes everybody happier—even the patients like it. He did a survey of elderly patients at one of our other properties in South Bend called Sunrise Home and they were fine about living there. But even here at ILLC you can go down the hall and ask the kids at random, "Do you like it here?" and every single one says yes. That's what that Joanne girl doesn't understand because some of these children came from abusive homes or their parents couldn't take care of them.

I also have to go up to the patient floors and inspect the supply closets and all that. I've never been up there, so I'm looking forward to it. If things are so terrible here maybe I can help make it better.

"Ahem."

It's her again. She's so juvenile. I say, "Are you talking to me?"

She says, "Yes. Will you be reviewing patient outcomes?"

So I say, "Patient outcomes?" I have no idea what she's talking about. I mean, that could mean anything.

"Right. The kids who live here. How are they? How is their health? How often do they get sick? Is that something you look at?"

"No, not really. I just get the information about how much everything costs, basically."

"Oh. Okay. I thought you might also be looking at the health of the children. You know."

So I say, "Like if they're healthy?"

She says, "Yes. How often they get sick? How many die and why do they die? How many of them go on to live in their own apartments in the community?"

So I say, "Those sound like good questions." Well, they did sound like good questions. "I'll bring them up to my supervisor and maybe someone can look into it."

Then she says, "You will?"

I say, "Sure."

She says, "Great. Thank you."

So that was the end of that conversation.

Maybe it was inappropriate for me to talk about her fingers

before. It's hard to know about that kind of thing because I don't want to act like, "Oh, I'm going to pretend I don't see it," so then I say something, but on the other hand it's not like I'd say something to Dr. Caviolini about the thing on his eyelid. Whatever it is. A mole or something.

Mía Oviedo

In class I jus' sleep. I so tire all the time. After class Mr. Sokolsky say, "Mia, why you so tire? You don't feel too good?" I say, "I don' know, maybe I got something, maybe a cold." He say, "You wanna go to the nurse?" I say, "No, I seen the nurse. She say everything okay." Mr. Sokolsky is the only one who ask.

In the night I keep awake. I watch the big bird with black feathers. He sit and watch. One night I in my bed and he whisper at me. At first I don't know what he say. He say over and over the same thing. Then I know. He say, "I gonna get you. I gonna get you." Sometime he lift up one of his foots and I see his claws. Sometime he stretching out his wings at me. He whisper, "*Puta. Puta sucia.*" He don' wanna wake up Fantasia. He very careful. Sometime he climb down from the closet and hold on my skin with his claws on me and whisper bad things.

"*Mi putita. Me gusta cuando me llamas Papi.*" I think maybe I going crazy.

Right now I don' feel nothing no more. I too tire. Only thing I feeling when I see Teddy and he so sad. Yessie say, "Why you make Teddy feel so bad? He looking like his dog die." Then I ask Toya or Beverly to take me to the toilet and when they close the door I put my hands on my face an' I cry. Beverly say, "You okay?" and I say, "Yeah. I gotta allergy a little." I don' cry no more.

But if Teddy know about—about it, you know what I saying? About Jerry. How he do bad things to me. Teddy think I making it up. He thinking I a *puta* too.

Joanne, she say I look depress. And I didn' tell her nothing about what happen. Joanne look at me and I bend my head down so she can't see but it don' matter. I think she knows. She ask me, "Why you not with Teddy no more? What happen?" Why eberybody asking me all the time? I tell her I don' know. I don' know why I not with Teddy. I just not. I can't talk about that. She say maybe I gotta talk to a counselor but why I do that? I not a snitch. *No le voy ha decir a nadie.*

Teddy Dobbs

Before Louie can get to me and take me out of drive, I smash my wheelchair into the wall and make a big hole. I back out and go as fast as I can to smash into the wall again and he grabs my handlebars and he's saying, "You retarded little shit," and he tries to get to the gears but I just keep ramming into the wall and backing up into his legs and I can hear Mr. Sokolsky at the door saying, "What's going on out here?" but I keep up ramming the wall and ramming Louie till Louie gets ahold of my gears and then my chair stops dead. I hear Mr. Sokolsky telling the class, "All right, all right now, settle down, it's all over," and the door to my class closes shut. Then Louie starts in pushing me to the time-out room.

He won't shut up. The whole way to the time-out room he's saying mean things to me. I ain't trying to hear him either.

Fuck him. And I don't care if he sees me crying because I ain't crying 'cause of him. I don't give two shits about Louie. I don't give a shit about nobody.

When he sticks me in the time-out room he goes into my pockets and takes my pen and pencil and a dollar I had left over from my allowance and two of my stamps I'm collecting. He says, "I'll just take this, retard," and I say, "Fuck you, dickhead!" He's laughing at me like I'm a joke. He says, "Fuck you, dickhead," like he's aping me and then every time I say something mean to him so he'll leave me be he says the exact same thing back at me. So I just stop talking. Then he makes like he's going out and he stops at the door.

"I can be a good king or I can be a bad king," he says, and I don't say nothing and he walks out the door and shuts it.

Now he's asking me how I'm doing in here. I can see his fat head in the little window they got there so they can keep watch on you.

It stinks like piss in here. They must've had a million cripples piss on themselves and on these ugly-ass carpet walls. They don't have to get locked up in here, so they don't care. You know what I want to do? I want to shoot Mrs. Phoebe up with drugs. I'm gonna steal drugs from the infirmary and sneak up on her and stick a needle right in her butt. Then I'm gonna get Bernard to help me drag her ugly self into the time-out room and lock her in here and leave her here and when she begs and cries to get let out I'm gonna say, "I'm afraid there ain't nothing I can do about it, *Phoebe.* I'm real sorry about it."

Me and my dad went to Mrs. Phoebe's office this morning 'cause she's telling us what the deal is with shipping me outta here. She says they're sending me to Maywood way far away in two months. My dad asks her can't they send me someplace closer to home? Closer to where he lives so's he could come visit easier and she goes, "I'm sorry. It's a very nice home. I think Teddy will be happy there." But I won't be happy. My dad's gonna have to take about fifty trains out there and he works all night at the restaurant and they cut his hours back, so he's trying to find a extra job, and I won't never see nobody.

And Mia *hates* me.

I don't know what I did, but Mia won't barely talk to me. She don't even look at me.

I want to stab myself in my stomach with a knife. That would feel better than what she did to me. I asked Fantasia if Mia was mad at me and she just shakes her head and won't say anything. I want to know what I did! Or maybe Mia loves somebody else. If she's got a new boyfriend, he's dead. What're they gonna do to me? They can't do nothing worser than I feel now. When I'm in prison Mia will know it's her fault and she blew it. She turned around her back on the one man who really loved her.

I don't care who sees me crying, this retarded Louie or nobody. He's more retarded than me.

One day when I'm out of here and I live on my own I'm coming back and burning this place down. First I'm getting the kids out, but then I'm gonna blow it up. With Louie and Mrs. Phoebe in it.

I cursed out Mr. Sokolsky. Maybe that was bad but I—Mia's in that class. She don't say nothing or pay attention. She closes her eyes like she don't wanna see me. She goes to sleep. I'd like to see Mr. Sokolsky try to sit in the same room as the girl who was his fiancée and then she acts like you better go forget it. She won't even tell me what I done. At least at Maywood I won't be in this place and I won't have to look at her no more.

I want to live with my dad again. I want to go home. When I lived with my dad it was better. It was more normal. He doesn't really know how mean some of them are here. He wouldn't never stick me in a room by myself. I'm sorry I told Mr. Sokolsky to get out of my face and threw chalk at him. But why'd he have to call Louie?

I'm getting out of here. I'm running away for real. I'll get a job and my own place. I'll watch TV all night. I'll eat at McDonald's.

Yessenia Lopez

I go to a counselor now called Mr. Bonelli. I told Mr. Bonelli about how Jimmie took me out to the lesbian party and how Jimmie is a singer and she sounds like Patti LaBelle except better. I told him that every female at the party was a lesbian and he says, "Are you a lesbian?" I just knew he would say that. So I say, "If I am or I'm not I don't see how that's any of your business." Well, I didn't! I told him one thing and all of the sudden he's all, "Are you a lesbian?" He don't ask me about Jimmie, he don't ask me did I have a good time. No. He just wanna know am I a lesbian. I see from that a little bit how a real lesbian must feel every day when the very first question people gots for you is, "Are you a lesbian?" And then I had a worse thought about my own self. Maybe I don't *say* it? But I think it. That's the same shit as how everybody look at me and say, "Oh, that girl's in a wheelchair, she can't do nothing." Even Tía Nene who loved me with all her might thought deep, deep down that poor Yessie wouldn't never be able to do a damn thing for herself.

Mr. Bonelli says he's sorry he ask. I say fine and for his information I am not a lesbian. I just want to be honest. Seeing as he write every itty-bitty thing down on my file. I'm only there in the first place because it's a condition on my parole.

I told my friends at Hoover all about Jimmie. Like Veronique who I see now that I can go back to classes. I told her how Jimmie wears jewry in her nose and her eyebrow and in her lip, and how she gots locks that hang down her back and she looks so, so, so cool. I even told her how her pants ride low on her butt so you can see her boxer shorts just like half of the males we see walking down the hall at school every day. I told her how much me and Jimmie talk all the time and how she misses her mama just like I miss my *tía* Nene and how I can tell Jimmie everything and she respects what I got to say. Veronique is my friend? But she thinks being a lesbian is bad. I can see right now how that could be infecting my feelings about her because I thought she'd be happy for me that I got someone I can talk to but she isn't happy. That's all right. Cheri is my friend now. Jimmie said that's how it is sometimes. You got some friends who are your friends for a while and then you got your friends who might be your friends forever and a lot of the time you never know which ones gonna last and which ones gonna just fall down on the side.

You wanna hear something that happened to myself and Cheri when we was just walking down the hall at ILLC minding our own sweet businesses? We bump straight into this female who it turns out was the person what talked Cheri's mama and daddy into shipping her butt off to ILLC. This chick is all "Hi!" and tossing her hair all over the place like she's Barbie in her Dreamhouse. "Hi! How are you! Do you remember me?" The look on Cheri's face could have stopped a bullet. I swear her face got so mad-looking and her good hand is clenching in and out and then she just let loose. "Don't you talk to me like we's friends! You are a liar! You get outta my sight before I beat your ass!" That was the first time I ever seen Cheri mad. I thought she might really jump on her for a minute. If I wasn't on parole I would've jumped on her my own self and pulled that bitch's hair out. Just so I could be a good friend to Cheri. But I'd have to catch up to her first. That girl's high heels clicked away so fast to Mrs. Phoebe's office that she left a trail of dust behind her.

Me and Cheri told Ricky the whole story when we was in the bus and he was mad for us. Even Ricky wanted to go kick that female's ass. He said how he was gonna tell Joanne. Ricky don't say so but we can all tell he thinks Joanne is the Queen of Sheba.

I can't hardly believe Cheri is a mentally ill schizophrenic sometimes. But two nights ago she woke me up and told me she was seeing patterns on the wall and she had some bad thoughts running through her head. I said, "What kind of bad thoughts?" and she said, "Bad thoughts," and I said, "What *kind* of bad thoughts?" and she said, "Just bad thoughts." Then she walked out the room—just walked right out in the middle of the night. So I real quick got in my chair and followed her out 'cause I was kind of worried for her but also I didn't want no maniac loose running the halls and I wanted to tell somebody even though Cheri is my best friend. I saw her get into the elevator, so I rushed and got in the other one. When I got downstairs I didn't see her, so I woke up the night nurse and told how Cheri was running loose, so we went looking for her which didn't take too long because she turned on the TV in the TV room and it was *loud*. It was *loud* loud. The nurse told me to go back to bed but I said hell no and when we got in the TV room the nurse says to Cheri did she know what time it was and Cheri said, "Uh-uh," and the nurse said, "Three thirty in the morning and it's time to be in bed." And Cheri said, "Okay," but then all of a sudden she screams and my heart flipped around and the nurse jumped up like she just been goosed by King Kong. The nurse said, "What's the matter?" and I said, "She keeps seeing patterns," and Cheri said, "I'm feeling very agitated." The nurse said, "Did you take your medicine tonight?" and Cheri said, "I ain't sure." Then the nurse said, "Well, do you think you did?" and Cheri said, "I probably didn't because I'm feeling so agitated." So we went back to the infirmary and Cheri took her pill.

I said, "What's your name?"

"I'm Nurse Jackson," she said. "But you two can call me Lorraine."

After that Cheri did go to sleep for real.

I never seen that nurse before because she works graveyard shift. You know how a smell sometime make you think of something? Well, Miss Lorraine smelled like my *tía* Nene, and I had that good smell in my nose when I went to sleep.

Joanne Madsen

The more I rely on Ricky, the more complicated things get. Not that he minds. He loves driving around in the bus together. In the beginning everybody loves doing everything for the other person but then one day it's not convenient and then it turns into something you *have* to do all the time or you're just not in the mood to see the person every single minute, and before you even notice, you've become the white man's burden. Or in this case, the Puerto Rican man's burden. And there goes the romance.

Ricky is picking me up at the AutoMex on Racine at six o'clock, but I have some time to look through the file of a kid he's been asking me about. His name is Pierre Washington and Ricky is frequently called upon to put him in the time-out

room for crimes against humanity such as whistling or jumping out of his seat. I've seen Pierre in the halls a lot but never
had a conversation with him. He's almost always alone.

The way these files read is very bare-bones, just an accumu-
lation of forms really. Here are the highlights: When Pierre
was five, he was picked up by the police when they saw him
looking for food in a grocery store Dumpster. It was snow-
ing and he wasn't wearing a coat or shoes. They found his
younger brother at an apartment that looked like it had been
abandoned. The kids were taken out of the apartment and put
in custody of Family Services. Pierre was put into foster care
but there's nothing in the file about what happened to his little
brother. Pierre had at least three different foster care place-
ments. No details are given. When he was eleven—God, this
is so fucked up—he was transferred to a residential treatment
center. He was diagnosed with cerebral palsy—which is weird
because according to Ricky he doesn't even have cerebral palsy.
He also has learning disabilities and attention deficit/hyper-
activity disorder. ADHD. So he was a hard-to-place, disabled,
African American eleven-year-old and he was lost in the ma-
trix. I'm filling in the blanks here. Poetic license. Somewhere
there should be medical test results and psych evals but not
in this particular file. They transferred him to a residential
treatment center called Moreland Estates in Indiana where he
stayed for three years. I don't know anything about Moreland
Estates but their website listed lots of very good activities and
services. Pierre was transferred to ILLC after one of the staff at

Moreland Estates hit him in the head with a wrench. Nothing about whether there was long-term damage.

The most informative document was from Pierre's case-worker, Clarinda Cummings at Family Services. She must have been the one to get the call from Moreland. Clarinda called Pierre's Guardian *ad litem*—GAL is what they say for short. A GAL can represent a ward in court and is supposed to make sure the kid gets the best placement. Even a guy can be a GAL. Ha-ha. From what it looks like in the little narrative, the guardian went over to Moreland and asked to know the name of the person who hit Pierre, but the staff closed ranks. She must've brought a camera too because it says she took pictures of everything—Pierre's room, the rooms in the institution, the hallways, et cetera—but none of those pictures were in the file. There was one of Pierre which was taken at the hospital. It shows the gash in his head. She must have found out who hit him because at the bottom it says he was charged with a felony. She's the one who had Pierre transferred to ILLC.

When Pierre came to ILLC they did another psych assessment that broadened the description of his disabilities. The cerebral palsy had already been changed to rickets on some form I didn't have, he still has the ADHD diagnosis, and they added post-traumatic stress disorder, PTSD, and oppositional defiant disorder, or ODD.

I Googled ODD and it's—well, it's got a lot of behaviors listed. And the problem with looking any health condition up online is you get lots of words and scary acronyms that give you only a tiny sliver of true understanding about a particular human being. I looked up my own disability once and it scared the crap out of me. I could hardly recognize my own experience. Some of the technical descriptions were totally creepy and they had no relationship to my real life. I think doctors use the worst-case scenarios in order to be published. In my opinion.

I Googled ODD anyway. It sometimes develops in kids with ADHD, like Pierre, and sometimes not. The articles don't talk about the nature-versus-nurture aspect, at least the ones I read. It seems to me that if the nurturing is bad, a kid is more likely to develop some symptoms of ODD. The symptoms are basically the symptoms of an extremely angry kid. I can understand why Pierre might be angry. Even without being hit in the head with a wrench.

I tilt back in my chair and look at the spiderweb in the ceiling corner in my office. It's a big, fresh-looking web but the spider is AWOL. You see that a lot. Web minus spider. Where did it go? I have an irrational fear of spiders. Even seeing the word *spider* on a page scares me a little.

At quarter of six I go into the bathroom and empty my leg bag, wash my hands, and brush my hair. I look in the mirror. I look good. I go back to my office and fold up some notes about Pierre's file and put them in a file folder and stick the folder in my satchel, and put on my coat and scarf and earmuffs and mittens.

In the hallway I see Demetria and Patricia, who want to give me a beauty makeover. Demetria says, "First we'll give you a facial and then we'll do your hair—"

"You gave me a facial last month." My whole face broke out into one megapimple.

Patricia says, "Hey, Joanne! Hey, Joanne! Joanne—we, we could, we'll do your hair. We'll straighten it and we'll dye it—"

"But my hair's already straight."

"No, we'll make it real straight. Like flat."

"Okay. No hair dyeing."

"Not all of it, just streaks."

"And Joanne, Joanne—I'll do your face, okay? I'll make you beautiful."

"I can't do it tonight though. I have to go. Can we do it some other time?"

"Tomorrow?"

"No, next week, okay? I gotta go." I start heading toward the lobby. "No hair dyeing. Everything else would be great but no hair dyeing."

"We won't."

"Joanne, Joanne—"

"I gotta fly! See you tomorrow. Bye."

It's dark outside. There are a few streetlights and one of those big blue light thingies that the city installs to scare the gangbangers. The night is clear and brittle and the air feels refreshing after the stifling confines of the center. You know what people say when I tell them I work a few blocks from the old stockyards? They ask me if it still stinks. I don't get that. They closed it in the early seventies. But almost everyone asks.

I take my earmuffs off. It feels a little bit like spring. All winter I feel two-dimensional and when the weather loosens up I get my third dimension back. When there's no traffic I like to get on the smooth pavement, so I'm pretty much flooring my chair down the middle of the street. It feels wonderful.

I pass the Meat Authority and turn the corner to meet Ricky at AutoMex.

And there he is, waiting for me.

"Hey," he says.

"Hi. You waiting for me?"

"Uh, yes." Except he says "yes" real long and drawn out, like some comedian, but I can't remember who. We turn the corner and start walking toward the parking lot.

"Hey," I say, but just then there's a big gust of wind and he doesn't hear me. "Hey!" I yell this time, and I stop.

He turns around. "What?"

"Come here."

"Why?"

"Come over here, okay?"

He walks back and looks down at me. "What?"

I reach out and grab his jacket with my gimpy hand. "Let's go home and go to bed."

He bends down and smiles. "Really?" he says.

"Yes."

"Really?"

"Yes, definitely."

Then we kiss and kiss again. Then we look at each other.

"You have no idea . . . ," he says, grinning now.

"But first, dinner," I say.

It feels so good, kissing his warm mouth in the cold air.

Ricky Hernandez

After I unload all the kids from Hoover, I run into Jimmie. She wants to talk to me. We walk over by the cafeteria, sit down. The place is empty but the food-service people are cooking something for dinner. Smells like cheese sandwiches.

"Okay," Jimmie says, "I know you keep an eye on Pierre and I wanted to give you a heads-up on something. You know he keeps food up in his room?"

"I know he has a thing about food," I say. "I know he worries over it, like if he feels he might not get enough, he might snatch some extra. What happened?" I'm starting to get a sick feeling in my gut, and I think I better brace myself 'cause I'm about to hear something I don't wanna hear.

"This is just what I heard," Jimmie says, sighing. "Okay. Toya told me that Louie changed Pierre's treatment plan because

Pierre's been acting out, like, you know, stupid stuff, like Pierre took off his shirt when he wasn't supposed to and he wouldn't go to his room or something—just the usual. So Louie's been getting Pierre's meals withheld. This afternoon Louie found some food under Pierre's mattress—"

"Where's Louie?"

"Ricky! Chill, chill, okay? You need to be cool or I can't tell you this."

"Where's Pierre? Time-out room?"

"Well, yeah, but there's more to it. Louie lost his cool. Like he went looking for Pierre and when he found him he dragged him up to his room and sorta—he was Louie, okay? He was a pig. Toya said it was not cool. Pierre just—he just shut down, you know?"

In my head I'm sorting through what Jimmie's saying, but at the same time I'm thinking of tearing Louie's nose off.

"So Toya goes in there while Louie's going off on him," she says. "Now Pierre's on the floor, sitting on the floor, and Louie kept telling him to get up. But Pierre won't do it. Louie starts shouting in Pierre's ear, 'Get up! Get up!' but Pierre won't budge. Toya said she tried to butt in but Louie was screaming, you know, like Pierre not getting up was this big thing and he had to get up. But the more he yells, the stiller Pierre gets. So he grabs Pierre up by the arm—"

"That fuck! I'm okay. I'm okay."

"—and he's walking real fast holding Pierre's arm and Pierre's just—he couldn't keep up. Toya said she followed

but she couldn't take on Louie. Of course. I mean, of course.
When they get to the time-out room Louie puts Pierre inside
and leaves. Toya went over and looked in on Pierre but he
didn't want to come out."

"Did Louie hit Pierre?"

"I really don't know," Jimmie says. "I don't think so. Toya's
up in Pierre's room cleaning up, so maybe you want to talk
to her."

I take the stairs. I don't wanna run into anyone. All I see on
my way down the hall to his room is a few of the boys. Tony,
Michael, DeLeon. In Pierre's room, his roommate José is in
there putting on shaving cologne. He probably has on half
a bottle already. José is thirteen years old and looks like he's
about eight. He looks up at me when I walk in and says hi.

"José, you seen Toya?"

"No, she's gone somewhere. I'm going to eat dinner. You
wanna come with me?"

"Not today, man."

José rolls outta the room. I walk over to Pierre's bed. The
mattress is gone. Toya's probably off looking for a replacement.
There is a frozen hamburger box under the bed that has a stink
rising up off it like old diapers. How can it be stinking in here
and no one noticing it till now? Three of those little minimilks
under the bed. The room smells like a combination of ripe
garbage and Brut. A bunch of Pierre's stuff is scattered on the
floor. These little cards he collects, size of baseball cards but
they have pictures of old-time TV shows, one of Barney Fife

tied to a tree and it says "Stumped" on it, and one of Aunt Bee and Andy, a Ted Baxter card from the *Mary Tyler Moore Show*—all sorta stuff like that. About thirty or forty cards. I gather them up. I look around in his closet and find a couple bags of Fritos and a dusty taffy apple. I grab the Fritos.

When I get to the time-out room, I knock on the door. Not hard, just a tap. "Hey, Pierre? It's me, man. It's Ricky. Okay I open the door a little bit?"

Nothing.

So I tap again. I say, "I'm just gonna open it a little bit, okay?" Nada. I'm sweating now. I can feel my face bead up and a drop runs down my chest. I ain't hot, I'm scared. I open the door real slow. He's balled up in the corner. I crawl in and sit down next to him, reach over, and pull the door shut.

"Jeez, it's cold in here. You cold? You want I should put my coat over you a little bit?" He's not talking but I put my coat across the front of him because I'm not kidding, it is fucking cold. For a while we just sit there not saying nothing. Then I take out his cards and we sit awhile looking at them. He has a few really cool Three Stooges ones. Real collector's items. He could probably get some decent money for these on eBay. I guess we sit in there for an hour or so. I don't know what to do. You can hear noise and kids talking a little bit—must've been coming from the cafeteria. I nudged Pierre awake—he had went to sleep—and we end up walking down to the cafeteria and eating dinner together. I didn't want to leave him alone in case Louie showed up.

I told Joanne about it later in bed.

"Whole time we're in that room, does anybody come looking for him? Do they wonder, 'Oh, where's Pierre?' Hell no. And when we get to the cafeteria, guess who's working the shift on the boys' side that night?"

She's running her fingers through my hair and stroking my face and it feels good. It feels unbelievable.

"Who?" she says.

"Jerry," I say. "And I know I can't deal with Jerry. Because I wanted to tell whoever, 'Look, keep an eye on Pierre tonight, okay? He's a little sensitive tonight.' You know, whatever whatever. But I don't want Jerry around Pierre. Jerry's not responsible. Guy leaves a trail of slime behind him when he walks."

"So what'd you do?"

"So I get the idea to go by the infirmary, see if I can give the nurse a heads-up. There's this—"

"Good idea."

"Yeah. And there's this nurse Lorraine who's there nights— do you know her?"

"No."

She's rubbing her nose against my cheek a little. She has this real soft little nose.

I say, "She's gonna check up on the kid and make sure he gets a clean mattress."

"Mmm," Joanne says.

"Come here."

"I am here," she says.

"Come closer."

"Like in your nostril?"

"You feel great," I say. "Oh, man. You feel amazing."

"Ow. You're on my boob."

"Can I kiss it and make it better?"

"Uh-huh," she says.

And after that we don't do much talking.

Maybe I'll call the nurse later. Check on the mattress situation.

Jimmie Kendrick

By the time I got home and parked, I think I walked to my apartment in my sleep. I took a shower—last shower I had to give that day—and lay down on my bed and closed my eyes. But sleep wouldn't come.

It was just me and Beverly on the girls' side today. Toya, Anthony, and Louie on the boys' side. But Toya called in sick and they didn't even try to find a replacement. Normally, Toya would float between both sides, but when she's not there, I don't like asking a male aide to help out because the girls don't like it and I don't blame them. But Beverly's cool. I like working with her, I really do. But seven, eight kids apiece is just—uh-uh. It's ridiculous. Day like today, I had eight kids. Seven need help with pretty much everything. They have to use the toilet and get showered and ready for bed. But all of them need your time. I don't care who the kid is, he or she is going to want to talk about their day, ask you questions about any- and everything. They might be upset about something or not feeling well. I mean, it's more than just going through the motions. You have to be there, be present.

Then you have to clean up. Wipe down their shower chairs with alcohol, pick up, collect the laundry, collect the garbage, all of that. There are not enough hours. No, that's not true. There just aren't enough aides.

Right now my back aches, my *feet*, oh my God—just throbbing, in Technicolor and surround sound. It's bad enough when you have two other people but—I don't know, it's like they're trying to get us to quit. I don't know what they're doing but I swear to God, they are working . . . us . . . to *death*. I guess when they can't work us any more they'll hire new people. Work *them* to death.

Yessie lied to me today. One of the younger kids here, Heaven, has like six dollar bills folded up into an empty box of Raisinets. And she told a couple of friends which was a mistake and word got out. Now, I was up on the third floor at one point looking for some tape and nonstick gauze, and who do I happen to see coming out of Heaven's room? I say, "Hey, you, what brings you up here?" Yessie says, "I was just looking to see if Heaven was here 'cause I wanna give her one of my teddy bears. From my collection? 'Cause I said I might and she's not here, so I'm going now."

I can already tell from, you know, everything . . . that she's telling me a story. And it's fiction.

I say, "Why you want to give one of your teddies to Heaven? I didn't know you and Heaven were friends."

She says, "I just wanted to because I was thinking I didn't like my teddy bears anymore, so I was gonna give one of 'em to one of the kids. I probably won't 'cause she's not here, so I'm just gonna go see can I find Cheri."

I say, "You can give it to her at dinner."

Yessie says, "Okay, that's a good idea. Bye, Jimmie."

Like Yessie's planning on giving her prized possession to a kid she never said a word to in her life. This is not the first time either. Just a few little incidents, but coincidences add up. This time I decide to do something about it.

Half hour later I track down Heaven and bring her to Yessie's room. I mean, Heaven is young. She's eight years old. Real good kid and no pushover. She keeps that Raisinets box tucked into her undies. Yessie's laying on her bed reading the *Enquirer*.

I say, "Look who I found."

Yessie looks at me like, blank faced. I bet she's already forgotten the whole thing. She looks at Heaven like she's never seen her before. Then you can see the lemons on the slot machine sorta line up in her mind.

And I'm waiting to see, is she gonna come clean or is she gonna keep up the lie? She says, "Oh, hi, Heaven. I'm so glad to see you."

She's keeping up the lie.

Heaven says, "What you wanna see me about?"

Yessie says, "Nothing. I mean, I thought I might give you something but I changed my mind. Sorry."

Heaven says, "What do you wanna give me?"

Yessie says, "Nothing. I told you. Thanks for coming over though. It was so nice of you. Thanks, Jimmie."

But I keep standing there with Heaven who can't go anywhere because she's in a manual chair.

Heaven says, "You want me to come back and see you?"

Yessie—who is already back to reading her *Enquirer*—says, "No. That's okay. Bye."

So me and Heaven start to leave. But before we do I say to Yessie, "I'm onto you." Yessie says, "Huh?" and I say, "Never kid a kidder." Then Heaven says good-bye to Yessie and we start on our way to the cafeteria. I hear Yessie call after me, "I have no idea what you're talking about," and I call back, "Oh yes, you do."

My mother could see right through me. All us kids, and there were eight of us. Knew we were lying before we did. And oh my God, I used to tell some ridiculous lies. One time she told me to be home before dark and I got home late. I said, "But it's still light out. See?" and she looked at me and said, "You're grounded," and I said, "But—" She was already walking away by then.

I'm not Yessie's mom. But I couldn't let her get away with it. I can't ground her, I mean, it's not my place, and anyway, around here the way they punish you is . . . not my style.

I want her to know though. Don't lie to me. I won't tolerate it because I am on your side.

A kid, a teenager like Yessie, ward of the state, I mean, I don't know from personal experience but she must wonder sometimes, like, "Who *is* on my side?"

Yessenia Lopez

Me and Cheri was on our way to get some Pepsi out the pop machine and when we passed Joanne's office we stopped in to say hi. I like her office. She decorated it with little pretty bowls and she got some pictures up on her wall. She had some new pictures up since last time I was here. One of 'em is of the hottest, most handsomest male I think I have ever seen. Oh my *God.* Who is the boy and what is he doing up on the wall in Joanne's office? I wanted to ask but Cheri was telling Joanne about how all she wound up at ILLC.

Cheri says, "I wouldn't even be here if it weren't for that Michelle girl."

Joanne says, "What Michelle girl?"

Cheri says, "The girl who talked to me at the shelter that time. I just thought she was being my friend."

I say, "Cheri told that Michelle girl that she got schizophrenia and then Michelle called Cheri's parents and talked them into shipping Cheri off to here and now she can't get out. I told Cheri she's going to have to stop telling everyone and they mama she gots schizophrenia. People gonna think she's crazy."

Joanne says, "I met her."

I say, "Who?"

Joanne says, "That Michelle girl."

Cheri says, "Can you get her to talk to my parents and say they should let me come home?"

"I'm—well, I'm not sure. I don't really know her, I just know who she is."

I says to Cheri, "If anyone can help you get home, it's Joanne."

"Wait a second. I doubt I can help," Joanne says. "Even if I talked to her it's extremely unlikely that she would be willing to turn this around. To help you get home, I mean. Her job is the opposite of that. She gets people into nursing homes and other institutions for a living. She got paid for convincing Cheri's parents to send her here."

Cheri says, "Can you call my parents?"

"Oh, Cheri, I . . ."

Joanne starts in shaking her head and looking down at her hands and shaking her head some more.

Then she says, "I will try to see if there's anything I can do. But listen, shh, shh, now listen. I probably can't do a thing, I just want you to understand. But I'll speak to someone I know about this. And I'll get back to you as soon as I can.

"One more thing," Joanne says. "You cannot say a word about this. Not one word. If you talk to each other about it, make absolutely sure no one is listening, okay?"

"Yes, ma'am." Me and Cheri both said that practically in the same second. Then Joanne asks Cheri to tell her about why she got into a homeless shelter in the first place and Cheri tells her about the naked T-Mobile guy in her bedroom and all that and Joanne asks her when she got diagnosed with schizophrenia. Cheri says, "Um, when I was in grade school my mom heard me conversating with myself in my bed and laughing."

I say, "She sees patterns sometimes and sometimes the patterns is covered in blood and she gets so, so, so scared."

"Yes, sure, I can see why," Joanne said. "I promise to do my best. Just don't get your hopes up."

"I won't." But Cheri was smiling when she said that, so it was too late not to get her hopes up.

It looked like they was stopped talking, so I says, "Joanne. Girl. Tell me who is this hunk of man meat you got taped up on your wall?"

"Him? I don't know. He's some random crip at a crip-rights protest. I found the picture in this little magazine I read called the *Plumed Serpent*. It's a cool picture, don't you think?"

"Oh my God, this boy is beyond hot. Cheri, come look at this succulent male. Why's he got chains on him?"

"That's part of the way they protest when they're really mad about something. He's trying to shut down a building where—well, it's complicated—okay, in this building they have senators and other politicians who support nursing homes. He's chained up to the doors so no one can go in or out and the police can't pull him away."

"You don't want to play with them po-lice."

"I know. Do you want to look at the article that goes with the picture?" Joanne says.

"No. But can I have the picture?"

"Absolutely. Take it. I'll bring more protest pictures. Mrs. Phoebe will love it."

I say, "She will?" and Joanne says, "Sarcasm."

When I get the picture of the angry, succulent brother down off the wall I look at him closer and I swear my heart starts beating straight out my chest. He has long locks to his shoulders and I can imagine myself braiding them and looking into those big, fierce-looking eyes. I fell in love then and there.

When we get by the pop machine later, Cheri says, "Why do Joanne call disable people crips?"

I say, "Oh, that's just Joanne."

She says, "Do she think we're crips?"

"Yeah, probably," I say. "I hope so."

Mía Oviedo

Beverly push me to the infirmary. When we come there Beverly say, "Okay, let me get back up there. Ask the nurse to call up there for me when you're done, okay?"

She put me where you wait for the nurse. I can't stand no more how bad it hurt. Down there, you know? Is like burning and hurting so bad. I feeling hot.

Beverly say, "You need anything? Drink of water? Have the nurse call upstairs when you're done now."

I saw him. He come after dinnertime. I keeping my head down but I see Fantasia go away from me real fast alla sudden. I pray I am too sick to go back in my room after. Maybe the nurse let me sleep here. Please, please, God, let me sleep here.

"What's the matter tonight?" the nurse say.

"I feeling sick," I say.

We go in a room. The room got wallpaper with bunnies on it and little blue and yellow and pink eggs. Easter. I don't want to tell her how bad my coochie hurting me. She take my blood pressure. She go, "You don't have a fever, so it's probably nothing too serious." I feeling so nervous and I am afraid. She say, "What hurts?" and I say, "Down there," and she say, "Your vagina?" Oh my goodness! I don' wan' her to say that. I am so embarrass. I nod my head yeah. Yes.

Nurse Donna take me to a different room. It got a kine of a bed with the place for the feets. And she sit next to me an' she pet my shoulder. I know I not suppose to cry but the feets on the bed making me nervous and worrying and my belly hurting and I crying a little—and she asking me, "What's wrong?"

I say, "I don' feel so good."

An' Nurse Donna say, "Shhh." And she pet on my back and she say it gonna be okay but I think I gonna throw up, you know? And I can't breathe. She put her hand on my hand and she say, "Stop crying. Stop crying."

And I tell her, "Please, can I sleep here tonight? I am so stress out, you know?"

Nurse Donna say, "But I don't know what's wrong with you. Let's find out the problem and go from there. Can I examine you now?"

An' I say, "Please don't exam me. Okay? I think only thing I need is medicine, you know? Please, Miss Nurse."

She say, "Mia, I have to examine you. There's nothing to cry about. Don't act like a baby."

The feets remine me of—they scaring me a lot. I say, "I change my mind. I feeling better."

Nurse Donna say, "Mia, I'm going to help you." And she get all kine of stuff out the closet and she moving me to the table with feets and she slide me on it an' taking my shoes an' I just wanna stay here and she taking my pants and eberything.

I say, "Can I stay here after?"

She say, "Shh."

She listen to my heart and make me breathe. I say, "Please, can I stay here after? I be quiet, okay?" Maybe she not gonna look. Maybe she only listen to my heart. I not gonna say nothing.

"Mia? I'm going to take a look in your pelvic area, okay? When was your last period?"

"My last period? Not too much time. Not very long, okay?"

Then alla sudden she taking my foot and put it in the thing and I don' want her to. I feeling hot. Stop it! "¡Déjame! Please don' do that!"

"Mia, just relax and I won't hurt you."

She put my other foot up there. I trow up in my mouth.

"Just relax."

"I tryne."

"I know it's cold but I am not hurting you."

"Please, please," I say.

"Just relax. Do the houseparents wash your vagina?"

"No! I don' know. Yeah, they help me."

"Well. You have a discharge."

I look at the wallpaper and it got seals on it. At the circus.

She say, "I'm just taking a little sample here."

I wanna say, "Shut up, Nurse Donna." I say, "I gonna trow up."

"Don't tense."

"I gonna trow up."

She looking at a microscope. The seals clapping with their paws.

"Can I stay here now?" I say.

"Just be still."

"I still," I say.

She say, "Mia, are you having sex with somebody?"

My head hurting. I trow up in my neck. I say, "No."

She say, "Don't lie to me. You've got a venereal disease. Do you know what that is?"

"I—no."

"Well, you have a parasite that is usually passed through sexual intercourse. I took a sample to be sure. Let me clean you up."

Miss Donna get a—the thing, from the closet, to trow up in it, and a wet towel and wipe my face and neck. I shut my eyes.

Nurse Donna say, "I'll have to tell Mrs. Phoebe. Who did you have sex with?"

"Nobody."

She say, "Who? Mia?"

"I tell you, nobody. Nobody."

"Your boyfriend?"

"I don' got no boyfrien'."

Then she get mad. She say, "Mia, I'm not stupid!"

"He will be mad."

She say, "Who?"

"I feeling sick. I—please, please—"

"Well, I'll just have to test everyone here. Because I will find out."

Snitches get stitches.

"Answer me, Mia."

I say real, real soft, "Jerry."

She say, "Are you sure?" She say, "If you're not telling the truth, that's a very bad thing."

I don't say nothing.

Nurse Donna say, "I'll try to find someone to dress you now. I'll be right back."

She leave. She didn't cover me down there. The wallpaper got little seals. Seals from a circus. And the seals doing all different things like one seal got a big ball on his nose, another seal clapping his paws. I want my feets down. I hate Nurse Donna. I wanna be cover.

"Nurse Donna!"

The ceiling got yellow squares. They look old. Like they be here a long time. Like I be here a long time.

Joanne Madsen

I took a sick day today. My new driver is taking me to see Elaine Brown at the Center for Disability Justice, or CDJ. I finally posted an ad on Craigslist for a driver and he had the best response. Any response with any variation on the theme "I really love helping people who are less fortunate" gets an immediate delete. Do they not understand that this is a job? That I am paying them money? And do I really need to know if the person driving my car is a Christian? In fact, thanks for pointing that out so I can delete you. Bye, have fun at the Rapture.

The guy I hired wrote just the facts. Very *Dragnet*. He lives near my neighborhood and is flexible because he has a small side business that allows him to work out of his apartment. He's been on the company payroll—me—for about a week and we get along fine. So far. It's a work in progress.

One time I hired a guy who honked at other cars constantly. If we were at a stoplight, he'd start honking a moment before the light on the cross street turned yellow. He'd honk if we were stopped at the light but he perceived the car ahead of him could be a few inches closer to the intersection. He'd honk at people if they were going merely the speed limit. And he dressed like a pirate. Not once in a while, but every day. He had his pants tucked into his boots with a puffy effect at the knees and he had long, greasy hair and wore a bandanna around his head. I fired him. You might ask why I would hire someone who arrived at the interview in a pirate outfit. All I can say is, guilty as charged.

My new driver's name is Leo.

I don't want to rely on Ricky for rides. Now that our relationship is on somewhat solid ground, I'm staking out my independence. His too, in a way. I'm a believer in keeping your relationship person clearly separated from your employee person. I don't want to be Ricky's job.

Leo drops me off a few minutes early at CDJ. The office is nice. Small lobby. A few *People* magazines, back issues of the *Nation*. Brochures. And a *Plumed Serpent*—very auspicious. The receptionist is behind a sliding glass window, so I can see behind her into the office. The walls are painted with a big mural of people shouting and protesting about something. Some of the people in the mural have disabilities. But they're your basic generic-looking crips—one white guy in a manual wheelchair, a black guy with a white cane and black sunglasses, and a white woman signing to her friend. The Big Three. Someone said to the muralist, "Okay, we want disabled people to be represented," and the muralist went home and got his inspiration from a McDonald's commercial. He should've shown Mia in her crappy, broken-down manual chair and Cheri trying to shut out the mean voices.

Only a few of the staff at ILLC are supposed to know about what happened to Mia, but everyone seems to know something already. The kids were there when the police arrived at ILLC and arrested Jerry on his way in to work. A few of the kids watched the police cuff him and actually cheered. Fantasia has been questioned by the police and apparently she was awake and terrified during all of the assaults. No one noticed that she's been suffering herself all this time.

If most of the kids don't already have a clear idea of what happened to Mia, they do have a vague notion that Jerry did something to her and whatever he did shouldn't be named.

Yessie's been trying to spend more time with Mia. She and Mia came to my office together once but Mia didn't bring the matter up. She didn't say much at all. Then yesterday Yessie wheeled Mia over, disconnected the bungee cord, said, "Mia wants to talk to you," and left. The moment the door closed behind her, Mia burst into tears.

I put my arm around her and passed her a tissue from time to time. After she calmed down a little I asked her if she wanted to talk and she shook her head no. So I asked her if she would stay and keep me company and she nodded her head yes. When lunchtime came, I went to the cafeteria and brought her back whatever I could carry and we ate lunch together.

There's a therapist that comes to ILLC once a week to meet with various kids and she saw Mia once before leaving for a vacation. The therapist told Mia she'd be back in two weeks and in the meantime to "think happy thoughts." I'm not making this up.

What Mia needs is some hard-core psychotherapy by someone who knows what's she's doing. I'm going to emphatically bring it up to Mrs. Phoebe. I mean, I've seen Mia's file, I know she was sexually abused and tortured by her father, and here comes that slime Jerry resurrecting the whole experience and Mrs. Phoebe knows it too. Of course, why would Mrs. Phoebe bother to listen? I'm the data-entry clerk.

Ricky has figured out a way to blame himself for what happened. He feels he could have prevented all of it. So does Jimmie. They think they should have seen signs. Maybe we were all criminally oblivious. But in a way, I think it was bound to happen.

The elevator door opens and Teddy and his dad come into the lobby. I tell Mr. Dobbs how nice it is to see him again and he shakes my gimpy hand without getting flustered. He's been around gimpy hands before. He's wearing a brown, kind of crumpled suit—though not as crumpled as Teddy's suit.

Elaine Brown comes out to greet us. She's tall and really beautiful. A little older than me, I think. We follow her back past the murals and into a conference room. When everyone finds a spot to sit, Elaine says, "I'm a lawyer. My job is all about protecting the rights of people with disabilities in Illinois. Any disabled person. Now Joanne here told me a little bit about your situation. Let me see if I have this right. Teddy, you're about to turn twenty-two?"

Teddy says, "On June twenty-eighth."

"Okay. And ILLC wants to transfer you to a nursing home in Maywood, is that right?"

"I ain't going there," Teddy says.

"Tell me where you see yourself living instead."

Elaine led Teddy and Mr. Dobbs into a conversation about their options and Teddy's rights and the law, taking her time, answering questions, making sure everyone was keeping up. It was an education for me too. I had no idea people actually had any choices.

Here's Teddy's vision of his future: He wants to live in an apartment, get a job, decide where he wants to go and when he's going to bed. Hooking Teddy up with Elaine Brown was the only worthwhile thing I'd done since I started at ILLC, and if anyone found out I did it, they'd probably fire me.

Elaine says, "It means you have a right to live in the community, with caregivers you hire and fire yourself. Or there are living situations that are not nursing homes or institutions but have more round-the-clock help if you decide you need that. Meanwhile, we can get an injunction to stop ILLC from transferring you."

Teddy says, "Why didn't Mrs. Phoebe let me do that?"

Elaine says, "Well, maybe you can ask her."

Teddy says, "I want to live in a apartment."

Elaine says, "Okay. But first there's a lot of work to do, for me and for you. I want you to start spending time at Access Now and sign up with the Mi Casa Project. Learn some good skills, talk to other people there who moved out of institutions back into the world. It'll take some time and you have to be really committed to working on it. Just so you know."

We stayed awhile longer. When Teddy and his dad went to the bathroom, Elaine says, "You know, we don't see too many nursing-home employees bringing kids around here."

"Yeah, I bet not. I'm actually home sick today."

"Of course," Elaine says. "Look, here's my card. Feel free, okay?"

"Thanks. I saw an article about a case you worked on where an entire institution for disabled kids was shut down."

"Oh, a lot of people worked on that. We're still working on it. Making sure the kids who were in that hellhole get resettled somewhere better, which isn't easy."

"Also," I say, "I should tell you, in case it makes any difference, that Whitney-Palm owns the nursing home in Maywood where they want to send Teddy. Same company that manages ILLC."

I waited on the sidewalk with Teddy while his dad got the car. I risked asking Teddy if he'd talked to Mia lately.

"I ain't even thinking about her no more. That's all over."

"Oh, Teddy. I'm sorry to hear it." He must know something about what happened, but what he's thinking about whatever version of events he's heard is unclear.

"Don't be."

I say, "That's too bad. I bet she could use a friend now more than ever."

He just stares at the sidewalk. He shakes his head but looks like he's afraid he'll cry if he says anything. I put my hand on his shoulder and squeeze a couple times. I shouldn't have brought it up. It was such a good day so far. I should have let the feeling last a little longer.

Teddy Dobbs

Bernard says, "Jerry was a freak. You know that just as good as anybody in this place."

"If she didn't like him, then why didn't she tell nobody? That's what I would do. Why didn't she tell me?"

Bernard says, "Not everybody does what you do. Did Yessie tell you anything?"

"She said I'm a asshole. But if Mia don't say nothing—"

"Well, maybe she didn't know what to do," Bernard says. "Maybe she just didn't know."

Bernard never gets mad. I'm mad 'cause now everybody's ganging up on me for being mad at Mia when she's the one who didn't talk to me or say nothing all this time.

"She never thought how I could feel," I says, "so I ain't trying to be worrying about her."

"Well, maybe she was afraid you'd go all crazy. Like you are right now."

Bernard threw his ciggie butt into the empty swimming pool. I ain't trying to be crazy. I don't wanna feel this way. But Mia was my fiancée and she should've told me if she had a boyfriend, especially if it was Jerry. I can't even believe that part. All I know is I feel bad.

I says, "Yessie said Jerry forced her. You think that's what happened?"

"Yeah, man. That shit happens to girls. They don't want it, but dang." Bernard lit another ciggie. "You wanna puff?" he says.

"She didn't want Jerry to be her boyfriend but he made her be?"

"Yeah, man. There's no boyfriend-girlfriend thing about it."

I says, "You think Mia wants to get back engaged with me?"

"Just talk to her."

"Just say, 'Mia, I wanna talk to you'?"

"I don't know. Yeah, I guess."

I says, "She probably could use a friend right now more than ever. Is that what you think?"

"Yeah, man. Can always use a friend."

"Maybe I could talk to her."

Bernard says, "I probably have to move back in with my mom. Her diabetes is getting worse."

"But her place ain't even assessable."

"I didn't say I want to. I said I have to. She needs the money from my check real bad to buy medicine."

"How are you gonna get in and out? How you gonna go to school?"

"I don't know. I guess I could go sometimes if one of my sisters or brothers can come and bump me down the stairs." Bernard shrugs his shoulders like he don't care. His mom's place is up three flights and his brothers and sisters don't always like him asking them.

I go, "When you gotta go?"

"It ain't set yet. Pretty soon, I think."

"I don't want you to go."

"Me neither," he says.

"Bernard, when I get my own place, you gotta move in with me."

"Can you do that?"

"It'll be my place. If I want you to move in it's okay."

We sat there for a while and then we left.

Ricky Hernandez

There's this girl at the place. She's like eleven. Ten or eleven. Cleo. Little girl. Little ponytail off to the side of her head. They always put it in a ponytail. You know, the houseparents. Her head is a little pointy on top—I don't mean she's a pinhead or anything. That ain't what I'm saying. But I think they put the ponytail off to the side to—whatever—to draw your eye away from the way her head is shaped or whatever. Which is cool. Accentuate the positive and all that. I don't know Cleo too good but from what I do know, she has friends, you always see her with her little group because most of them have their friends they hang with. She ain't a standout. She ain't a leader-of-the-pack type. She's a little shy. And Mrs. Velasquez who is a sub, a substitute, but she's around a lot because the teachers get sick—she has me paged to come and take somebody out of the class, I get there and it's this Cleo. Fine. Whatever. So I get in there, they're all in the gym or they call it a gym but it's more like a minigym, everybody's playing catch with this—a beach ball. It's therapy or phys ed or something. Cleo is sitting by herself, she's a chair person so she's in her chair, not acting out, not making trouble, just sitting. So I'm like, "What's the problem?"

Teacher says, "She's not playing."

I'm like, "And?"

She says, "Cleo has to learn that she can't come to gym class and sit on the sidelines whenever she wants. Gym is just as important as any class."

The fuck do they find these teachers?

I say, "Okay, well, what do you want me to do with her?"

"I think she might like spending some time thinking it over in the time-out room. Would you like that, Cleo?"

I'm just standing there thinking, "You are an asshole," and little Cleo is still deadpanning it. Here's a kid, she's not doing a damn thing, so what do they want? They want to stick the kid, by herself, into a stinky room, size of a doughnut hole. Kid is either—either doing too much of something or too little of something. Fuck you, Mrs. Velasquez. So I say okay and I take ahold of Cleo's chair. "For the rest of the class period," Mrs. Velasquez says. By then I'm at the door and she says, "Did you hear me?" so I just act like, "No, I didn't hear you," and keep on pushing Cleo down the hall.

I'm wiped. Up half the night helping Consuela move.

Something went down in her neighborhood, a shooting, a drive-by, two blocks away, two people killed. So she can't stay there and I don't mind helping. My sister's helped me out more than once. It works two ways.

Consuela got me a job at a loading dock once. She worked there in the office and she got me a job loading and unloading trucks. First day I'm there this guy, Joe something, is showing me around and I'm thinking like, "No problem," but the second day is my first full day, right? Get there at the crack of dawn and start unloading these semis which're, oh, man, packed solid with boxes. We're talking big, heavy mothers, you know, like boxes from Panasonic filled with TVs or all this electrical equipment, or bicycles which Panasonic actually makes bicycles which was news to me. Lots of different companies though, Foot Locker, Levi's—huge boxes of Levi's. Boxes filled with microwaves, office supplies, Sealy mattresses. The mattresses were brutal. But everything you could think of. We'd be unloading these things with nothing but solid muscle, one after another. You'd have ten boxes going to wherever, like Eau Claire, Wisconsin, you'd separate out the boxes, load them onto a two-wheeler, and pack them into another semi. Forty boxes to Rensselaer or Joliet or Wauwatosa. You know, Timbuktu. End of the first day I'm crawling up the stairs to my apartment. I hated it at first. But it got better. After a while I was the go-to guy. They wanted to know where whatever boxes were going, they'd ask me. This one guy, Bill? He used to get Joliet and Beloit mixed up. He'd say, "Hey,

Enrique, where's fuckin' Boliet?" They called me my real name there. I'd say, "You dyslexic prick, it's Beloit, not Boliet." It actually turned into a pretty fun job. I stayed there seven years. Laid off in '06.

I feel bad putting Cleo in the time-out room. It's not right to put a kid in here when it's dirty like this. Especially a girl. Or a boy.

"Which way do you want to face?" I say to Cleo. "Not like there's anything to see, but do you have a preference? Of which way? I tell you what. The only thing to look at is smelly carpet. But if you face this way, see that little window? You can see my handsome face. Ha-ha. No, just kidding. But if you look up. And I can wave at you now and then. How about that?"

Ta-da! She nods her head. All right, Cleo!

So I say, "If you need anything, just wave, okay? Or just say, 'Hey, you.' I'll be right at that window."

Then I go out and look through the window, and sure enough, she's looking at me. I give her a little wave and she waves back. Next thing I do? Genius that I am. Is fall asleep.

I must've been out—maybe ten or fifteen minutes? It was so quiet I didn't know where I was for a second. I'm thinking, "What time is it? Is it time to pick the kids up at Hoover?" Then I realize I'm by the time-out room and I have to remind myself what kid is in there. Pierre? Vernell? Cleo. I look in the window and the first thing I see is this person and it—it doesn't look like Cleo. So I go running in.

I say, "Cleo, Cleo, what happened? What'd you do? What'd
you do? Oh—oh, baby!"

She must've had a Magic Marker in her pocket. She's covered with purple ink. She colored herself in. Not just her skin
but, like, everything. Her hands, her fingernails, her face—
her whole face. She colored her eyelids, her ears, her *teeth* even—
she colored her teeth.

I say, "Cleo, why'd you do this?" But she doesn't say nothing. Just that same deadpan as before.

So that was how my day started.

I'm parked over on—I don't even know—Ogden. I'm waiting here before I go pick up the kids by Hoover. I'd park by
the school itself but you can't breathe over there. Every day,
just before school is over, maybe a half hour before it lets out,
there's about five or six school buses that line up in front of the
place, and they all keep the motors running the whole time
they're waiting. Diesel fumes everywhere. The whole place is
like a mushroom cloud. Most times I try and pull up right as
they get out so I don't have to breathe in that crap for too long.
After I get my ten or twelve kids in the ILLC bus I pull away
fast and stop a few blocks down so I can help two of them with
their inhalers. That's how bad it is. I don't give those two a hit,
they're in the ER with a breathing attack.

I can't remember feeling this bad. Jo and me were in bed a
couple nights ago and I'm telling her I don't like myself. All I
do all day is punish these children. It used to be I could more
focus on the driving part, and when we're in the bus—when

me and the kids are in the bus everything's cool. We got our own little kingdom, you know? But more and more all they want me to do is lock them up or hold them down and I hate it. I hate it.

And Joanne says to me, "Maybe you need to think about getting out. Doing something else."

I'm like, "Yeah, but then I think they'll get some other gorilla instead of me and at least if I'm doing the job it's one less psycho they got in there messing with them, you know?"

"Raping them," she says.

Neither one of us talks for a while after she says that.

I say, "I have these fantasies in my head. All the time, I'll be walking down the hall at ILLC or driving the bus or brushing my teeth and the whole time I'm dreaming about killing Jerry. But slow-killing him. I want him to suffer. Smashing his head into a concrete wall over and over till his brains start coming out. Pretty fucked up, right?"

Joanne says, "No, it's not fucked up. I can understand that."

I say, "You think that's normal?"

She says, "I think you're normal. If you were someone who would really do that, that would be bad."

I say, "Is that your foot?" and she says, "I don't know," and I say, "You can't feel that?" and she says, "Not really," and I say, "I'm gonna try harder to not leave my shoes around the house," and she says, "Good. Are you saying that because I can't feel my foot?" and I tell her, "Because I got big shoes and I'm leaving them around too much and I saw you tonight, you didn't

see it was behind you and you rolled over it, and the chair—
your wheelchair kinda tipped." She says, "I love you," and I
say, "I love you too."

She says, "You do have giant shoes. They're like pieces of
furniture."

I can hear a bunch of kids' voices in the distance now. They
must be letting them out of school. I open the window to let
some cold air come in, help me wake up. Why does my sister
always need me to help her move the night before I gotta work
the next day?

Maybe I'll stop off at the Dunkin' Donuts and get some
coffee on the way back to ILLC. A "coffee creation." Box of
doughnut holes for the kids. They'll love that. Grease-and-
sugar balls, just what they all need.

Michelle Volkmann

A girl died at Riverwood again, one of our IMDs. In Illinois that stands for institution for mental diseases. I don't know what other states call it. Anyway, a girl in Riverwood that Whitney-Palm runs, she died under weird circumstances. They found her sitting in front of the TV like six hours after she died and by then she had rigor mortis. The thing is, she was sitting in a wheelchair, but she could walk. Before she died she could walk, I mean. So why was she sitting in a wheelchair? I thought that was weird. She was tied into the wheelchair. One of my co-workers, Margo, and I were talking about it and we thought maybe the girl was on really, really strong meds, medicine, and she kept like falling over so they had to tie her. But she was tied really tight and she suffocated from it. That actually happens, especially if a person's breathing is slow from the meds. Another way it might have happened is—and this would be horrible but not unusual—is if someone was sitting on her and she suffocated. Sometimes if a patient acts up they make him or her lie on the floor facedown and sit on them until they calm down, and if the aide isn't careful the patient can die. But since the patient was on meds already she probably wouldn't have been acting up. And if she died from being sat on, they would have had to put her into the wheelchair after she was dead. When you work around these places too much? Your mind starts coming up with all kinds of crazy theories. Anyway, it took six hours before someone even noticed her in the wheelchair. I guess they thought she was sleeping. I don't know what they thought. Honestly? I wouldn't say this out loud but I don't think they cared.

Tim is furious. Whitney-Palm will probably have to pay another fine because the girl's parents told the state they wanted an investigation. They're going to do an autopsy. Autopsies take a long time because the coroner's office is so busy. They have a bunch of pathologists who all they do is bodies from nursing homes and IMDs. But even though that's all they do, they're still really backed up. When they do an autopsy faster it's because the death is under mysterious circumstances, so you're more likely to get a big fine. To be honest with you, I don't know why Tim is as mad as he is because it's not like anyone ever pays the fines anyway. At the most Whitney-Palm will end up paying 20 percent of the fine, and the state will be completely thrilled to just take whatever money they can get. That's how desperate they are.

I was looking in Whitney-Palm's annual report and the company donated $765,000 last year to politicians. I remember meeting two of the politicians because they both stopped by the office over a year ago. State legislators. At the time I thought it was strange, I mean for a Democrat and a Republican to be together like that. Whitney-Palm must give money to their campaigns so the politicians won't do anything that would be bad for companies that run nursing homes and IMDs.

Today is the day we have our big meeting with the staff people who work directly with the nursing facilities we manage. Three different people including me gave reports on what we found from our research at three different Whitney-Palm contracts. My report was on ILLC and I made charts showing how much each area cost, for example medical supplies or food. Then I showed how much on average each individual resident used of each area, in other words cost per resident. Also I had charts showing number of aide hours on average per resident and cost per aide and all the other staff too. Then I made recommendations for streamlining and creating higher efficiency by implementing more up-to-date technology.

After I was done, Tim said it was very good but he wondered if we could think out of the box more about creative strategies for increasing revenue. He said did I visit the patient floors and I said yes. He asked how many beds were in each room and I said two. He said what if we increased the number of beds per room?

Wow. I never thought of that.

I said, "Well, the rooms don't have much extra space. Some of the space has stuff in it already like medical equipment. But even if that wasn't there, I don't think you could fit another bed in very easily."

Tim said, "Okay. But think about it. There may be a way of reconfiguring the beds so an extra bed could in fact fit comfortably in the room. Sometimes it's simply a matter of looking at it from a different angle."

I said, "Okay." I disagree but I'm not going to stress out about it. There's nothing I can do anyway. Not if Tim wants it that way.

Tim said, "Why don't you get the actual dimensions of the room and the beds and look at it again. Sound good?"

I said, "Yes. I'll do it this week."

Tim said, "Good girl. Let me know what you find."

Then he said that was the kind of creative thinking he depended on. He said I was a great example and everyone should learn from me. I'm not sure if I was an example of good or bad, but he was smiling.

There really is not any more room for beds.

After all the reports were finished, Tim led a very serious discussion on the outcome of the Pine Hills case. That's another of the facilities we oversee where there was a big mess. Pine Hills looks like a giant castle from England, at least that's what it looks like from outside. I've only seen pictures. Anyway, it's another place for developmentally disabled children. It's not where the girl who got suffocated was. This is a different facility. But it's a huge deal because what happened there was in the newspapers and Whitney-Palm will have to pay another fine and some politicians said it should be bigger than what we usually pay.

The story is that Whitney-Palm agreed to take over at Pine Hills because it already had a bad reputation and Tim thought we could do a better job and really clean the place up. We've only been in charge for a little over a year now, so Tim is pissed off how the newspapers keep assuming it's his fault what happened.

The first thing was that Pine Hills has this extra-higher than normal number of deaths and that was attracting attention but that started before Whitney-Palm took over. But the deaths kept happening. The thing that led to the fine was really sad. At Pine Hills the residents are teenagers and young adults and some of them are even below teenagers in terms of age. And what happened is this one kid who is a sexual predator, he was sup*posed* to be in a room by himself because his mother told them, "Put my son in a room by himself because he is a sexual predator," but they put him in a room with a little kid and he raped the little kid. And that's how they did find out was from this one aide who was passing the room and he noticed something was off so he goes in and sees another aide watching while the boy who is a sexual predator was molesting the little boy. He—the aide who was watching—wasn't doing anything to stop it. Then on top of everything, the little boy hung himself. I would never say this to Tim probably but we deserve to pay a big fine.

Tim said the media is biased against business and the really sad thing about doing this kind of work is that people die. He said if it weren't for places like Whitney-Palm taking care of all the people no one else wanted to take care of, a lot more people would die, but they never put that in their newspaper articles. He said when those reporters put their mothers or their children in nursing homes they'll be grateful if that home is run by a caring place like us where their people will receive the highest possible quality care. He said death is a natural part of life and unfortunately in our business we have to accept that there is going to be a lot more death than usual because the people are frail and what happened to the little boy was a tragedy and his heart went out to the family. He said if we were contacted by anybody like reporters or anybody we should not say anything and let him know immediately.

He also said how we should all feel proud of the work we do and be confident we were good people doing a good thing. Then he invited the whole staff to go on his boat next Saturday. Tim has this huge sailboat and it has a little kitchen and bathroom and kind of a bedroom and it's so amazing. He even has this guy to sail the boat for him. I'm not going. My stomach has really been acting up lately and the last place I need to be stuck is on Tim's boat throwing up in the one little tiny bathroom where everybody can hear every single sound.

Tim said, "Any questions?"

I said, "If the mother said her son was a sexual predator, why did they put him in the room with the little boy?"

Tim said he had asked that very same question himself and the person who did that had been fired.

After the meeting I decided to ask Tim if I could see him for a few minutes. And I told him about that thing that woman Joanne at ILLC told me, that we should find out more about the health of the kids there and what happens to the children after they leave ILLC. I said I wasn't sure if there was data on it but maybe he could look into it and if there was a problem he could fix it before something bad happened. He said I was absolutely right to tell him. And then he said he would begin a personal investigation next week.

I'm trying to say "woman" instead of "girl" all the time. Also, I don't believe Tim will investigate.

He said, "I'm very glad you mentioned it. We really have each other's backs here, don't we?"

I said, "Yeah."

Yessenia Lopez

When I got back in my room after school today Cheri was gone like—she was just *gone*. No clothes, no nail polishes, no nothing. I ask where she is and Toya says, "She's in a better place," and my head starts in buzzing and I feel real hot in my face and I say, "Did she die?" and Toya laughs out loud and says, "No, no, she's not dead! She just got moved to a different place for a while." And I put my head down on my knees so I could take a breath and Toya says, "I'm sorry I scared you," and pats me on the back and I like Toya but at that moment I just wanted to grab her hair and pull her face down where I could reach and slap the shit out of her. But I didn't. I say, "Where'd they send her?" and Toya says, "She went to a hospital where they can take better care of her than we can here," and I say, "How long'll she be gone?" and she says, "Yessenia, if you got questions you're going to have to ask Mrs. Phoebe because I can't go around telling everybody personal information about patients," and then she walks out the room.

They sent Cheri off to *el manicomio*. *El manicomio* is the nuthouse. You know how I know where she is? Because they told her they was going to send her there if she run off again. That's where they always send the runaways, to let them know they better not run away from this place ever 'cause they mean business. Mrs. Phoebe and all them don't play fair and I hate them and I don't mind telling them right to their face.

Cheri was homesick. She wanted to see her mother and father. They came to visit her a couple times but she wanted to go home. She wanted to go home for real. I mean for *real* for real. And she has a little brother and she missed him. Sometimes when Cheri gets sad she says all the things she's gonna promise to her whole family like she won't never bring a strange male into the house again and she won't never drive somebody's car again until she knows how to drive and she won't never be picked up by the po-lice again and she's gonna turn a new leaf over. But I met them the first time they came to visit and they didn't look like they was in a hurry to take Cheri home anytime soon.

She told me she was taking off. The first time she waited till she got her thirty dollars' allowance. They caught her the next day or two later, acting crazy because of course she didn't have no meds with her because they keep them locked up in the infirmary. Cheri gots to have her meds or she starts hearing people telling her stuff. But they won't let her at her own meds! She knows she's got to have them and she'll take them but they treat her like she's a two-year-old child and she can't even keep her own medicine. They know she runs off every now and then but they don't care if she gets sick. The neighbors saw her walking around and around in her own backyard and they called the po-lice. She never did see her parents.

One time she was walking out the door and they caught her right then and there. When she got back in our room she cut the inside of her leg with a stray piece of wood. Jimmie was there that night, so we was able to talk her out of taking Cheri to the nurse but first Cheri had to promise she would tell the psychologist all about it.

One thing I know for a fact is all you gots to do when Cheri is depress is talk to the woman! Talk to her, find out why she's feeling bad, and she starts feeling better. She snaps right out of it. That's the thing about Cheri is once you talk to her? It's like that's all what she needed in the first place.

This time she ran she must have been more careful to go when no one was looking because it took them two days to find her. Next thing I know is all her stuff is gone and she's gone with it.

You could see the dust bunnies under her bed now 'cause there's no blanket hanging off it. There's all sorts of crap down under there. A used-up towel looking real stiff like it been under there since before the Flood, a lid from a peanut-butter-with-grape-jelly jar, a squished-up, empty box of tissue, a slipper which isn't mine and it isn't Cheri's, so I don't know who it comes from, lots of used-up cotton balls and dried-up nail polish all over the place.

They didn't even think to give us a opportunity to say good-bye. Cheri is the best friend I got here, not counting Jimmie. But I don't even know where they sent her.

It's time for dinner but I can't look at no food. I'm a lay down and close my eyes. But every time I close 'em, I think of Cheri in *el manicomio* and I get scared like my first night at Juvie. I hope she don't hear the mean voices in her head. I always know when she doesn't get her meds for a couple days 'cause she talks to somebody when she's in the bathroom. You can hear her answering questions and apologizing in there like somebody's giving her a hard time and she's just trying to get that person to shut the fuck up. I say, "Cheri, you take your medicine?" and she says, "I don't think so," so we go down to the infirmary to see Nurse Lorraine. We love Nurse Lorraine and after Cheri takes her pill pretty soon she's her old self.

I have to lay in my bed facing the wall because I can't stand looking at Cheri's empty part of the room. I'm gonna be sixteen next week. Laying this way I like to look at the picture on my wall that Joanne gave me. The one of the hot brother with pretty locks sitting in his wheelchair chained to that glass door. He has a look on his face like he's thinking, "I'm not afraid of you. There isn't nothing you can do to me and nothing you *ev*er can do to me." His eyes are looking right out of the picture. Right back at me.

Jimmie Kendrick

I'm working a graveyard shift tonight. They needed someone and I don't mind because I could use tomorrow off. I have a gang of errands I've let slide.

It's quiet. Only noise is all four washing machines on rinse. Normally that's the type of thing that'd put me right to sleep, especially late like this. But I had a couple cups of coffee. Couldn't sleep if I wanted to.

I know whose clothes belong to who now. Demetria has her striped leggings, Krystal has her pink and purple everything, Teddy's suits, of course. Mia's things. I know her stuff because I just know it.

The thing is, when I washed her up, had to be a couple mornings, at least that, I could smell that something was wrong. That she had something going on. And I did say something about it, to her, to Mia, I did, but I moved on. She'd say, "No problem," or she was going to see the nurse or she had already seen the nurse or you know, various answers. And I'd say okay, and I'd move on. It was like I was glad she acknowledged it and said she was on it so I didn't have to do anything. Like get involved, spend the time to really talk to her. Go *with* her to the nurse. I was about finishing one person, moving to the next person. Like in a factory. Another part coming down the assembly line. And I've always thought to myself how I'm a better houseparent than the rest, that I'm—all the kids love Jimmie, but that was just until one of 'em had an issue that would require me to step up.

Except for Yessie. She's the one I'll do things for and all the kids know that. "Yessie is Jimmie's favorite." "Jimmie already has a favorite, so don't bother Jimmie." Oh *God*. Please don't let them feel that way.

Joanne said it wasn't my fault. I can't even let myself go there right now. I'm just too angry at myself.

If I'd been thinking about the kids, about Mia . . . it just . . . this is what kills me, okay? It's—it did not *have* to happen. I mean, she threw up in her bed. There was blood on the sheet. What part of that did I not see?

Joanne's thing is, we're none of us responsible. Or we're all responsible. I couldn't figure out which one she was saying. No, but for real, she says—you know, we were just kickin' it at her place last weekend and fell into talking about, what else, the job, and Joanne has this whole other way she thinks about it—she says that what happened to Mia is not, like, an isolated incident. It happens in a lot of, or Joanne said all, institutions. Her idea is it's the System.

Joanne always thinks it's the System. And I a*gree*! But the thing is, to me—does that, like, erase that people are responsible for their choices? Seems like we go back and forth about that every time we see each other.

I say if it's not an individual person's fault, like you say—I'm talking to Joanne here—then what about Jerry? Are you saying it's not Jerry's fault either? She says, "Yes, of course responsibility for the *act* lies with Jerry." I say, "Then it is the fault of the individual," and she says, "There are Jerrys everywhere but the System lets it happen." I'm like, "It would be a whole lot easier if you would stop saying 'System' because you use the word like it's something people can see and it's not." I say, "It's not like you go into a building and it says SYSTEM on the door."

I think we were both a little buzzed at that point. And she says, "Well, it should say SYSTEM on a whole lot of buildings, like Whitney-Palm and ILLC and St. Theresa's Hospital." I'm like, "St. Theresa's Hospital? Raped Mia? Really?" Joanne says, "On the front of every prison, police station—" and now I—I mean, she knows I agree with her down the line on that. I guess I'm just thinking about my own, whatever, part in this. I can say to myself, "It's the System," but does that mean I couldn't do anything about *any*thing? To change things? To me, the two things go together. You can't change one thing without changing the other thing.

And the truth is, Yessie is special to me. Sometimes I—wow, I just hate leaving her here at the end of the day. Because in a way it's like she can take care of herself, she's nobody's fool. But part of that—that "you can't mess with me" deal, that attitude—I recognize that from myself, okay? I was just like that at fifteen and sixteen and on up. But I wasn't in a wheelchair. I could put a beat-down on any thug that had the lack of judgment to step to me. So I'm just like—little Yessie has a very big mouth. She could tick somebody off. And ILLC—I mean, if I'm not here and something happens to her . . . I can't even *think* about it.

I told all that to Joanne too. I tell Joanne everything. She asked me did I ever talk to Yessenia about it. And I should do that, I will do that, but I'm just going by what I would do if any adult would tell *me* to zig, you know? Because I would definitely zag. So I'm hesitant to even bring it up. But Joanne asks me—this was funny, I mean, if you know Yessie, it's really funny—Joanne asks did Yessie ever tell me why she was in Juvie. And I say no. Joanne says how she doesn't know the whole story but, like, Yessie is not your average girl in a chair. She can do some serious damage. She can fight.

In a way, that made me feel better.

It's just that I know, underneath all that, that public Yessie, is someone else. Someone who's hurting and mad about it and doesn't know which way to turn. Just like everybody else. Just like Mia.

Ricky Hernandez

By mistake I leave my notebook at work, just some of my writing, like when I'm sitting in the ILLC bus waiting or in a traffic mess, you know. Thoughts, some doodles, you know, stuff no one cares about except it has forty-six dollars stuck in it. A little notebook thing, spiral notebook. It has some paper shoved in it like a gas bill, some receipts, and the cash. If it's lying around, it's first come, first served. So I'm in the Neon, heading back to ILLC again.

I'm 99 percent sure I left the notebook on a chair by a table down by where the juice boxes are. In the cafeteria. I can hear the voices and smell the cigarette smoke the second the elevator door opens. When I get closer I can pick out the voices. Louie and Candy. The Dynamic Duo. Taking a little break together.

At first I'm walking toward the caf but then I hear Candy talking, so I decide to slow down. Something, something, "spray in the face with cold water."

Louie says, "Disrespect me," something, something, "no." Then he says something else but I can't pick it up.

That's a big thing people tell themselves—they can't be disrespected. I hear that all the time. Problem is they always think they're being disrespected. To the point where the one who always thinks he's getting disrespected, it doesn't matter what you say. That person has a hard-on for you and they feel like, "I'm the victim." The kids ain't the victim. No. The grown-up is the victim. See. And some jerk like Louie—you know, ex–prison guard, shaved head, scary motherfucker—he's the victim. You gotta really do some deep self-deluded backflips in your brain to see yourself as the victim when you're the pig with the truncheon beating some guy's head in. It's a whole psychology they got, some of these people. I don't know. That's how they get off. Maybe once when they was little they really were the victim and they just kept thinking that. But you know what? I don't care. Fuck you anyway.

So I stop walking. I'm still like twenty feet away from the open cafeteria door. I stand there kinda leaning up against the wall. I'm James Bond now.

Candy says, "Children will manipulate you if you give them a chance. They'll play you off against each other, they'll lie. And these ones'll do worse than that because they know off the bat you're gonna feel sorry for them."

Louie was agreeing. You could hear him saying "Uh-huh" and "I hear you" like he's at a revival meeting. Then she says, "That's what kills me is we see that. We see that. But they got everybody else eating out their—"

"Fucking Hernandez." That's Louie talking now. "Treats Pierre Washington like that's his pet puppy. Guy's an asshole. When I worked at Stateville, that's the kind of guy, you'd shit if he was on your shift, because you're in a situation? Something jumps off? Guy like that ain't gonna have your back. Guy's a liability."

See? This is the kind of thing. Louie has beef with me? Fine. He wants to step to me? Fine. But he doesn't do that. He's too busy telling the kids he's the king or whatever. I'll king you, you prick.

Then Candy says, "When was you at Statesville?" but I can't stand it no more and I walk in just then, so I don't get to hear the story. I stop at the doorway and let them look at me. Then I smile and say, "Hey, guys!" I take my time walking over by the juice counter to get my notebook. Which is right where I left it. Oh, man, you coulda heard a pin. Then I turn around and walk back to the door. Just taking it slow.

I say, "Forgot my notebook."

Louie's looking at me and I'm looking at him. I wish he'd get it up and bring it but I'm almost a foot taller than him and I guess he don't have his Taser handy. Candy's not looking at all, just dragging on her cigarette and staring off into space like she's thinking up the cure for cancer.

So I'm back in the Neon. I gotta admit, I feel a little bit stupid. Looking back at my whatever. The Notebook Caper. Why challenge the guy? He's just another cop, right? Stupid guy crap, you know, you learn it coming up, and that's the way you do things. You defend your manhood or whatever bullshit you tell yourself.

It just bugs me that some people are even allowed around kids. Louie, a guy who couldn't even make it as a prison guard. "Oh, he's too big a creep to deal with prisoners? Let him take care of kids." And Candy. I could more see her in a job like, you know, mortician or toxic waste cleanup. Something like that, where she could use her people skills.

Something like that.

Yessenia Lopez

I was sitting with Fantasia, Amber, and Ree Ree after we four had got our trays. It was lunchtime. Jimmie was there too because she was cutting up Fantasia's meatballs and spaghetti. Ree Ree is my roommate since Cheri got sent away. I don't like Ree Ree and I don't hate her. She's just there. She's four-teen, two years younger than me, but she looks like about ten years old on account of being small for her age and she *acts* young. Like she's always asking questions. "Yessie, will you put makeup on me?" "Yessie, can I go with you?" "Yessie, can I sit next to you?" And she laughs a little tinkly laugh at every damn thing I say and I know I'm funny but I'm not *that* funny. Jimmie told me just be patient 'cause I don't know nothing about her yet, so I am trying to give the child a chance. Lord knows, I am trying.

One other thing about Ree Ree that I don't like—and I know I'm being bad to say so, but I can't help it—the girl has something funny in her eye. Funny like disgusting. Just one eye only. It looks like somebody dropped a blob of snot right on her eye. Not on the white part? But on the eye, on the brown part. The eye itself. It just rubs me the wrong way. I don't wanna look at her because I don't wanna see that one eyeball staring out at me.

But Ree Ree ain't the reason I'm telling about being in the lunchroom eating meatballs and spaghetti and garlic bread and waxy beans or waxed beans or whatever that crap is.

It was Jimmie, Louie, and Mr. Hudson was the adults. Mr. Hudson teaches the kids what can't go to school on the account they might be too sick or have to stay in their bed. I love Mr. Hudson. He's the nicest, least strictest teacher in this whole place and he always stops and says, "Hi, how are you, Yessenia?" and jokes around with you and he's just really, really cool.

So we was all—us four girls and Jimmie—talking and just minding our own sweet businesses when all of a sudden there's a whole lotta yelling going on like three tables away. And I see Louie is grabbing at Pierre Washington's tray of food and Pierre won't let go of that sucker even though Pierre is little and skinny and Louie's big and reminds me of a damn skinhead. You know who he reminds me of? This guy called Meatstick that used to work at the Chili Shack near Hoover. Anyway, hunks of food start falling offa the tray, like little meatballs go flying through the air and waxy beans just plopping down all over the floor. Then Louie got the tray away from Pierre and Pierre says, "You fucker!" and Louie says, "Pick up that mess! Pick up that mess right now, you little freak!" and Mr. Hudson like breaks in and says, "What's the problem here? Louie! You got to calm down. Louie!" and Louie says, "He's on a de-layed lunch and he don't belong in here and he knows it!" and Pierre says, "You a liar!" and Louie says, "You're outta here, you stinking little shit!" and he grabs Pierre on the arm and Pierre hollers and Mr. Hudson—he grabs onto *Lou*ie's arm and says, "Louie! Calm down! Let go of that child!"

So Louie lets go of Pierre but he more like jerks him away than just letting him go and Pierre falls down and Mr. Hud-son goes, "Louie, I am supervising here today and they give me the list of who gets what kind of lunch"—he meant because some kids can't eat regular food, okay?—"who gets what kind of lunch and Pierre's name is right here and they would've told me if he was on a delayed lunch, so why don't you just let him eat."

That only made Louie more mad, so he says, "Get off my dick!" Right to Mr. Hudson's face! Louie done lost his mind. He must have realized at that same minute that he went too far 'cause he did back off then. He even helped Pierre up offa the floor and gets him to sit down. There's practically no food left on Pierre's tray, so Mr. Hudson sends Jason Remke to make him a new tray and Mr. Hudson sits down and everybody goes back to what they was doing and Ree Ree is up in my face asking what happen and why'd he do that and am I scared and every other stupid thing and I says, "You're sitting here seeing the same shit as I am, so why you asking me?"

And just when I'm saying that, Pierre must have had him a pencil. Or he grabbed up somebody else's pencil, but before you even know what's happening Pierre is up and racing with his ricket legs at Louie and he *sticks* that pencil right in Louie's chest. And Louie let out a scream like a pig just got stabbed by a butcher knife. Oh my Lord Jesus, it was *the greatest thing* I seen at ILLC since I been here! But now Louie's really mad and he stands up and the pencil is still in him wobbling around and he raises his arm up over Pierre's head and *wham*! He slams Pierre so hard that Pierre's feet go right out from under him and it look like he's just hanging in the air for a second till all of a sudden he goes *down*. But Louie wasn't done yet. Pierre was all curled up in a itty-bitty knot on the floor and Louie looks like he's gonna kill him.

I guess my eyes were all on Louie and Pierre because I swear I never even seen Jimmie coming. First thing I see is her big paw clamping onto Louie's neck and—I can't explain it—it looks like she's dancing with him, like they're just gliding along until Louie's body slams up against the wall and she's holding him there with her one hand on his neck and her other arm pulled back in a fist the size of a bear paw. Her face didn't even look mad.

All of us kids started in cheering and screaming, "Jim-mie! Jim-mie!" You could see that Jimmie was saying something to

Louie too, real close-up so nobody else could hear, and Louie's face was real red and his eyes popped out and looked all still and straight ahead, so whatever it was Jimmie said, it must've been good.

They hadda send for two ambulances, one for Pierre and one for Louie and his pencil. It had fell out of him when Jimmie pushed him up against the wall but he was still holding his chest like he was dying even though there wasn't even any blood. He only got a couple stitches and that was that. Just a little scratch. Why they even bother threading a needle? Let the Meatstick bleed is what I say.

Pierre got hurt bad. Louie broke that boy's jaw. When I broke Mary Molina's jaw they put my ass in prison, so I bet Louie's gonna get a whole library of books thrown at his ass.

Everybody's talking about it with everybody. I got a picture of Pierre getting beat down in my brain, and it keeps playing over and over in my head. Pierre's a runt and Louie has big muscles like a redneck con. Then I think of Cheri being took away and put in *el manicomio* even though I wasn't there, and that girl Maricela at Juvie when she come outta the Hole and she couldn't even talk.

I found Jimmie after she came out from being talked to by the po-lice about what happened at the cafeteria. I wanted to talk to her but I didn't want to go to my room because Ree Ree was there. So we went out to Jimmie's car in the parking lot and I got out of my chair and we sat in the front seat together. It makes me feel like I must be doing something right to have a friend like Jimmie. I got a picture of Jimmie in my brain too, the part where she pins Louie up against the wall with her one hand on his fat neck and she has her other hand ready to break his face whenever she felt like it. I said, "Jimmie, girl, what the hell did you say to Louie when we couldn't hear?" Jimmie says, "Oh, nothing much." Do you believe that woman? I kept on asking and she just kept on saying, "Nothing much, nothing much." Finally she said, "Really. I just told him not to mess with any of you kids anymore. Or something like that."

I won't never forget how Louie looked. And I won't never forget what Jimmie did. None of us children or young adults will.

Michelle Volkmann

Ever since the little boy killed himself and they printed up all those horror stories about Pine Hills and the rapes and stuff, Tim has wanted us to all be extracareful to make sure we know what's going on at the different places we—meaning Whitney-Palm—manage. So yesterday I had to drive out to Riverwood Juvenile Mental Health Hospital and stay overnight at a Days Inn in Aurora, Illinois. Kill me right now if I ever end up living there. On the drive over I'm thinking how Tim should really give me a raise because this was not in my job description. The thing about recruiting is that I can make a big bonus every time I get a new person and now I'm just on my salary which is not that great and I'll probably have to move because my lease is up in two months and I know my landlord is going to raise my rent and two nights ago my engine light went on.

Plus my best friend Ariel is getting married to this guy—his actual name is Guy which fits him perfectly because he is so generic—they fight constantly and he throws stuff at her and she calls me up crying. I say, "Ariel, why would you marry someone who throws a cell phone at your head?" But I'm the maid of honor so I have to get a dress plus the wedding itself is in Duluth so I have to buy a plane ticket and there's the present which has to cost at least a hundred. I can't afford to do that on my salary.

I practiced asking for a raise out loud in my car. I said, "Tim, I know the company is going through a really hard time right now." Which is a lie. Maybe I'm wrong but it doesn't seem like it's that hard of a time because Tim bought a house in Florida which I saw a picture of online and it's huge and his wife is decorating it, so he bought her a Lexus so she could drive around while she's there. So that's real nice for her but why do I have to hear about it when my car is a piece-of-garbage rusty gas-guzzler?

Today I'm supposed to be at Riverwood by 7:00 a.m. to see how things are when the shift changes and stay there all day and answer questions on a giant checklist. But first I'm having the continental breakfast which is just coffee and a croissant which was obviously frozen and they nuked it.

I'm sure it will be depressing. I mean, it is a mental hospital, so. Also, they don't know I'm coming. Usually if they know someone's coming they clean up a little better or as this guy Kevin at Whitney-Palm says, "They hide the bodies," but that's not really funny anymore. They probably won't go haywire if a Whitney-Palm person comes by surprise. They only get upset if it's someone from Family Services or the public guardian's office.

Believe it or not, I've never been to Riverwood before. It's just this beige brick building near some old train tracks that must not get used anymore because they have weeds and grass and stuff growing around the tracks. There are some stores too, like a Denny's and a place you can buy giant spools of wire if you happen to need a giant spool of wire, and a shoe repair store with dusty shoes in the window.

Along the way, there are places with FOR RENT signs on them, like a hardware store and a bridal store with naked female mannequins in the window and other places you can't really tell what they are or used to be. There aren't very many people around but that could be the area. I go into the beige building and of course I have to get buzzed in because this is a mental hospital. There's a little tiny room behind glass with wire in it where I show them my ID from Whitney-Palm, and then this African American guy has to unlock the elevator for me to even get on. Then he takes away my purse and cell phone and my scarf and makes me go through a metal detector. I asked him how come he needs my scarf and he said because someone could come up behind me and strangle me.

There's a room where they make the parents wait to visit their children. There's a sign with the visiting hours which are Tuesdays or Thursdays between six o'clock and seven thirty. Only one visitor is allowed at a time.

Finally I get to go in the main hospital. The walls are this tannish color and they have those fluorescent lights that keep buzzing and buzzing.

It's real quiet except for the buzzing, so I guess the patients are still sleeping and the staff is doing their switch-over to the next shift. I go to the nurses' station and there's another African American guy sitting there and he looks exactly like the first guy. Because he's big, I mean. He's wearing a T-shirt and he has really developed muscles. I tell him I'm from Whitney-Palm and ask where the nurses are meeting and he just ignores me like I don't exist. So I say, "Excuse me, can I ask a question, please?" and I tell him again and he says, "I need to see ID," and I tell him no problem, but hello, the first guy took my purse with my ID in it, so he waits there for about a minute and neither of us says a word and then he gets up and walks away like nothing even happened. Well, thanks. Finally he comes back and starts walking in another direction. Then he turns around and says, "Are you coming or not?" God! He unlocks the door to another room where there are these two women sitting having coffee.

I introduce myself and ask if I'm in the right place for the report session. It's just a head nurse and a Hispanic nurse. The head nurse asks if I have ID, and I'm totally exasperated and I explain—again—so they start going through the list of patients and reporting how they were last night like did they sleep okay or did they act out, what meds they're on, all sorts of things. Then I hear the name Cheri Smith and I'm thinking, "This is weird," and I know it can't be the same girl because she's at ILLC but maybe she had her schizophrenia act up and they sent her here. Oh my God, I really hope not. Smith is a very common name but not Cheri, but they pronounced it like "cherry," so maybe it's a different person. I'm going through my checklist and under "Shift Change" I check "Orderly and efficient." I asked them where are the other nurses and they look at me and say there aren't any. But the head nurse says they have a lot of assistance from the patient-care techs. So I say, "Oh, where are they?" And she said the guy who unlocked the door was one of them.

I'm supposed to walk down the halls and look in the rooms now, but honestly? I feel uncomfortable. So I stay in the TV area until they come out. I look at my checklist and for "Condition of the Common Area?" I check "Clean" but I put a "No" by "Cheerful." It's really not. It's ugly and almost bare. There's some random books and games like Scrabble and Trivial Pursuit. There's a poster of a hot air balloon and another one of three hot air balloons. And one about being courteous, but that's about it. I'm pretty sure they have the exact same hot air balloon poster at ILLC. Maybe all these places get the hot air balloon poster. There's a couch with orange-and-blue plastic seat cushions and the TV is on even though no one is in there. One thing about these kinds of places is the TV is always on.

After a while the patients start coming out. It's pretty slow because I guess all the rooms are filled but they only have those two nurses. And the seven patient-care techs or PCTs. Next to "Ratio of Staff to Patients" I write, "Enough nurses?"

I haven't seen Cheri yet, so that's a good sign.

Some of the girls here are very young. It starts at twelve. A PCT guy, who isn't as big as the first two guys but almost, is giving them trays and they eat the food but kind of slow and they talk to each other a little bit. The TV has *Supermarket Sweep,* so they like that. Every now and then another girl comes out and sits down. The PCT guy gives each girl a tray and says, "Good morning, ladies. How are you this morning?" and they say fine but most of them are still pretty sleepy. They look normal, not that I was expecting them to look abnormal, but they really do look normal. I don't know what I was expecting. I guess they take strong meds which makes them walk slower and only talk a little but they basically look normal, like I said. When the guy talks to them individually they perk up. So that's good. I still haven't seen Cheri, so I go up to him and say, "Are these all the patients?" and he says, "Not all. Some of them take breakfast in their rooms." At least this PCT talks to me.

Well. I guess I should go look in the rooms. I put "No" next to "Do the food handlers wear hairnets?"

There are windows in every door, so I start looking in the

windows a little bit at a time. The rooms are small. There's a decent-size window in the door but in the room the windows have wire mesh. There's a little dresser and a closet that's anchored to the wall and not much else. There's a sink but no mirror and no place to put personal things like shampoo. The showers must be someplace else. Most of the rooms have two beds. Some of the girls are still in bed. There are names written next to each room. Coleman. Elston. Gomez. Garner.

The rooms aren't too cheerful, so I cross that word off the list. They look clean. But the lights keep buzzing so loud and my head is beginning to pound. I hope I'm not getting one of my migraines. In one room there's a teenage girl brushing her teeth really slowly and a female PCT folding some clothes. In another room there is a girl lying on her bed in her underwear. In another room there is a girl sitting on her bed with a helmet on her head.

When I get to the room that says "Cheri Smith," I admit that it must be my Cheri. I can't really see at first because she's still lying on her bed. There's a tray of food on a hospital table and the PCT is sitting there and he's that asshole from before. "Eat your breakfast, Cherry. Turn around and sit up now, please." But she doesn't move. So he pulls her into a sitting position. It's Cheri but not Cheri. Her eyes are almost closed and her mouth is open. When he lets go of her she slides back down in her bed. I move back from the window and turn around and start walking. Someone says, "Miss? Are you leaving?" And I walk a little faster to the elevator and press the button but it's locked. I look around for help and get the nice PCT to call someone on his walkie-talkie. Then he fiddles with his key ring for a while and unlocks the elevator. Downstairs the guy at the desk gives me my things and I walk as fast as I can down the street, past the giant spools of wire and past the closed diner and the shoes and the Denny's, and then I get in my car and drive.

Teddy Dobbs

Most nights I can't get to sleep. Things keep going around and around in my head. I try waking up Bernard and asking him to go get us some pop or something but he don't wake up for nothing. He sleeps real heavy. It don't matter how loud you yell for a houseparent most of the time either. Even if all you want is some water. If Anthony's working he'll get me water and sometimes he brings food like once it was Ruffles potato chips with ridges. Beverly always gets me water 'cause she said she knows what it's like to not go to sleep easy. Candy came a couple times but she said I was the boy crying wolf, and I don't know who that even is. My dad says don't bother any of them because he don't want me to get in trouble. But sometimes they get mad and sometimes they don't and I don't know why. That's how the turd plops around here.

Tonight I'm lying in bed like I do in the middle of the night and I hear somebody in the hall outside my room making noises like they using the wall phone they got out there. I say, "Hey, who's that out there?" Then it gets real quiet, so I say it more softer. "Hey, who's out there?" Next thing I see is Yessie sitting in the door of my room.

"That you, Yessie?"

"No, it's the Queen of Sheba." She's whispering. "Will you shut up before you wake up everybody in the damn place?"

"C'mere."

"If I come over there will you be quiet?"

"Yeah."

So she rolls over to my bed and asks me what I'm doing awake, so I says, "Well, what're *you* doing awake and who're you calling?" She says it ain't none of my business and I says, "Okay, but you wanna stay in here and talk to me awhile? Because I ain't tired." She says, "Okay, but we have to think up a good reason for me to be on the boys' side in case we get caught."

"Just say you heard me yelling and screaming, so you came in here to see was I okay 'cause none of them heard me. And how you was awake anyway 'cause you was going to the bathroom."

"I will beat your ass if you tell them I was on that phone."

" ain't gonna get you busted," I says.

"I know," Yessie says. "If you must know, I was calling up this dude I met on Facebook. He gots a fire-breathing-dragon tattoo on the back of his neck with the fire coming around a little itty bit to the front. So he said to call him. And can you believe who answered tattoo boy's phone? His mama. And she did not sound happy, so I just hung up."

Yessie looks at me. "This must be the first time I ever seen you not wearing one of your raggedy-ass suits. I'm glad you don't wear 'em to bed too."

"You're not suppose to wear suits to bed."

"Thanks for telling me. Hey, is it for real you're getting your own apartment?"

"Yup. I go to Access Now to learn how to do stuff on my own. Joanne took me to get a lawyer and the lawyer's real cool and she's gonna get me set up. And it'll have a elevator so people can come see me."

"Is that Bernard? It's a shame a child that age can snore that loud."

"You want I should introduce you to my lawyer?"

"They won't let me outta here till I'm eighteen years old and not no sooner than that. But I'm happy for you 'cause I didn't like thinking about you in a nursing home for the rest of your life. You're a badass but you ain't no criminal."

"Yeah, I'm a badass. I'm a *bad*ass."

"Shhh! Never mind. I thought I heard something. You know who needs a lawyer? Cheri. They up and moved her to the nuthouse."

"Pierre too," I says.

"Pierre? I thought he was in a regular hospital. Ricky had a card for him and we all signed it when we was on the bus."

"Yeah, but they're sending him to Riverwood after that."

"How do you know everything?"

"I heard Mrs. Phoebe tell Joanne to send his file."

"Ain't that a bitch? Pierre gets a beat-down from Louie, so they send Pierre off to *el manicomio*. Is that where they sent Cheri?"

"Yeah," I says. "They always send 'em to Riverwood. You wanna hear something cool? When I was at my lawyer's, I saw all these pictures of people and they were pissed off and holding signs that said DOWN WITH NURSING HOMES."

"I got that same picture. With the succulent disabled brother? All chained to the door?"

"I don't think so. On the wall?"

"Taped up by my bed."

"Yeah, but I'm talking about a whole big wall. Like all these people? It was like a drawing?"

"We're talking about two different things."

"We should do that! You wanna?"

"Wanna what?" Yessie says. "Chain myself to something? Where we gonna get chain at? Hey, when you get sent to the nuthouse, then what happens? Do they ever come back?"

"Sometimes. Louie use to be a prison guard before," I says.

"You told me."

"I'm glad he's gone."

"Louie isn't fired," Yessie says.

"Is too," I says.

"Is not. He's suspended till they decide what punishment he gets. He might get fired or he might not. Jimmie said if a houseparent beats down on one of us and gets suspended they might could come back. If they—Mrs. Phoebe or somebody— think it's not their fault. You got a caseworker?"

"Nah. I got my dad."

"Oh yeah. I forgot. Where your mama at?"

"I ain't her favorite person."

"Oh. My caseworker's Tanya Epstein. She's nice. I asked could I get moved to some other place with less stricter rules but she said there's no such place. But I wouldn't go nowhere now anyway on account of Jimmie."

"You and Jimmie are friends."

"Why you acting so stupid about Mia?"

"I ain't acting stupid," I says.

"She misses you."

I say, "She does?"

"What do you care?"

"C'mon, Yessie," I says. "Do she?"

"What you two doin' up?"

George ain't exactly in but leaning up against the door. He took Jerry's place when Jerry got fired. He's okay, I guess. But George—one time I was sleeping, sleeping real good, and I wake up and the light is on and there's George talking on his cell phone right in my room. I guess that's better'n what Candy does which is she's not never around.

Yessie says, "What you doing, George? Lurking?"

George says, "You're not allowed in here. You better get back in bed, Yessie."

"Bye, Teddy," Yessie says. "And Bernard with your pitiful snoring self. Move out the way, George, so I can get through the door."

George says, "I'm gonna have to tell on you for breaking the rules," and Yessie says, "I was just going to get some water for him because you all ain't doing your job." Then George says, "I'm supposed to believe that?" and Yessie says, "I don't care what you believe, I got my story and I'm sticking to it," and George says, "Get to sleep, Teddy," and then they left.

I called out, "Night, Yessie," but they was already gone.

Ricky Hernandez

They took Pierre to Children's. I was surprised it wasn't St.
Theresa because that's where Mrs. Phoebe always says to take
the kids but it was an ambulance so the paramedics didn't
know that, lucky for Pierre, so they took him to Children's.
Poor little guy has his jaw wired shut. He has to sip everything
through a straw. I stopped after work and got him a smoothie.
Banana and strawberry. I got a extra shot of protein put in
there too. I don't want the little guy to go hungry. Knowing
how he worries about food. And I know the kind of crap they
serve up in hospitals, so I can just see them trying to give him
pureed liver through a straw. Which is how he has to eat for
a while.

I had an appendix incident as a kid where I got sick as a dog.
And in my family for you to go to a hospital, you had to be

near death. My folks were immigrants and where they came from if a person got sick, they didn't go to a doctor first, they went to a doctor last. Puerto Rico's not just San Juan. It's not just what the tourists see. It's your basic poverty-struck island. My grandfather, you know what he did? He mixed cement. I don't mean he pushed a button and the machine started going around. I mean *he* mixed cement. With his arms. Stood there for hours working it and working it. Guy had arms like tree trunks. My grandparents lived in a little cement house, no upstairs, just the one floor—I mean, they're dead now, they died when I was about nineteen or twenty—but the house was, I'm gonna say . . . not real big. Me and some of my siblings went there, lived there a couple summers. They raised hens. There were always ten or twenty hens running around in the yard and we'd toss corn all around for them. Then there was nothing to do at night, right? No lights. The big excitement was the roosters shut up for a while. Of course the second the roosters quiet down you get the *coquís*. I got one on my key ring here, a little green frog. Clicks too, this noise it makes which ain't really what they sound like but for a key ring it's not bad. But what I was saying was what happened with my appendix is it burst and I ended up at a hospital. I ended up at Children's Hospital, where Pierre is now. And I remember—I must've been eight or nine—my parents telling me I had to go to the hospital and I kept telling them, "No, no, I'm okay, I feel better," but they weren't hearing that, of course, so off we go. And it was a cool place. You know, for a hospital, but I mean it's set up for kids, that's all they do, and they do it really good. So I'm relieved that the paramedics brought Pierre here, like, automatically, instead of the usual thing with kids from ILLC which is St. Theresa. At least here I know they're really giving him good care. You know, for a hospital.

I saw him sleeping in the bed and I almost turned around and left. Pierre's face was pretty bad. It's like I suddenly felt really tired just standing there. Here's the thing. I don't know if it's such a great idea that I came. I don't know if I wanna get involved like this. I don't want him to start thinking I'm gonna be around for him, because he's not my kid, you know? But I had the smoothie, so what the hell. He opened his eyes when I pulled the chair up to his bed. One of his eyes he couldn't barely open at all.

"Don't worry, I ain't here to throw you in solitary," I say. "I just wanted to see how you were doing. I brought you a special drink. I got it right here and it's all for you. Here, let me put the straw in there. Don't worry, I washed my hands a couple days ago. No, I'm kidding. I just washed them. They're pretty clean."

I shake up the smoothie and then I bring it up to his mouth. He takes a little sip and I swear, as banged up as he is, he opens his one eye up a little wider and looks at me as he drinks it, like he never had nothing so good. He looks like a baby bird. I wish he had somebody to be his parent and really take care of him. But that's not the reality.

All I ever do anymore is feel like crap. Like Jo tells me last night—and we're in bed and we're just beginning to relax a little bit, you know, and she seems like she's not all that sleepy and I'm not all that sleepy and I'm hoping we're gonna get it on because we've both been worn out, right? Just tired from the job. And I am never too tired to have sex, always ready to make some good love. No matter what job I've been doing. But ILLC fucks with your head.

And she says, "Ricky, I have to tell you something," and I say, "What?" and she says, "It's not good," and I'm like, "Oh, crap," you know, like, "Please don't let this get in the way of us making love because—just please," but I didn't say that out loud. She says, "They're transferring Pierre to an institution for mental diseases."

I get like a sick feeling in my gut. Just want to—I don't know. Cry? She says, "I'm sorry I'm telling you now but I just remembered I was going to tell you when we were making dinner but I got distracted and it flew out of my head."

We just laid there for a minute not saying anything.

She says, "You know who we should talk to? Pierre's guardian. I bet if you went over there—the public guardian's office is in the same building as Juvie. His guardian is the one who can legally protest his placement."

"So maybe we can do something. You think?"

She says, "It's possible."

I say, "Thanks."

She says, "You look tired. Maybe you should try to compartmentalize it and we'll talk about it in the morning?"

Joanne loves this whole thing about "compartmentalizing." It doesn't matter what it is, she thinks if you can't deal with it, you should put it in a—like a, you know, a compartment in your mind. Like a glove compartment and think about it when it's a better time. The weird thing about this is I have no problem doing that. I do that automatically. Jo's the one who can't compartmentalize. Like when she told me how they were gonna put Pierre in the IMD, I freaked. I guess my first reaction was like shock, you know? But I still had my hard-on. I mean, are you kidding? That's compartmentalizing. She's says, "Are you okay? I know this is hard for you," and I say, "Yeah, well, this is hard for you," and I kinda rub up against her and get busy, and she says, "You are unbelievable," but she says it kinda laughing, like, "You are unbelievable," and I say, "You told me to compartmentalize."

Pierre keeps looking at me until he knows I got the system down. Here's the system. He sips for a while and then he stops but he keeps the straw in his mouth so I know not to take it away. Then he sips a few more times. Then he rests. As long as I don't take the smoothie out of his mouth, he's good. He's gonna drink the whole thing. Which may not be so great for him because he's such a little guy. In the hospital bed he barely takes up any space at all. So we do the system for about fifteen minutes and he starts to nod off like that. I pull the straw out a little bit and his good eye snaps open and he starts sipping again. He's really fighting the sleep monster. But pretty soon he nods off for real.

There's a picture on the wall by his bed. A crayon picture he drew. It looks like a picture of him, of Pierre, sitting in a cave. Or a—there's a doorway and a big lock or bolt on it. Then he drew stuff that looks like food, like a box of Oreos and there's a big pizza and candy canes and all that kinda thing. It's a good picture, good artwork, you know? Pierre alone in a cave with his food. I seen the picture before or versions of the picture. There's one like it on the wall in one of the classrooms.

Idiot that I am, I told him I'd come back tomorrow with another smoothie.

Mía Oviedo

The bird won' go away. He's gone, Jerry. He not aroun' no more. The police arrest him. Yessie tol' me. But the bird don' go away. He still show me his claws.

Teddy an' me was at the class with Mrs. Schmidt. She teaching about going to the bank, how the bank give you money, how you fill in the book an' they give you money. Teddy tell the class about his apar'ment, an' he gonna be having his bank account an' eberything.

Teddy look at me sometime. He don' say nothing, but he smile at me.

Yessie tell me, "Don' worry, don' worry, eberything gonna be okay," but I can't help it. Yessie say I alla time espec' bad things to happen. But I hoping for good things too.

Mrs. Schmidt always talks. I don' listen to her. I don' know what she's talking about mos' of the time. Like she jus' say something to me an' I din' hear it. She say, "Stop daydreaming," an' I say, "Okay," but I thinking about Teddy. Maybe he smile at me again.

I seeing the therapist they got here. She's nice. I'm all finish with the pills. She asks me about the bad guy but I don' wanna talk about that. She keep saying his name but I don' like to say it. His name scare me.

The therapist wanna know about all kinda things. She say, "You tell me about the scars on you arms?" an' I tell her I don' know what she mean. She say, "The scars on you arms," an' I say I don' know, I was little, I don' remember, I don' know what she talking about. She say, "You don' remember who do that to you?" I don' mind going to see her but I don' like talking too much to her.

In the class, Mrs. Schmidt put a picture on the wall. It has pictures of all differen' kinds of food on it. Apples, bread, meat. I can't see too good from where I sit. The picture is call "Eating Right." Like you should eat bread an' milk an' eggs an' vegetables an' eberything. Mrs. Schmidt say, "What kind of bread is good to eat? Like healthy to eat? Who gonna give a example?" An' Teddy say, "Pop-Tarts." The whole class laugh so much. Mrs. Schmidt laughing too. Everybody laughing an' cracking up. Mrs. Schmidt get more serious an' say that Pop-Tarts not good for you. Pop-Tarts not so good for you body. An' she say, "What else is good, is healthy to eat?" an' Teddy, he say, "Pizza," an' alla the kids jus' cracking up an' I cracking up an' Mrs. Schmidt cracking up also. But she say how pizza not so bad. It not too bad because pizza is jus' bread an' cheese an' they got those things in the picture. An' then she say if eberybody do very good in the quiz, she bringing pizza for eberybody, and eberybody clap. An' Teddy look at me an' he's smiling.

After class I have to wait for Jimmie to push me to the bathroom an' then we go to the cafeteria. Teddy is talking to DeLeon. He's not wearing his jacket today. He only wear his blue shirt tuck in his pants. I love his blue shirt. The blue shirt is his mos' favorite shirt an' my mos' favorite. Then alla sudden he come to me where I am sitting.

He say, "Hi."

I say, "Hi."

He say, "You going to the cafeteria?"

I say, "Yeah. I going to it."

He say, "You wanna ride?"

I say, "Okay."

Then he tie my chair to his chair jus' like always, an' he take me real slow to the hallway an' I remember—Teddy is my friend. An' he say, "You not heavy. You don' weigh nothing." An' he smile at me an' I am so happy. I din' know what to do, I jus'—happy. I say, "Oh, Teddy, I missing you very much." He say I miss you too.

Thas jus' how it happen.

Yessenia Lopez

Joanne talked to a lawyer to see could she get Cheri out of *el manicomio*. She said the lawyer helps disable people but she couldn't help Cheri. I said, "Did you tell her Cheri is fine if she takes her meds? Did you tell her they only sent her there 'cause they was mad she ran away?" Joanne said she told her alla that. She said the lawyer said they just run out of lawyers. Illinois won't pay for them no more. I said, "When am I ever gonna see Cheri again?" and Joanne said she didn't know. I asked her what was the lawyer's name and could I talk to her and Joanne said she thought that was a good idea and she wrote down the lawyer's name and number. Elaine Brown at Center for Disability Justice.

I finally tried reading some of Joanne's favorite magazine, the *Plume Serpent*. I fell asleep before I finished the first sentence. But every night before I close my eyes to sleep I look at the picture of that fine-ass brother that I taped to my wall. He's at a protest of a nursing home, is what Joanne said. He's chained around and around his waist and arm to a big glass door of a building. And the chain even weaves in and outta his wheelchair. And the look on his face is "Do not fuck with me." He's a brother but he has light-colored eyes and real pretty long locks. The boy is fierce. Oh my Lord Jesus, he is so, so, so succulent. Sometimes I pretend in my mind that he's here for real and we're all chained up together and after we're done being chained we go off together and we tell everybody we know the story of how we met.

I liked some other pictures in the *Plume Serpent* too. There's pictures of a picket march with a lot of disable people. They got signs. All the people in the march got signs and they're all disable people. Almost all of them. The signs say things like OUR HOMES! NOT NURSING HOMES! That means they want to live in their own homes. One day when I bust out of this bitch I'm gonna find out where they marching and I'm gonna find that brother. I hope he don't already have a girlfriend.

But my favorite picture is—not counting the fierce brother— there's this line of people in chairs just sitting real stone-faceded in front of a door, and right across from them, in another line, is the po-lice and them po-lice look mad as hell. But they can't beat on a bunch of challenged people with a camera aimed on 'em. It makes me laugh.

Cheri didn't put anything new on her Facebook page since

she been gone. I try to check every day but how'm I gonna do that when they only have two computers in this whole place and we each get one hour a week to use it? I don't really wanna touch them though 'cause you cannot believe the greasy, germy, boogery little fingers been all over them keys. Last week every single child almost on the third floor had diarrhea on account of a germ they been passing ever since one of them got home from the hospital. Not just any diarrhea. I'm talking dia-*ree-ah*. You better take some strong antibiotics to kill that mother. All the teachers had to wipe off anything those children ever touched which was just about everything, including those computers. But even if I could get on Facebook like everybody else in the entire world, Cheri probably don't have a computer at *el manicomio*.

My new roommate Ree Ree is still a pain in my be-hind. I think they put that child in with me as a experiment to see how long before I wrap some duct tape on her mouth. I am serious. I had a teacher once in fifth grade? Her name was Miss Finkle and she was mad at this kid in my class called Angelo 'cause he had a brain challenge and he had a loose tooth and he kept wiggling and wiggling that tooth so Miss Finkle duct-taped Angelo's hands behind his chair so Angelo started tapping his feet so Miss Finkle duct-taped his feet to the floor so he laughed at her and damn if Miss Finkle didn't duct-tape Angelo's mouth and all around his head and his whole body to the chair. When they finally pulled that tape off from Angelo's head it pulled most of his hair out too and his mama was mad.

Ree Ree starts in asking me questions soon as I get on the bus after school. I told Ricky, "Please, please, unless you want a murder on this thing, do not let that skinny little milky-eye brat sit near me. *Please.*" Ricky just laughed and he put Ree Ree up by him in the front and now she's in love with him and driving his ass crazy.

When I get home from Hoover and she is in our room, I know I gots to get my ass to Joanne's office and close the door because it's the onliest place I can be alone. Not counting if Joanne's there.

Today Joanne's not here. I don't know where she's at but I hope she gets back soon. She always lets me sit here and talk to her and help her with things. Joanne asked one time why don't I do my homework, so I tell her I don't got no homework. And she asked what kind of high school they sending me to and I don't have any homework? And I tell her the truth. I go to cripple school. You don't get no homework in cripple school. She said how you children gonna learn? and I said I wish they did give homework because then I'd have something to do. Joanne said she wishes she could give me a job with the filing but all the papers she has is confidential. Sometimes when she's not there I'll dust her desk or her shelfs or clean out her garbage or anything I can think to do.

Maybe I'll leave her a note.

"Dear Joane I am leaving this note for you. I tried to read the Plume serpent. It was boreing. I miss you. Sincerly xxxxoooo Yessie."

And I drew hearts all over the place.

Teddy Dobbs

Beverly's supposed to get me up today. Usually Beverly's not here on Fridays but Vicky's sick and Toya quit. Beverly said they ain't gonna get a new person 'cause they're cutting back and I heard her and Anthony and Vicky all talking about how mad they was 'cause they don't got enough help and now they got more of us they gotta take care of.

I'm glad I got Beverly today because she and me get along perfect and me and Vicky—even though she's new, we already don't get along so good. She told Fantasia she wouldn't never get a job because she was retarded. That's not nice to say and I'm against the R-word. I put Vaseline on her cigarettes.

Beverly asked was it okay with me if she got me up last because they was running real late. She said they didn't have enough houseparents today and she thought maybe if she left me to be the last person on her list I wouldn't mind because I might like a little extra time in my bed. I told her that was fine with me. I didn't sleep much last night anyway. Also I got lots of cool stuff to think about like how Mia and me is in love again and how we're gonna get married and we'll live in my new apartment.

Bernard's long gone because he can get his own self up. He got his arms and when you got your arms you don't really need your legs for much. I got my arms enough to do some stuff, like eat and write and all that, but Bernard can sit himself up in bed and pull on his pants and socks and get in his chair by himself.

By the time Beverly gets to my room to get me up, I had went back to sleep again. I must be the last guy on the whole floor 'cause it's quiet. I guess everybody is at breakfast or school or someplace. Beverly says it's her son's birthday and I say how old is he and she says eleven. She gets me up out my bed and sticks me in a shower chair. She says that she is tired and can't wait to get home and relax her feet but she's still gotta cook her son's favorite dinner. I says how I'm wide awake from all that extra sleep I got and she says it took her a long time to get to me because she had to get three extra kids up that day because one of the houseparents for the little kids' floor hurt her back, so Anthony had to spend part of his time up there. She thanks me for being so patient and I says it ain't no big deal and I'm wavy-gravy and she says she's glad I am. She rolls me into the hallway and we start going to the shower room down the hall.

I say, "Hey, Beverly, did you hear about me and Mia?" and she says she sure did hear about it and oh, boy, isn't that the best news. She says she knew we'd get back together because we was like two peas in a pod and I say I know. I say, "You're invited to the wedding. And we ain't inviting all the house-parents, just the ones we really like," and Beverly says, "Oh my gosh, I'm gonna have to find something pretty to wear." When we get to the shower room I'm the only guy in there. I like it empty because you get more hot water that way.

She has to run out for a second to call her husband to make sure did he get the birthday cake and she says she'll be right back and I says that's okay with me. She turns on the water and runs out. First thing I notice is the water is hot. I know I said I like hot water but the water is *real* hot. Bernard always says how the water in here has two temperatures—freeze or burn. I yell out for Beverly but she don't hear me. I yell out for anyone because I see my skin on my hip and my leg get-ting all red and I try to move my shower chair but it has little wheels at the bottom and I can't get at 'em and even if I could I probably couldn't push. It feels like there's fire coming outta the shower top. I keep screaming for someone to come get me. I try to push myself, push real hard on my balance to push myself out the shower chair, and finally I do feel myself falling and then I'm on the floor. They got a hard floor there, so it should've hurt, but right away I feel better. Ain't that funny? I didn't even feel hurt by landing on the hard floor. I feel a little sleepy then but I think I'm probably still in the water a little bit because my foot and leg feel hot, so I know I better get away from it. I crawl away. I think I did, because I didn't feel burny anymore. I never knew I could crawl like that. I'm stronger than I thought. I saw this show once and they had a guy on it and his son was stuck under a car and even though the guy was just average, he was so worked up that he lifted the car right up so he could save his son and he did.

I feel nice and warm. Not hot but just comfortable. There's some blood going down the drain and I know it's mine but I ain't worried because it ain't much.

Then I could hear people in the hall making noise. I ask this girl if they found me and she says yes. I tell her I got burned and she says I'm gonna be okay. I can't see anybody's face because I'm facing down. I hear a guy on a loudspeaker. It's Louie. It can't be Louie because he's suspended and the girl is there and she says, "You're gonna be okay," and I say, "Am I bleeding?" and she says, "Not too bad," and I say, "Did you call my dad?" and she says something and I say, "Did Beverly's husband get the cake?" and then I can't remember.

Next time I wake up I'm *cold*. I'm in a hospital. I ain't surprised. One of my legs hurts real bad. I open up my eyes and I must be on my side because I can see the floor next to my bed and I see Mia's feet in her footrests and one of her shoelaces is untied. Hey, Mia! Somebody's yelling and Mia's foot goes away and I know this is real and I know I'm me, so I know I'm gonna be okay. I hope they ain't yelling at Mia. They might think I'm still mad but that's all done.

Next time I wake up it's real loud. I got a machine in my mouth and my whole body's going up and down, up and down, and I ain't doing it. It's the machine. It's a vent. Michael Jackson has a vent. It kinda hurts but I don't know if it's the vent that hurts or something else. Can I have some pain meds? Can I have some pain meds? Dad? Dad, my back hurts and my neck. And my legs. Is my dad here? Fuck this!

Then I see a nurse. Finally! Where you been? She says, "How are you?" And I say—but then I remember I can't talk. All this time I thought I was talking but I was dreaming. The nurse is real and I wanna say how bad it hurts and I want my dad. And then my dad comes, so maybe I did say it. And he pets my forehead and my hair and he's crying and smiling all at the same time. Then the nurse says, "This will help him with the pain."

Next time I wake up I'm real tired. I can't open my eyes up. I'm trying to but it don't work. Somebody's holding my hand. It's my dad.

Next time I'm awake all I can hear is the machine making me breathe. It's too loud. My dad says I love you Teddy. I love you too Dad. I love you so much. Tell Mia I love her. Tell her I say bye. Tell her she's my hot Mexican mama.

I'm gonna go to sleep in this bed. It feels like being in a soft black cloud.

It ain't how I thought it would be.

Yessenia Lopez

At Teddy's funeral there was pictures of him when he was a little baby and then a little boy like five years old on up. All the way to now. And do you know that boy started up dressing in a suit back when he was a itty-bitty child? I said to Mr. Dobbs, "Mr. Dobbs, how old is Teddy in that picture and is my eyes deceiving me or is he wearing a suit already?" and Mr. Dobbs says, "He was eight years old in that picture." The boy definitely had his own style. If you can call it that.

I told Mr. Dobbs, "Teddy loved you very much, he told me alla the time," and he started crying right in front of me even though I was making it up that Teddy said that but I think he would have said it if the subject had came up. Just burst down crying like his heart was broke. I said, "It's okay, Mr. Dobbs, it's okay." But I know it's not okay and it don't matter what I say or what anybody say.

Beverly and her husband sat all the way in the back row even though there was about fifty empty rows between them and everybody else. I didn't want to say hello to her because I was afraid Mr. Dobbs would see me and he'd get mad. The ambulance people said Beverly was most likely only gone for two or three minutes and that's all it took for Teddy to get burned. Later I saw Joanne was sitting next to Beverly and they was talking. It made me think. In a way it must be worse to kill somebody and it be a accident than for that person to just die from being sick. You might be just as sad as anyone that the person is passed? But everybody hates you 'cause it's your fault he's dead. And no matter how hard you pray to go back to those two minutes or whatever and do them again? You can't. And nobody knows how sorry you feel.

But Mia was worse of all. The girl could not stop crying and crying her eyes out. They had to give her pills to make her sleep last night. The girl is a wreck. Just when she started back feeling kinda normal. I feel so bad for her but at the same time I wanna tell her to stop crying and shut up for two minutes put together but then I remind myself what a hot mess I was when Tía died, so I decided it'd be best to keep my distance so I don't bust out with something nasty by accident.

After the priest gave his sermon and blessed everybody he asked did anybody want to come up there and say anything about Teddy. Nobody said nothing at first and then Mrs. Phoebe got up and walked to the microphone and started in talking bullshit about how everybody at ILLC gonna miss Teddy and that Teddy is a part of our ILLC "family" and how bad she miss him and I almost hurtled up my breakfast right then and there and then she went back to her pew and sat her fat ass down.

It was Tuesday but we didn't have to go to school on the account of Teddy's funeral which I bet made Teddy happy from up in heaven if he was paying attention. Ricky drove some of us that went to the funeral back to ILLC. Jimmie couldn't go 'cause they made her work but Joanne was in the bus with us because they let her offa her job to go to the funeral. Joanne don't believe there's a God. She *really* don't believe it. I says, "So you don't believe there's a heaven?" and she says, "Nope. Or hell." And I says, "Well, where you think Teddy's at right now?" And she says, "I think he's nowhere. He died and now he doesn't exist anymore except when we think about him and remember what he meant to us." I says, "So he's just dead." And she says, "Yes." And I says, "You think when you die you're just gonna be dead?" And she says, "Yes. I think everybody's going to be just dead someday." So I says, "That's depressing. Who told you that?" She says, "Do you think cows and lizards and insects and fish go to heaven?" and I says, "They don't got souls," and she says, "What's a soul?"

Whatever. I know there is a higher power up there somewhere because it makes sense. How else did alla us get here?

And I know Tía Nene is watching down on me. There's only one good thing about not believing in God which is you don't never have to worry about going to hell but I never do worry about that anyway. Well, sometimes I do. Sometimes I do when I do something really, really bad. Like the time I stole five dollars out of Tía Nene's purse and she caught me and held my hands over the hot stove to teach me a lesson but it didn't really work even though that fire hurt like hell. I never did steal again from Tía Nene though. Just other people.

And the times I got jiggy with the CDT driver. One of them guys who takes the disabled from your door to whatever other door you have to go to. I don't feel like I gots to go to hell from that because it wasn't too serious. He was married and I was only fourteen, so it's not like it was going anywhere.

If anyone's in heaven it's Teddy.

I ask Joanne, "If I believe in God and you don't, do it mean we can't be friends no more?" and she says, "Only if a booming voice from the sky yells down that we can't." Ricky laughed but I didn't appreciate it.

Ree Ree was in school because she didn't get to go to the funeral. She didn't hardly know Teddy. So when I got back to ILLC I could just go to my room and have it all to myself. I put on my pink top that says "Baby Girl" on the front and I put on different eye makeup because mine got messed up from crying. I want to look good in case they got cameras. I put on some red, red lipstick that I'm keeping for Cheri when she comes back if she does. I had a valentine Mia gave me that

I saved up and I stuck that in my fanny pack. I didn't have nothing from Teddy or Pierre, so I wrote Teddy's name on my arm and put a heart around it and I wrote Pierre's name on my other arm and drew a pencil like the one he stabbed Louie with. It didn't look like a pencil that much but it was a pencil. I took three belts I found from the lost and found at Hoover and attached them one to the other and my lock from my locker and put 'em in my bag hanging offa my chair, and I got my sign I made from under my bed. Then I went down the elevator and out the door.

It was nice outside. Kinda warm and sunny and it felt like that feeling you get when it's spring, but it is spring, so I guess that's why. I rolled out to the middle of the grass right in front of ILLC, but I didn't see no place good to attach myself to. I always thought there was a tree out here or something but all I see now is two skinny baby trees and a whole lotta bushes. How can you see a place every single day and not know what the hell it looks like? Damn. So I wrapped my belts around one of the baby trees and then I wrapped the rest around me and my chair, and I put my padlock around some spokes on my wheelchair wheel and held up my sign and waited for the fur to start flying.

Nothing happened for a while.

One thing I didn't remember to think about is nothing never happens around here. ILLC's in the middle of nowhere. Some cars drove by and the drivers looked at me? But they didn't look at my sign. They just looked at my cleavage or my wheelchair. I hope it's my cleavage. A truck from the meat-packer place come past and the driver waved and he read my sign but he didn't give a shit. I started to feel stupid just sitting there holding a sign and belted to a little tree and people driving by and thinking I'm some crazy cripple person.

If Cheri was here she'd be out here with me and then I'd have somebody to talk to. But if Cheri was here maybe I wouldn't be out here in the first place.

Then Ricky drove up with more people he picked up from the funeral. First he honked at me like he was saying hello. Then, the Lord strike me dead if I'm lying, he must have read my sign because the boy's mouth just dropped open like someone smacked him in the face.

THIS PLACE ABUSE AND KILL CHILDREN.

That's what my sign says.

Ricky let down the ramp for the straggles from the funeral. Bernard and Fantasia and Mia and Michael Jackson was some of them. After they all got out they come over to where I was. Ricky and them and a couple other of the inmates came over to me by my tree and the first thing Ricky says is, "Did Joanne see this?" and I says, "She gonna be mad?" and Ricky says, "Hell no, she ain't gonna be mad. But I'm surprised they ain't had you arrested."

"That is not funny."

"Yeah, yeah, no—this is great. It's great. Let me go get her though, okay?"

I'm like, "Hey, the more the merrier."

Bernard says, "You gon' get in trouble."

"Won't be the first time," I say.

Michael say, "Dag." He don't talk much.

Bernard says, "They gonna kick you outta here."

I say, "That'll suit me fine." Even though that was the first time it popped into my mind that I might get my ass into real trouble.

Fantasia says, "I don't wanna get in no trouble."

Bernard says, "I bet Teddy would've liked it though."

I say, "Why you think I'm sitting here for?"

And Bernard wheels over right next to me and puts on his brakes. Fantasia can't stand for Bernard to do nothing without her, so she wheeled over by him and stayed put. Bernard got Fantasia dickmatized. Then Mia says, "Yessie, what it say? The sign?" Not on account that she can't read but because Mia's blind as a bat.

So I read it off for Mia and she asks Bernard to push her over to sit next to me. She took up my hand and held it real tight.

A guy in a car stopped and asked were we selling lemonade. Can you believe that shit? They see a group of teenage people standing together anywhere else, they'd be arrested for being gangbangers. They see a bunch of disable people and think we're selling lemonade. Where is the respect?

I yelled, "Can't you read?" and he drove away.

Pretty soon more people from ILLC came back from the funeral and Dominique and Chris and José all said they was gonna stand there with us, but they had to first go to the bathroom. That was the last we seen of them.

When Ricky came back from Joanne's office he had Joanne and she almost fell out her chair when she saw my sign and she hugged everybody in our line and then she started calling all over the place on her cell phone. She called the place where Teddy's lawyer is and she called some other places and Ricky went to pick up the kids getting out from school at Hoover and to get us some food. I told Joanne to call Jimmie and Joanne said Jimmie knows we're out here but she can't come because she might get fired. I says, "Ain't you worried about you getting fired?" And she kinda shrugs and just shakes her head no. I says, "And after you done calling Jimmie, can you take my picture on your cell phone? I want a picture of me wearing this top all chained to my tree."

When Mrs. Phoebe got back from the funeral and stepped outta her car is the first time she seen any of us and she came to stand in front of us. She's with a old guy in a suit and he don't look too happy.

Mrs. Phoebe says, "I understand you're all upset and disturbed about losing Teddy but this is not the way to show it. Teddy's passing was tragic. It was a terrible accident. This is a time to grieve and remember what a treasured friend he was to all of us. I don't believe he would want his friends to be turning this sad time into a circus."

Bernard says, "It ain't a circus."

Mrs. Phoebe says, "Please, all of you, please come inside to my office or wherever you want and we can talk about this. No one will be punished. Nothing bad will happen to you. Believe it or not I do understand how you might feel angry about Teddy's death. I'm angry too. But I must remind you that this is private property and what you are doing is illegal. I'm on your side, but there are those on ILLC's board of directors who may not be."

I say, "But we live here, so why can't I sit here and hold a sign?"

Mrs. Phoebe says, "Yessenia, that's a very hurtful sign. I don't know what you're trying to prove and I don't know who you think is going to read it. I hope you know there are consequences to your actions."

So I says, "You said no one here'd be punished."

I can hear Fantasia out the corner of my ear saying, "I'm going in. I don't wanna get in trouble."

Then Mrs. Phoebe looks at Joanne and says, "Are you coming back to work?"

Joanne says, "No, I don't think so."

Mrs. Phoebe turned around and walked back inside after that. We all just sat there. Bernard said, "Maybe we should go inside. There ain't nothing happening here." Fantasia said how she don't care, she's going inside, but I know she won't make a move till Bernard does. Then here's the part that surprised me. Mia says, "I staying. I staying. I stay here with you."

Then Joanne says, "Hey," and pointed down the street. You could see there was some disable people walking down there, like there was two people was in chairs and a person with a dog because he was blind and another girl who rocked when she walked like she had cerebral palsy. When they got over by us they told us they was from Access Now. They heard what we was doing and they came to help. Somebody Joanne called told 'em.

They said there was more people coming too. One of 'em in a wheelchair named Cal started in calling up people on his cell and asking them to come and telling everybody how we was a awesome group of young people—except he called us "youth," like on the six o'clock news when they say, "The police are looking for a youth who got himself in a mess of trouble."

Right about then Ricky came back from Hoover with a bunch more "youth" and most of them went inside, but Tony, DeLeon, Krystal, and Dawn all four joined up with us. And Amber. I was happy and also not happy because Ree Ree was there and all I kept thinking was, "Please, please, please don't make Ree Ree want to stay with us, *please.*" But the girl planted herself right near my tree and said, "I wanna stay! I wanna stay!" She didn't realize we were involved in serious business but that's Ree Ree. I felt better though because she attached herself to one of the females from the Access Now who didn't know that with Ree Ree you gots to be a bitch or she'll never let you alone for the rest of your sweet, succulent life.

Ricky had to be with us on the down low. He was with us, but he couldn' *look* like he was with us, so he had to leave and go inside the ILLC building and be a spy and see what all was going on in there. I don't know what was happening with Joanne—was she fired or not? Either way she was busy talking to who knows who on her cell phone, telling them all about our protest, and she looked like she was having a good time and she didn't give a rat's ass about her job.

And since Ricky was on the down low Joanne had called him and told him he better not bring us any food, so we still didn't eat since before the funeral and it was three o'clock and we was hungry and my bladder was about to burst. I didn't think ahead too much after the part about attaching myself up to the tree. We couldn't go back in ILLC no more to use the toilet because they wasn't letting any of the youths back out the building once they was in, which was why we never did see José and the others after they went to the bathroom. But it seemed like everything was going to be okay no matter what happened to get in our way. Even Fantasia stopped bitching. I wouldn't never say this to Joanne but I think Teddy really was watching out for our asses because a van drove right up to us with a whole big bunch more disable people and they brought sandwiches and chips and any of us what had to go to the bathroom got a ride to a gas station. They was all from that same Access Now and they acted like friends and they treated us like we was friends too. One of them had a camera and he took my picture a bunch of times and said he'd make sure I got copies.

When Mia and me got back from using the toilet at the Citgo station, there was another big van with a big TV camera on top of it and Marjorie Davies from channel 5 had her microphone right up in Bernard's face! Oh my sweet Lord, Marjorie Davies! Joanne come racing over to me saying, "She wants to interview you," and "Come on and get ready," and I was so, so, so nervous plus I had to hurry up and get my ass belted back up to that tree so it'd look good for the camera.

I cannot believe I am getting on TV with Marjorie Davies. She is so nice you wouldn't believe it. Her makeup is perfect and her body is hot even though she's old. My girl Marjorie gots some junk in her trunk, okay? But I mean, we hit it off right away. We just talked about this and that, and she went to high school right near my old neighborhood and I told her about Tía Nene and about my disability and then she starts asking me questions for real, like that camera was right on us and she wanted to know how I liked it living at ILLC and who was Teddy and why I come to be out here today chained to a tree and everything. Just everything. And I told her, "Marjorie, what I'm saying is us youth come to these places on account of we got no place else to go and the least they could do is to take care of us and make sure nobody gets beat up or gets raped or left in the shower by mistake and killed. And don't send people off to the booby hatch just because they homesick and didn't take their meds. We are teenage youth, and I mean, what do they expect?"

Marjorie said that I did real good and I was gonna be on the news that night. She stayed to interview Teddy's lawyer—the same lawyer that told Joanne she couldn't get Cheri outta *el manicomio*, so she's on my shit list—and she, the lawyer lady, Elaine, who is also gor-*geous* and I am not kidding, I mean she could be a ex–fashion model, like a old Tyra—anyway, Elaine was saying how nursing homes are a very bad place to live and they gonna be investigating ILLC to see about violations and abuse. She said some stuff I honestly didn't get and Cal from Access Now tried to explain it to Mia and me. Cal is so, so nice and he's gay. I'm just saying. Well, he said so first! And Elaine said how it signified stuff when a person in a nursing home attaches her ass to a tree. So she's not on my shit list no more.

I forgot to say how there was these two guys who was lawyers from ILLC that come after Marjorie got there and she talked to them too. Only part I heard is she asked them was these children, meaning us, going to be let back in tonight without needing to be afraid of getting a concussion. I mean a repercussion. She meant was Mrs. Phoebe gonna kick us out, I guess. And I am glad she asked because she had a point, you know? I sure didn't want to get locked up in no time-out room tonight. Hell, I wanna see myself on TV.

'Course it turned out I didn't have to worry because Joanne and Jimmie was on it. Jimmie already decided she was working a double shift just so she could be there tonight and watch over us and call the lawyers if there was repercussions against us youth. And Elaine said how they couldn't fire Joanne so easy either, so she should just come to ILLC tomorrow like usual. I don't see why people always saying such bad things about lawyers.

It was almost dark when everybody was gone, so it was late 'cause it stays light longer now. Joanne and me was the last people to go in. I was so tired I almost couldn't remember the combination to my padlock. Ricky unbelted the belts from around the little tree. I love the little tree. Joanne asked me how in the world I ever got the idea to hook myself up to that tree in the first place and I told her, "It was your fault. You gave me the picture." She says, "What picture?" I say, "The one offa your wall. Of that fine-ass crippled black brother all chained up to a door. I fell in love."

Michelle Volkmann

There's an emergency board meeting at ILLC. Not for the whole board but the ones who are the most important, like the lawyer and the public relations person. The president of Whitney-Palm is there too. His name is Howard Anderson but he's barely ever around. Everyone knows Tim is the one who runs the place. And Tim is there, of course, and me. Tim wants me here because he thinks I'm familiar with the staff and the children, but I told him I really wasn't that familiar and if I know any of them it's just a little. Then he said he needed me to take notes which is the real reason he wants me, I'm sure. I thought I might see that Joanne woman because she has been at every meeting so far, but she's not here. Dr. Caviolini walked in like twenty minutes after everyone is in the middle of everything and he goes up to Mrs. Phoebe who's the director here and says something in her ear and laughs and everybody's looking at him, so he says, "Sorry I'm late, everyone. Patient emergency." Then he sits down next to me and writes something on a piece of paper and slides it over to me. Guess what the note says? It says, "When ya getting married? The first or the second?" *God*. Shut *up*.

It's really hot in here. The only thing there is to drink is coffee which I expected so I stopped at a 7-Eleven and got an orange soda Big Gulp and there's a fruit tray but one of the lawyers keeps coughing all over it. Of course Dr. Caviolini picks pieces of cantaloupe and orange wedges off the tray with his fat fingers.

The reason we're all here is for damage control. Believe it or not, another kid died here. It was this boy who got left in the shower by accident and the hot water pipes started—I think they must've been broken, but anyway, this boy got burned with third-degree and fourth-degree burns. And he died. Because he had his legs amputated and got pneumonia. None of this was that big a deal—well, it was a huge deal for the boy, of course, and his father who is suing but what I meant to say is it wasn't picked up by the media at all until one of the girls here decides to sit in front of the building one day with a big sign that says THEY ABUSE AND KILL CHILDREN HERE. I recognized the girl in the picture as one of Cheri's friends. All of a sudden it's like all over the newspapers and the TV news and they say the boy was neglected because of dangerous understaffing and this never should be allowed to happen, and to be perfectly honest? A part of me is really happy that the media covered the protest.

I still see why Tim is angry though. It's not like the media really knows what happened or knows how hard it is to run a place like this. I'm not saying the boy wasn't neglected. But I'd like to see one of those reporters try doing what Tim does.

The main subject at the meeting tonight is how they're going to get some better media coverage. The lawyer is talking about how we have to find a way to "frame it in terms of the fragility of the population we serve. Take the emphasis off the small number of children who die but the very large number of children who live."

Since I'm taking notes, I write down, "Most children stay alive here."

The PR guy says, "What about a press conference?"

The lawyer says how that's "too fluid and there's too much room for inadvertently saying something that could complicate our legal position." So the PR guy says but what if Dr. Caviolini had a prepared statement and that was it? The lawyer says that Dr. Caviolini is "too vulnerable." Then Dr. Caviolini says, "Please, call me Roman."

It was like at the moment I could hear Dr. Caviolini start to talk, something in my brain said, "I bet he's going to say, 'Please, call me Roman,'" and when he actually did say, "Please, call me Roman," I guess I was really losing my self-control because I couldn't help bursting out laughing, not a

big loud laugh or anything—it wouldn't have been very noticeable but I had a mouthful of orange soda at the moment
and it spurted out of my mouth and there was some on my
chin and a few small drops on Tim's watch. And a little might
have gone on the fruit. They all looked at me like an alien just
burst out of my chest.

When Tim comes back after wiping his Rolex, he says,
"There is no way any of us can speak to the press and hope to
get unbiased coverage. However, we do have natural, sympathetic allies in the parents. There are parents out there who are
the final authorities on how difficult it is to raise these children
at home. The last thing they want is the prospect of ILLC and
other residential institutions being closed down."

Then Dr. Caviolini says, "Closed down? Why closed down?"

Howard Anderson says, "No, no, Roman, don't worry.
ILLC will not close. We have marvelous staff, such as Michelle
here, who do a brilliant job recruiting new residents, and the
need for ILLC will always be there. We're one of the few businesses for which there will always be a need. We're like funeral
directors." And then I swear he laughs out loud, like "Ho, ho,
ho," like he was going to go ride off with his reindeer.

The lawyer says, "That may not be something you'd want
quoted on the front page of the *Tribune,* Howard."

Howard Anderson says, "Of course not, Ed. Of course not.
All I'm saying is the entire situation is absurd. Does anyone—I
mean any rational person—really believe our society would be
able to function if places like ILLC were suddenly no longer

available? Imagine the death rate under *those* circumstances. It's exhausting to confront this question over and over again every time there's a natural or accidental death."

Then Tim says, "I think we can pursue a measured, proactive strategy with the press, such as employing the parents as spokespersons. Encouraging them to come forward as volunteers on their own behalf and on behalf of their children."

Mrs. Phoebe says, "I can identify some parents who would be good candidates."

The PR guy says, "That's terrific, Phoebe. When can I get that list?"

"Thank you, Phoebe." Tim's talking again. "That's an important first step. Reporters with kids of their own will sympathize. If we can keep sympathetic parents who have children here or at other facilities writing letters to the editor, contacting their legislators about the need for facilities like ILLC, acting as spokespersons, it could have a profound impact."

It is so unbelievably hot in here. I feel like I'm melting.

Then Mr. Anderson says, "Yes, and get some children too. The wards, the ones with no place to go. They can carry posters too. ILLC IS OUR ONLY HOME or some such thing. WE LOVE OUR HOME. I think it's obvious someone put that sign in the girl's hands last week."

Mrs. Phoebe says, "One staff member that we know of participated in the protest. But we wanted to consult with all of you before taking action against her."

Howard Anderson says, "Well, I say get rid of her."

Mrs. Phoebe says, "Well, there might be legal problems if we do. Certainly a possibility of damaging publicity. She is our one disabled employee."

Dr. Caviolini says, "Holy shit."

I cannot believe Dr. Caviolini. If I'm ever fighting for my life, and the only doctor available in the entire world is Dr. Caviolini, I'll take my chances with no doctor.

Tim says, "What was the name of the child who died?"

I say, "Teddy Dobbs. He was twenty-two." Pause, pause, pause. "I mean, so he wasn't exactly a child."

Howard Anderson says, "Yes, well. If they live at ILLC, they're all children. Under the law."

"If not physically, then certainly mentally," Dr. Caviolini says.

Tim says, "For now, Phoebe, take no action against the employee who participated. Our primary goal is, first, to get some sympathetic publicity that tells our side of the story. Agree with the public. Yes, the death was tragic, but under the circumstances, a reasonable number of deaths is justified."

The PR guy says, "How many deaths are reasonable? Is there a number?"

Mr. Anderson says, "However many of them have died. That's the number."

You know what would be funny? To give a copy of my notes to some reporter. Ho, ho, ho!

I won't really do it. It doesn't matter. I'm so over everything.

Joanne Madsen

Ricky pulled the last of the weather stripping from around my kitchen window, jerked the window up from the sill, and let the fresh air blow in.

I appreciate the luxury of having someone to pull off my weather stripping. And under the heading of "Weather Stripping" I include tightening the pipes under the sink, unjammimg the paper shredder, catching stray spiders and introducing them back into the wild, and the rest of the very large family of tasks I'm unable to do for myself. The thing is, all these things, except the spiders, were getting done before Ricky came into my life. I don't want to forget how long it took for me to become self-sufficient again after being injured. I always want to be self-sufficient. You never know how long anything might last, relationshipwise.

I just—I don't like asking anyone for a favor. I'm on top of the situation.

He says, "What do you want me to do with this stuff?" holding up the filthy, mangled weather stripping.

"You can just toss it," I say.

"You can use it again next year."

"Okay," I say. I was sitting at my kitchen table, sipping a cold *horchata*. "It's really almost summer. Any minute now. Are you going to sit down ever?"

It's Saturday. We've been a little slow getting started today, so we've mostly been sitting around talking about work, or in my case the place where I used to work but got fired. The whole protest thing that Yessie came up with has erupted into an investigation including newspaper articles with pathetic titles like "Squeaky Wheels Get the Grease?" Even I, Joanne E. Madsen, went to a protest against nursing homes downtown. I think my social skills may be improving.

"The whole thing keeps mushrooming," I say. "Not a poison mushroom but a good mushroom. Like a truffle."

Ricky says, "So are you gonna be a deadweight now that you don't have a job? Am I gonna have to give you money all the time?"

"Oh yeah, definitely. I accept traveler's checks."

"No, but really," he says, sitting down across from me. "You gonna be okay till you find something?"

"Yeah, yeah. I have money, remember?"

"I know you got enough for the shrimp burgers and the chauffeur—"

"He's not a chauffeur, he's a driver."

"Oh, right, right, your *driver*—"

"Maybe if we were French he'd be a chauffeur, but we're not, so he's just Leo the guy who drives me around. And I wouldn't be able to afford a driver unless the CTA was paying me to make up for hitting me. So I consider my driver a form of public transportation."

Sometimes Ricky will burst out laughing at me. In disbelief. I don't mind. I can see his point.

Meanwhile I still feel burned about getting the ax. First Mrs. Phoebe made a big deal about how they weren't going to fire me, and then she fired me. I wanted to say, "Why, you can't fire me! I quit!" like they say in old movies. Apparently even when you hate the place where you work and you have to call your boss something as stupid and treacly as "Mrs. Phoebe," it never feels too good to get dumped. And some of those kids—I've grown attached, and now, like just about everyone else in their lives, I've disappeared in a puff of smoke.

I say, "The prospect of returning to my former state of unemployed limbohood makes me queasy. I can't even list ILLC on my résumé."

Ricky says, "You'll find a job."

"Yeah. Maybe. You know, before this job I figured no one would ever hire me again. Now I can't imagine not having a job every day. I don't want to go back to those empty days."

"You're smart. Who wouldn't want to hire you? What about you could work at Center for Disability Justice?"

"You have to be a lawyer to work at CDJ."

"Come on, they gotta have secretaries, or you could work at Access Now. What about them?"

"I'm not sure that's what I want to do. I know I don't want a job just because it's a job. Not again."

He laughs at me and says, "It'll work out. Everything's gonna work out."

"I was thinking I might write an article about ILLC and send it to the *Plumed Serpent*."

"You gotta do that."

"Well, it's just a little article. But I want to. I'm a little bit excited about it. I don't have any idea if it'll get accepted, but—"

"That's not the point."

"Right. It's not the point."

We just sat there for a minute.

"You know what else I was thinking?" I say. "You should probably start looking around too."

He took a big sigh then and leaned back. He says, "We got any more *horchata*?"

"Fridge."

Sometimes things just pop out of my mouth, like a broken jack-in-the-box. Ricky's not the kind of person you need to say things like that to. But if I apologize he always acts like he has no idea what I'm apologizing for. So then I have to tell him *why* I apologized and he looks at me as if my eyeballs are twirling in their sockets like pinwheels.

I say, "Jimmie said that Candy told her that Louie got a new job. He's working at a group home for boys with psychiatric disabilities."

He puts his head between his hands and says, "Fuuuck."

"I know."

"Don't they do background checks?"

"Yeah," I say. "They're supposed to. Maybe the charges were dropped. Maybe—I have no idea. I checked the name of the place though and it's definitely not where Pierre is. How's Pierre doing?"

"I'm supposed to drive down and see him at the new place his guardian put him. You wanna go?"

"Yeah. Road trip!"

"It could be hard finding something," Ricky finally says. "Finding another job right now. I can't quit. I'll look around but for now I'm gonna have to stick. See what happens."

"I know. And the kids love you."

"I love them."

I drank the end of my *horchata* and blew in the empty bottle to hear the noise. I shouldn't push him. I'm the one who didn't have a job for all those years. Maybe he doesn't feel pushed, but this type of thing can have a cumulative effect. One day I'll find a note on the fridge: "You're too pushy." He'll have moved on. Not that I can't handle it, but it's not optimal.

He says, "Another thing is, I was thinking maybe—go back

to school. Get a degree in something. Maybe something working with kids but not like what I'm doing now. Maybe work at Juvie."

"*Ju*vie? Are you kidding me? That's—*Ju*vie? I'm sorry. I'm overreacting."

"No, but really. What'm I gonna do? Get a job at Disneyland where everybody's happy?"

I sigh. "Well, even Juvie is less depressing than Disneyland, I guess."

"Don't you think I could, you know, get a job at Juvie?"

"I think you could absolutely get a job at Juvie."

"But you think it's a bad idea."

"No," I say. "I think you'll see a lot of sad stuff, but nothing you haven't already seen a lot in your life."

"You think I could help people?"

"I don't know," I say. "I think you could help some people."

"Yeah. Me too." He looked out the window. "You know, it looks nice out there."

"You know what would be great?" I say. "Let's go out and walk around and stop for lunch or dinner or whatever meal we're on. We can just wander until we end up somewhere."

"Let's go," he says. "How is Disneyland more depressing than Juvie?"

"Well, it's scarier," I say, putting my keys and my credit card in my pocket. "Have you ever been to Disneyland?"

"No. Have you ever been to Juvie?"

"Disneyland is scarier than Juvie any day of the week."

I love the warm weather. Of course, I'm seriously hoping for rain tomorrow. Ricky's family is having a picnic. There's no way I can get out of it. I've been feverishly checking the weather forecasts. I Google Earthed the dopplar radar for the area. So far, there is a chance of rain.

His family is large, and they are religious. I mean, they are Religious. Apparently, Ricky is the only non–Pentecostal Jehovian Catholic Witness among them. I'm just worried they'll think I'm an "invalid," or poor childbearing material, or the worst imaginable choice for their son, brother, et cetera. I am trying to compartmentalize and enjoying some success.

And even though Ricky and I don't know what might happen in the future, for now we're good.

Jimmie Kendrick

You wouldn't believe what's happening at ILLC. It is crazy. And it's all because of little Yessie.

They hired two new houseparents, for one thing. So that's a start. The grapevine is that Mrs. Phoebe might get fired or "retire" but that could be wishful thinking. They have a new psychologist and she seems very cool. First thing she did was get the wheelchair guy over to ILLC to measure Mia for a brand-new power chair. Her own power chair. Mia is—you would not believe her face. I mean, the chair's going to tilt like Joanne's and everything. And Joanne was so happy. First thing she asked was what color did Mia pick, and when I told her pink, she sighed really deep and said, "Perfect."

Now none of this would've happened without Access Now.

They told Mrs. Phoebe that it's against the law to deny power chairs to people who need them in nursing homes. So she didn't have a choice. They had a couple lawyers out here and everything. So I guess there are a lot of people who want to see ILLC changed or maybe even closed. But if they close it, that's a big deal. For the kids, you know?

There's just a lot going on and it's got me thinking about something.

I mean, the downside of closing ILLC is the kids know it might happen, even though the lawyers haven't said a thing about it. But the kids know it's a possibility and they're scared. I don't blame them. And of course ILLC and Whitney-Palm are stirring the pot by sending letters to the parents saying that, you know, "What's going to happen to your child?" Telling them the Center for Disability Justice is trying to throw their kids out on the street. The CDJ lawyers say if it ever happens that ILLC gets closed, the kids who are old enough will get the help they need to live in the community, if that's what they want. The younger kids, the minors, will go to places that are smaller, you know, better than ILLC.

Yessie's only sixteen. She doesn't have, like, a parent to cover her. I told her, you know, don't believe ILLC, 'cause all they want to do is scare the parents. And even if it does happen it'll be a long minute till the lawyers fight it all out and she might be eighteen by then and be her own guardian. But you know, that's too many "mights" or "maybes" for her and for me too. I mean she's been bounced from one place to another since her *tía* died. What I want to do is see can Yessie stay with me. As my foster daughter. If she's up for it, of course.

We click. It's like, I get where she's coming from and she gets where I'm coming from. And that's what's up, you know? That's what's up.

She may feel like—like she's not ready, she might not ever be ready to have anybody step in and say, "Hey, I want to be your foster parent." I don't want her to think my plan is "I'm gonna replace your *tía* Nene, I'm your mother now" or whatever because that is *not* where I'm coming from. I'm more, "This is a piece of paper, okay? Paper you fill out so Family Services will let you live with me and not in an institution. That paper has nothing to do with who we are together. That's—that's something we decide." You know? Whether we're mother and daughter or just friends or in between that, that's cool. I'll be there. She doesn't need to call me anything different than always. I'm still just Jimmie. That's what I'll say. And if she's not into it, that's not going to mess us up either. I'm still just Jimmie, either way.

I'm taking a day off next week and I thought I could work it out so I can pick her up after school and surprise her when she's coming out of Hoover and take her out for a little dinner. She's been talking about how she misses eating the food she grew up with, pulled pork and all that. There's this place that has Cuban sandwiches, the food is great and you can eat outside and I know she'll like that and—that's the plan. I'm going to bring it up to her then. I'll see. You know? I'll see.

I haven't told any of this to a soul, not even Joanne.

I admit some of it is selfish. I just love Yessie and I think I could finish raising her. I think I might be pretty good at it. But hey, if that's not comfortable for her, if that's not what she wants—I just want her to know she has options. I don't care if ILLC closes or not. If she wants out of this place, she's got a home with me.

Michelle Volkmann

I'm on my second day of having a really bad hangover, and right now all I want is to sit at my kitchen table with my tea and lemon. I can't think about food. Not like I have any.

On Friday after I quit my job at Whitney-Palm I went bar-hopping with my friend Farrah who I met when I used to work retail at Trilogy on Oak Street. Please, God, don't ever make me work retail again. My whole life practically all I ever wanted to do was work somewhere on Oak Street because in my mind that was The Place and let me say for the record I'd rather eat worms than work anywhere on that street ever again. The only thing that's worse than management is the customers. I could not believe what a snob your average shopper can be. They don't even look at your face. I mean, I'm happy for you that you're rich but were you raised in a barn?

The first bar Farrah and I went to was called Jericho's on Lincoln near Webster and we both had a beer and a shot and then this guy Octavio bought us another round. Then Octavio, Farrah, and I took a cab to Jelly's and on the way we each had a couple more shots because Octavio had a pint bottle of Southern Comfort.

Farrah is a total wild woman. You'd think her parents were fans of *Charlie's Angels* but she actually comes from a really strict Iraqi family, or maybe she's Iranian, so I bet that's why she's kind of rebellious and risk-taking. In the cab she took off her top and leaned out the back window and yelled, "One hundred percent American!"

I think we lost track of Octavio at Jelly's and Farrah and I took another cab to Humboldt's and I don't remember much after that.

I just started to feel weird about my job. I was all ready to ask Tim for a raise and then I never did. It was right around when I went to Aurora and stayed at that crappy Days Inn and visited Riverwood. After that I stopped thinking about getting a raise. And I stopped liking recruitment and my numbers went down. Natalie from Eli Lilly said I might have a vitamin deficiency which really could be it when I think about it.

I felt bad telling Tim I was leaving since he's going through such a hard time with the company and Whitney-Palm's legal problems and everything. He said I had been a valued employee of Whitney-Palm and of his personally and he wished me the best of luck wherever my path in life will take me.

You should see my apartment. I could apply for disaster relief. There's clothes and dirty dishes all over the place. And old newspapers from weeks ago. I'm not usually a big newspaper person but ever since the article about Dr. Caviolini and the kickbacks that he and the other doctors were getting from all those unnecessary tests he ordered, I like to skim it in case there are follow-up articles. There was even a picture of him in handcuffs and the police were putting him in the police car but I heard he's out on bail now. I put that picture on my refrigerator with my alphabet magnets spelling out CALL ME ROMAN.

The FBI had Dr. Caviolini on tape. He said a lot of obnoxious stuff as usual. Like he said he had a product to sell and the product was nursing-home patients. He says it like he's some kind of genius. I hope he has to go to jail. Forever. He made half a million dollars a year ordering fake tests as in tests they didn't need for nursing-home people including children. And then the nursing-home operators kept part of the money and St. Theresa's Hospital would keep part of the money and Dr. Caviolini and some other doctors who were in on it with him would keep part of the money. The money mostly came from Medicaid and Medicare, so everyone is really mad about fraud. But on the same page as the fraud article is a story about all these handicapped people who are mad because Illinois won't pay for them to have an aide come visit in their houses. So they have to get put in nursing homes. So Medicaid is still going to pay nursing homes all this money but they won't give it to people who don't want to live in nursing homes. So everything stays the same anyway.

And of course they're saying Whitney-Palm got kickbacks too.

Even though I have no memory of getting home from the bar, I remember waking up at five o'clock in the morning with another of my migraines. I did something then which I really don't need to be lectured about. I just didn't think I'd be able to sleep because my head ached so bad. And for some reason I had the idea that I had to work the next day and I still had to be recruiting new people. You know that feeling? So I took the twelve Dilaudid that I had left from getting my wisdom teeth out in February and the rest of that bottle of Xanax that I got from the Pfizer rep. I was actually pretty surprised when I woke up the next day. Or today, I mean.

I have five weeks of vacation and sick time saved up, so I'll be okay for money for about a month or more if I really cut back. I can probably get about eight or nine hundred for my car. Which I won't need so much now that I'm off the career track.

My mom is driving in to see me. She should be here by seven thirty or eight, so at some point I hope I can get it together to clean up. I'm really glad she's coming. She said she wouldn't even smoke in my apartment.

Not that I won't have a career someday. I just don't want the kind of career where you have to do things that—whatever. That you don't think you should do. If that's possible.

Mía Oviedo

On Thursday I go see Connie. I call her Connie. She is my therapist. Every Thursday at two o'clock. I like her. She in the same office of the old therapist who was fire. Thas where we meet in. She got flowers everywhere. Purple orchids. Yellow ones, all differen' color. I say, "Connie, you got a green thumb. A green thumb, you know?" She say, "It's not me. They grow good because they like to be together." Thas what she say. She wears big glasses and I can tell her anything I thinking about. Even if I not thinking of nothing, I can tell her about it.

Mos' of the time we talk about Teddy. I tell her the story of Teddy. About when I firs' meet him. One day a long, long time ago Teddy come to ILLC. Right away Teddy was nice to me and always talking to me and he has many friends. Every day he wear a suit and he was handsome. When I see him I am always very happy. He ask me to be his girlfriend and I say yeah. And I tell Connie so many things. I tell her about when we hold hands alla the time, about Mr. Dobbs taking us to a restaurant for dinner and giving me presents. If I am sick? Teddy sit nex' to my bed. He make me laugh alla the time. I tell her I was his hot Mexican mama and we laugh. Me and Connie.

You know what Connie say? She say, "Teddy loved you very much. But I'm thinking about when you said you're unlovable. Why do you think you're unlovable?"

I say, "I don' know."

She say, "Can you think why?"

I say, "I don' know."

Connie say, "You sure?"

I say, "Yeah."

Connie say, "Okay."

I say, "You think Teddy love me?"

She say, "Of course I do. The way Teddy felt and acted toward you shows how much he loved you. You can allow yourself to know that and feel it. You made Teddy very happy. He depended on you too."

Then I cry. I think I cry too much. But Connie say is okay to cry.

I ask Connie, "What I gonna do now Teddy is pass into the nex' life? What I gonna do without him?"

Then Connie say, "Now Teddy is gone, that doesn't mean

that feeling—of being loved—is gone. That feeling is not gone from the world. Okay?"

When I leaf her office, first thing I thinking is alla the things I forget to ask her. And I go write everything I gonna ask her. Nex' Thursday at two o'clock.

On Wednesday and Friday I go to Access Now. After we protest at ILLC an' eberything happen with that, Joanne say do I wanna go to Access Now. Before she get fire she say it. You not gonna belief alla the people work at that place. So many disable people. And they all working and busy and so nice. Now I go one time ebery Wednesday for the group to learn leadership, like learning to be leading. Las' week we taking the bus to Springfiel' to abdocate for rights for the disable people. The bus was so fun. I have one new frien' name Gloria and another friend name Trina. Every day I making a new friend. And I go one day for Pepe. Pepe Garcia Campos teaching me to ride on the bus by myself. Thas his job at Access Now. One time a week for that. Pepe in a willchair too. I not kidding.

Now I gotta 'lectric willchair. I love it! A pink one. I gotta sticker on the back. One of my friends gif me a big sticker and it say "Power to the People." I like it.

Sometimes I am doing something I like at Access Now and I think of Teddy. Alla sudden I just think of him. And I want him to be here so bad. I am so tire sometimes. I want to put my head down on his shoulder.

Joanne gif me a present! Ricky gif it to me but he tol' me

is from Joanne. She gif me a big pink pack for to hang on my
new willchair. With pockets and zippers. Ricky say to look
in it an' there's a box there. In the box is a picture of me an'
Teddy. We look so happy in the picture, and I remember the
day Joanne taked it. I ask Ricky can I call Joanne and Ricky
say to look in the little pocket and there she gif me a paper with
her name and number in real big letters so I could see. Ricky
say she miss me. Joanne miss me. Wow. I'm overwhelming.

I will show Connie my picture from Joanne. I read you my
list for Connie. Thursday at two o'clock.

I don wan tel abot the guy the bad one. i not redy thank you
Place i wan to go on a bus
A aparment for me I thinking mabe
When my mami press on my eye with a spoon

Yessenía Lopez

I been busy.

After I got famous from being on the TV with Marjorie Davies and Ramón Velarde that hot Ecuadorean from channel 26 and the *Tribune* newspaper that had a picture of me attached up to a tree what looked more like a bush, nothing happened. Okay, things happened? But to everybody else, not me. A whole bunch of people came to ILLC and they been opening everything and looking underneath everything and taking pictures of every damn thing too. Mrs. Phoebe looks like she's gonna have a heart attack and Joanne got fired and Jimmie's racing around like she's being chased by the po-lice 'cause she's training the new houseparents. She keeps saying how bad she has to talk to me like she's got a big thing to tell me, so she's probably quitting here 'cause she can't stand it no more. And now Mia's not ever here 'cause she gots her own wheelchair and she goes to Access Now whenever she wants and everybody there thinks she's the Queen of Sheba. So now I got no Mia, no Joanne, no Cheri because she's still in *el manicomio,* no Teddy because he's dead, and maybe no Jimmie. Maybe no Jimmie. I just couldn' take it no more, so I ran away.

Don't worry, I didn't run away the stupid way, I ran away the smart way. First thing I did when Ricky dropped us youth off at Hoover today was get me a bus into downtown Chicago. Ricky always drops us a little ways away from the other buses on the account that half the youth from ILLC gots asthma and might fall over dead if they get too close to the stink coming offa the school buses. I couldn't even walk inside a Hoover 'cause once you in? That's it, you in. They keep every single door in that place locked up tight so no youth could escape. And they make you go through a metal detector or search you when you go in. Just in case you got a gun and a Special Need to go shoot a teacher or a youth or whoever. So I moved real slow till Ricky drove away and then I snuck as fast as I could to a bus stop a few blocks away and caught the first bus to the Chicago Loop. I have never been downtown and that is a damn shame. Born and raised up in a place and you never even been to downtown. I like it. For real. I saw the buildings from far away a lotta times, but up close and personal was awesome. Everybody is walking real fast and wearing suits, even the females. And outside every building? There's more people in suits smoking cigarettes. Every corner gots its own bum too. Lots of them are disable people. Some of them are hypes and some of 'em just look tore up.

When I got downtown I took another bus to the Megabus station and bought a bus ticket to Milwaukee for five dollars. They all acted like they never saw a disable person trying to ride a bus before but they finally figured a way to make the ramp work and I got on and sat in the space they keep for wheelchairs. On the way to Milwaukee? I saw cows. And when I got to Milwaukee I called Pedro Nuñez my boyfriend I met on BlackPlanet and he came and picked me up after I waited on him for a hour. I didn't mind 'cause I needed some time to go to the ladies' and straighten my hair and do my face and put on my sexy new top I got at the Dollar Store that said "Come and Get Me" in gold glitter acrost my titties. I looked hot.

When the boy finally showed up he looked a little bit younger than I thought, so I made him show me his driver's license 'cause I wasn't about to get in a strange male's car without making sure he was the one he was suppose to be. When we got that settled he put my chair in his trunk and we went to McDonald's and he bought me a egg 'n waffle sandwich and a Sprite and he had him a Big Mac and chocolate parfait. We stayed in the car to eat and I had a chance to look at him some more.

First of all, he was kinda short. I was hoping he was gonna be taller. Like about a foot taller but he was still taller than me, so I guess it was okay. It was hard to believe the boy was twenty-one but I think that's 'cause he shaved off his goatee he had in his picture on BlackPlanet and all he left was a little bitty patch of fuzz right under the middle of his bottom lip. It doesn't bother me exactly? But it don't ring any chimes either. I guess males think it's sexy. He had dark brown hair, I think, but it was hard to know for sure 'cause it was short. Like shaved practically. You know what he looked like? A Indian. Like a cowboy-and-Indian kinda Indian. His skin was dark but it had some red in it but not like a sunburn red? It was like if he had long black hair with a feather in it, he'd'a looked just like an Indian. It just goes to show that even when they think they got everybody kilt off entirely, there is still a few gonna pop up here and there.

He asked me about the bus ride and I said it was awright and he asked what I liked doing for fun and I said I barely ever had no fun so I didn't know and he said that was too bad and did I like to party and I said it depended on what he meant by party and he said that was a cute top I was wearing and just about when I said I was glad he thought so, he put his parfait cup down in the cup holder by the ashtray and pounced on me and kissed me. But it wasn't really a kiss, it was more like he hit me on the lip with his face 'cause he jumped on me so fast. I'm lucky I didn't lose a tooth. I yelled at him to get the fuck offa me and I yelled it again and then I poured the rest of my Sprite on his head and he backed off. I said, "What're you trying to do, get jiggy in the McDonald's parking lot? Are you

stupid?" He said didn't I like sex and I said I thought so until
he hit my face with his fat head and he said you didn't have to
pour that shit on my head and I said I was sorry but he didn't
give me no choice and he said let's get outta here and I said
where we going and he said my place.

Right about then I got scared. I seen a lotta shows about
females being kidnapped and had all kindsa horrible things
done to them. Maybe I should push open my window and
scream for help, but then he said, "I guess I didn't expect you
to be so cute," and I felt better. That sounded more like he
did when we chatted online. I opened my window but I didn't
scream.

Milwaukee is different. It don't look like Chicago too much
but you could kinda tell it's supposed to be a sort of city. There
were a few tall buildings you could see that must be like the
city-looking part of Milwaukee. Where we was driving? Was
more in the "where people live" area. When we got to his place
it didn't look too bad from the outside. It had a lawn but the
grass was too long and messed up and there was weeds all over.
I said, "Is this whole house yours?" He said just the first floor.
I said, "Is the door accessible?" and he said, "Yeah, I guess,"
and I said, "What you think 'accessible' means?" and he said,
"Like you can get to it," and I said, "Just get my chair out the
trunk. You're gonna have to get me up those stairs."

His apartment was a hot mess. It looked like he didn't wash
his floor since before the Flood. The living room was bigger
than Tía Nene's and my whole apartment together but I could

see from where I was sitting I couldn't get in his bathroom. I asked him if he had another one and he said no. He asked me couldn't I get in there and I said no and he said I can help you and I said I could do it myself but I didn't need the bathroom now anyway. He went in his kitchen and brought out some beer and Cheetos and asked did I wanna watch some TV and I said okay.

He sat down on his couch what was all purple velvet but real ratty looking like he picked it up out of a alley. A brown stripe cat jumped on him and he started petting all over it and said, "You need help getting in the couch or you wanna stay there?"

"Does your cat bite?"

"No. She don't bite."

So I wheeled over there and transferred onto the couch. The stripe cat came near me and started in sniffing. I said, "He sure is getting personal fast. I guess you taught him."

"She's a girl."

"What's it called?"

"Gatita."

"That's original."

"You were nicer online."

"So were you," I said.

He shrugged and said, "You like soccer?"

"It's awright."

So we watched soccer and drank beer. I liked the beer. He kept going to the fridge and bringing back more of 'em too.

The more beer I drank the more Cheetos I ate and those was the best Cheetos I ever tasted. We started having a better time. He really was pretty cute. He had white teeth, like *white* white, and dimples when he smiled and even when he barely smiled. He told me about soccer which I already knew about because hello, I'm Puerto Rican, but that's okay. He said what team we were rooting for and in between that we just talked a little bit or watched commercials. The only thing was after all that beer I really had to use the ladies'.

I transferred up into my chair and I almost lost my grip. He said, "Where you going?" and I said, "The bathroom" and he said, "Let me help you," and I said "I'll be okay," and he said, "I could help," and I said "I'll call you if I need to but I'll be awright."

I was drunk. This was only my second time. The first time was when I was eleven and Tía Nene made *coquito* and when I got home from summer school one day I was real, real thirsty 'cause it was summer and it was hot, you know? An' I was so hot and thirsty and when I opened the fridge I saw the *coquito* and it looked so good and I had it before a lotta times but never very much, you know? *Coquito* has rum and coconut and sugar and all kinda stuff like that and Tía Nene wasn't home at the time 'cause she was still able to work then, so I had me a little sip but it was so, so good that I ended up drinking almost the whole thing. When I was eleven I only used my wheelchair part of the time, not all of the time because I used to use crutches more then? And I had my crutches that day. And I went into the bathroom, I guess, and when Tía Nene got home she found me passed out headfirst in the laundry hamper. That's what she said and I believe it 'cause I had to clean alla that *coquito* throw-up out from the bottom of the hamper and I had to clean the whole house for the next month. She was really mad at first but we ended up telling that story over and over again and laughing our ass off.

So I knew from the feeling I had when I drank the *coquito* that I was pretty drunk again offa those three beers. And the only way I was getting my ass on that toilet was if I transferred down to the floor, scooched over, and pulled myself up to the toilet. I was doing okay till I got to pulling myself up and started feeling like when I moved my head, the rest of the room started swinging around with it. I tried not moving my head and it helped but not enough. It's hard not moving your head. Damn. What was his name again?

"Hey! You! Hey! Dimples!"

When he came to the door he helped me to sit myself up on the toilet and got out the room so I could pull my chonies down and pee.

I have to say something now. I am sixteen years old and I am sick of being a virgin. That's all I'm saying.

Pedro helped me back out the bathroom too after I was all dressed and washed and the room stopped twirling as much. We went back in the living room and sat on the purple couch with the stripe cat. He was a nice cat. I mean she. I said, "That soccer game is still going?" And Pedro said, "This is a different soccer game." Then he looked at me in the eyes and I looked back. He kissed me but he didn't pounce on me this time.

Thank Jesus, Mary, and Joseph I am not a virgin no more. That's the truth. I mean the truth for real. And it didn't hurt like everybody says. I guess I been poked up in there by so many doctors there's nothing left to hurt on. I wish Tía Nene was here so I could tell her but she'd probably kill me if she knew. I do have a couple questions though.

Okay, here is my first question. How big is a *bicho* suppose to be? Pedro's *bicho* was . . . I wanna say . . . five inches? Is that okay? Could've been longer but I didn't really see it too much. And what the hell was that crinkled-up hairy bag of whatever hanging down back there? Do not tell me that was the balls. Is that what they talking about when they say "He got balls" or "He got sack" or "She's a ball breaker"? If that thing was really the balls, then I don't get why they is such a big deal. Males have been making out like balls is the greatest thing ever and anybody who don't got 'em is missing out but I'm glad I don't got one of those hanging between my legs. I liked the *bicho*, I guess, but no thank you on that crinkly bag of somethin' somethin'. Keep it.

You know what I liked though? The part when he put his thing up my punani and then he kept pulling it out and pushing it back in and pulling it out and pushing it back in a little more each time? It made me feel real, real, real, like, good, you know? I was sorry he stopped doing it so quick. But I guess he ejackalated because he was done. So that was that.

Pedro went to sleep but I got back in my chair and went to the kitchen and cleaned myself up with paper towels and sink water. I woke him up then and he drove me back to the bus. He stayed with me when I bought my ticket back to Chicago and then he bought us hot dogs. He asked me what Chicago was like. I said, "It's great. And it's big. Bigger than Milwaukee." He said maybe he'd come visit me sometime and even though I would like to see him again I gave him my address where I lived with Tía Nene. I didn't tell him I lived in a institution for disabled crip youth. I didn't tell him about all the bad things that happen there. I didn't say that I didn't have no place to go but back there and it was already 7:20 at night and I was afraid of what they might do to me to get even for my running away. Even if I told him he wouldn't know how it really is. Maybe when I'm eighteen and I can be award of myself I'll find him on Facebook or maybe I won't.

I told him he better go 'cause my bus was coming soon but I was ready for the boy to go, so he kissed me good-bye and I kissed back.

I lay my head against the bus window. I watched the white lines on the street get swallowed up by the bus and no matter how many white lines this bus goes past, there's always more white lines. Like how sometimes you're leaving one place and going someplace else but you're really in the same place all along? Not getting no farther away, not getting more closer.

And I was thinking about them cows earlier and the plants

growing and the barns and all of a sudden it hit me—this must be country. I wonder if Jimmie ever been as far as this. I wonder if she's worried about me and thinks I might be kidnapped.

I tried to think about other things, like not being a virgin and how much I liked kissing. I liked laying down with a boy with no clothes on and our arms around each other. Like he was my special person and I was his. I thought about getting offa this bus and turning around and going back to his house and him saying how happy he was that I come back and he loved me and would I stay with him. But I knew he wouldn't say that. And I knew I wouldn't get offa the bus.

The tears started falling outta my eyes and plopping down on my hands in my lap. The bus was so loud I didn't have to worry about nobody hearing me.

When I was at Juvie, they made me go see Patricia Flowers before I got out. She said, "How you feeling?" and oh my God, my tears just let go. Those bitches was just falling outta my eyes and they would not stop. Patricia just sat there and said, "I know, I know," and I go, "You *don't* know!" and she still stayed by my side till my tears finally dried up and stopped flooding the whole damn place. She said how all this is extrahard without my *tía* Nene by my side which was the exact thing I had been thinking of but I go, "*I don't wanna go there! I don't wanna go there!*" but she said, "You gots to go there. You're not never gonna ever feel better if you don't let yourself go there."

And after we talked some more, in a little bit of a way, I did feel my heart wasn't weighing me down like it had a hunk of brick stuck in it.

But I'm not crying about my *tía* this time. I mean, I am? But I'm not. Everything is all mixed up in me tonight.

I must have fell to sleep 'cause when I opened my eyes there were cars again and lights along the highway and signs. At the Megabus station I asked the way to the Halsted bus and the man said I had to take a bus just to get to the Halsted bus.

When I got offa the Halsted bus, there wasn't nobody in the streets. Every time my chair rolled from one square of sidewalk to the next you could hear it. *Ba-dump. Ba-dump.* It made my heart hurt thinking where I had to go back to.

ILLC looks real dark from the street. One little light in the lobby but nobody in there, not even the security guard.

I stopped at my little tree I was attached to that day. I thought about my friends. Cheri. Teddy. Mia. When I looked up I saw that somebody had come into the lobby. It wasn't the security guard.

It was Jimmie.

Acknowledgments

There are a few people who read at least one draft and gave me the confidence I needed to continue: my irreplaceable sister, Karen Nussbaum; my faithful playwrighting agent, Peter Hagan; and my treasured friends Jeanine Mt. Morick, Jim Charlton, Judy Dennis, Carolyn Gordon, Carrie Sandahl, Janet Leder, Aly Patsavas, Ethan Young, Tom Wilson, Jessica Palmert, Steve Remke, Sheila O'Donnell, and Tim Jones-Yelvington. Thanks, also, to Fannie Outlaw.

If I was a person who liked tattoos, I would tattoo Denisa Clark on one arm and Johnny Garcia on the other. Thank you both for your friendship, and for sharing your stories.

Many thanks to Lisa Koslowsky, Doug Williams, Rodney Estvan, and Deborah Kaplan for helping me understand how their pieces of the System work. I hope I succeeded in representing the oppressive reality for thousands of disabled kids in

Illinois, even if I didn't go into detail about the good people who work every day to protect the rights of those kids.

To Access Living, past and present: I'm only one of countless people who would not be able to imagine my life without you. Thanks for letting me print up a couple hundred articles and studies about institution-based abuse, even though it wasn't exactly my job. Thank you to the Empowered Fe Fes, and a big shout out to the tireless deinstitutionalization advocates who have helped liberate hundreds of people from the claws of the System in Illinois.

Thank you, Melanie Jackson, for taking a chance on me; Rosellen Brown and Margot Livesey for picking me; and Kathy Pories for being steadfast and stubborn.

To Barbara Kingsolver, for whom artistry and social conscience are seamless, thank you for your acknowledgment of me.

Thanks to my beloved family, most of whom read drafts without my even asking. Thanks to Jack Arlook for being my first reader, as well as Ira, Gene, and Norie Arlook. Thanks to Jack and Margaret Nussbaum, and to the three graces, Miri, Leah, and Elise Nussbaum. For their ongoing support, thanks to Julie Nussbaum, Aunt Ruth and Uncle Bob Berns, and Hernan Velarde. And to my hard-working and hilarious mother, Annette Nussbaum, who would have been so proud.

Dad, thank you for being such a healthy specimen. You can't imagine the pure pleasure it's given me to share this with you.

And to my darling daughter, Taina Rodriguez de Velarde, thank you for letting me call you at work every day to pick your brain for Spanish words, particularly insults and curses. You are my muse.

Good Kings Bad Kings

A Note from the Author

A Conversation with the Author

Questions for Discussion

A Note from the Author

I used to wonder where all the writers who have used disabled characters so liberally in their work were doing their research. When I became a wheelchair-user in the late seventies, all I knew about being disabled I learned from reading books and watching movies, and that scared the shit out of me. Tiny Tim was long-suffering and angelic and was cured at the end. Quasimodo was a monster who loved in vain and was killed at the end, but it was for the best. Lenny was a child who killed anything soft, and George had to shoot him. It was a mercy killing. Ahab was a bitter amputee and didn't care how many died in his mad pursuit to avenge himself on a whale. Laura Wingfield had a limp, so no man would ever love her.

This imagery fresh in my mind, my own future seemed to hold little promise. I had been in acting school at the time I was injured. As all of the theaters were now inaccessible to me, both behind the stage and in front, and the chances of any director in the world hiring me were remote, I decided I had no choice but to reinvent myself.

I joined the disability rights movement, barely organized in Chicago back then, and quickly came to realize that I was not alone. My surprisingly militant comrades and I addressed ourselves to the issues that were most pressing at the time— fighting and winning the right to wheelchair accessible public transportation, the remodeling of sidewalks, schools, stores, theaters, and the rest of the world, and protesting the systemic discrimination against us in every aspect of the bureaucracy we had become so dependent upon. My transformation from shamed victim to furiously rebellious crip (we took back the word that had oppressed us and used it in our own proud new vocabulary of defiance) was the foundation of my new identity. Still is.

As the scope of our movement broadened, so did my view of what was possible. I became a writer. If the dominant culture was saturated with backward concepts of who we were, I would answer back with my own collection of disabled characters. None of those people writing books and movies that exploited their disabled characters as "symbols" were disabled themselves. And who were these glamorous stars dying to catch that juicy disabled role, to do their best imitations and take home their Oscar? They knew little if anything about the experiences of real disabled people. I *knew* the world, the jokes, the words, the underground details. I knew all three dimensions, not the tired one dimension they put out there for the public to eat. I knew the struggles, the brutality of oppression, the love that held us together. I was the real thing, the authentic article. A genuine crip writer, writing about crips.

None of the characters I write about are particularly courageous or angelic or suicidal, bitter for their fate, ashamed to be alive, apt to kill anyone because they have an intellectual or psychiatric disability, or dreaming of being cured or even vaguely concerned with being cured.

I wrote plays. Having been an actress, that's how I saw and heard my characters. They were all produced, all relatively successful. All but one play. My last play and also my best play. I was sure I would break through the barriers with this one. Like African American writers who had to fight for their own authentic voices onstage—that would be me with disabled voices. I got a New York agent! But no matter how close I got, I couldn't get it produced, and I gave up writing. I think my heart was broken.

But eventually I decided to reinvent myself. Re-reinvent myself.

My book is about a bunch of disabled people who live in an institution for kids with disabilities. Some of the characters work there. Being trapped in one kind of institution or another is the fate of many of us. The characters in my book are dealing with a place that's not one of the worst, but abuse and neglect are rampant nonetheless. Some of them are sucked under by the riptide of repression, some of them bob to the surface against all odds, and maybe one or two find a way to fly away.

A Conversation with the Author

Susan Nussbaum's debut novel, winner of the PEN/Bellwether Prize for Socially Engaged Fiction, is, as Rosellen Brown says, "a celebration of strength, dignity, and the cathartic pleasure of telling it like it is."

Set in a nursing home for young adults with disabilities, *Good Kings Bad Kings* mines the lives of seven characters: a diverse group of young people and their caregivers. Nussbaum, who is an award-winning playwright, masterfully channels the voices of her characters, including a disabled Hispanic teen trying to find her way after losing the grandmother who raised her, a wheelchair-bound woman who is seeking new love and new meaning in her life, and a young man who wants to enjoy living and loving independent of any institution. They may inhabit a world unfamiliar to many, but the core of who they are, the heart of their joys and suffering, are intensely universal. Yes, this novel will make you ache, but in the very best way.

Good Kings Bad Kings is a marvel that does what the best fiction does. As Barbara Kingsolver, the founder of the PEN/ Bellwether Prize, explains: "Fiction . . . creat[es] empathy in a reader's heart for the theoretical stranger." Thanks to Nussbaum, the characters of *Good Kings Bad Kings* are strangers no more.

Here, she is interviewed by Heidi Durrow, the *New York Times* bestselling author of *The Girl Who Fell from the Sky,* which received the 2008 PEN/Bellwether Prize for Socially Engaged Fiction.

Heidi Durrow: What was the inspiration for *Good Kings Bad Kings*? Not just the spark of the story, but the wonderfully rich and varied voices of the seven characters who tell the tale?

Susan Nussbaum: For me, it's always been about letting disabled characters speak for themselves. The way disabled people are represented by the dominant culture is most always as a foil for the nondisabled protagonist. They're in the story so the nondisabled person "can become a better person." Once the disabled character fulfills that role, they're usually killed off, miraculously cured, or institutionalized.

Here's an example: The movie *Million Dollar Baby* is based on a woman named Katie Dallam who learned how to box and early in her career sustained a traumatic brain injury in the ring. The first thing Hollywood does is trade in the head injury for a spinal cord injury, making the character more accessible to a mass audience. Then they kill her. But first they lay in this very subversive storyline involving her begging Clint Eastwood to kill her, or "euthanize" her. That's big in Hollywood: *Now that I have a disability, I can't go on!* type of garbage. It's a strategy that solves that pesky problem of what to do with the disabled character once they've outlived their usefulness. Meanwhile, Clint Eastwood has become a better person, as opposed to a killer, because she begged him to do it. And they all win Oscars and live happily ever after.

Now the real irony here is, Katie Dallam is alive and well somewhere in Kansas, working as a painter. Not a house painter but a very gifted artist. Did she recover from her injury? No. She will always be dealing with the aftermath of that. Check out her work online.

So I'm always interested in giving a true voice to disabled characters, who are multidimensional, sexual, capable human beings with good senses of humor—and who sometimes become overwhelmed and depressed, like nondisabled people. But they are as unlikely to kill themselves as nondisabled people. What disabled people are up against is not simply the disability. If only that were the case! No, the really disabling problem is the oppression that rains down on us *because* of the disability.

And because I know lots of disabled people of all stripes and all ages, and live with a significant disability myself, and have a good ear for language, I feel like I could write characters that properly represent. I would be very surprised if there was another book out there by a disabled fiction writer that contains multiple disabled characters. Not to brag. Not at all. But that's how rare it is.

Durrow: I had no idea that was the story behind the movie. Wow. And yes, I'd say you have a terrific ear for language—each character's voice is distinct and also funny. Every character— in particular the ones with disabilities—has a healthy sense of humor and a certain optimism that I don't think I've seen in other stories about disabled characters.

You've also created truly memorable characters. I'm thinking specifically of Teddy—I swear I can see him in his rumpled suits so clearly—and Pierre. Those two characters stole my heart. I don't want to give anything away, but were the characters based on real stories you knew of or read about?

Nussbaum: No, Teddy and Pierre were total inventions. But I know it feels true, because Pierre is one of many thousands just like him. He's based on research and knowing people. The thing with Teddy is, when I first became a crip, I was surprised to learn how *totally* wrong, wrong, wrong I was about that entire group. I now know many people with intellectual disabilities, and I am often questioning the value of IQ tests. It's absolutely meaningless in terms of personal relationships. IQ impacts a person's learning, for sure, and their skill level, et cetera. But otherwise, they have gotten a very raw deal, public acceptance–wise. This whole "he has the mental age of a five-year-old" thing is pure vicious, ignorant horseshit. Yessie, however, is based on someone I know.

Durrow: You bring up something that I think a lot of people have a hard time asking. What is the right term to use when talking about someone with a disability? You say "crip," but all the characters in the book have a different way of describing themselves. I think the book is very much about the ability to name oneself.

Nussbaum: Yeah, I personally use "crip" in certain contexts, mostly with other crips. Here's the rationale behind it—like other minorities, we've appropriated some terms that represented a time when that term was used to denigrate us. For disabled people, the word "crip" is like a secret handshake. I went to Cuba once and met a bunch of disabled Cubans, and we asked them if they had a word in Spanish that was equivalent to crip. They told us *cojo,* which means "lame," roughly. So one of my disabled American friends started the Cojo Club. We had this ridiculous gimpy wave. We were fairly drunk at the time.

But I totally get your deeper point about naming oneself. It's all about claiming identity. And that very thing is so important, especially for people who might think their identity as a disabled person isn't such a great thing. Yet, however much we would like to name ourselves, we have already been named many times over by the dominant culture. "Cripple" turned into "feeble-minded" turned into "handicapped" turned into "handicapable," "differently abled," "challenged," et cetera. I mean, I would hate to think I'm "handicapable." If that was the vogue term for disability, I'm pretty sure I'd call up Clint Eastwood and ask him to come over and euthanize me, ASAP.

Anyway, it's understandable that people are afraid of saying the wrong word and pissing off some disgruntled crip. I often hear people describing a "handicapped disabled" person, trying really hard not to offend anyone. Just covering all the bases. So the characters in the book mirror that confusion. Even the disabled characters get confused.

But, to answer your question at last, if I were a nondisabled person, I would refer to disabled people as "disabled." Just "disabled" is good.

Durrow: What does the title of the book mean? I know it's used in the book, but is that a saying?

Nussbaum: The title comes from an article I read while doing research for the book. A young boy lived in an institution somewhere in Illinois, I think. I don't remember the name of the place. The boy was in the institution's van, accompanied by two aides; one was driving, the other sat in back with the boy. The boy kept trying to stand up out of his seat. So the aide put him facedown on the backseat and sat on him. This kind of "takedown," as they are called, is quite common, although they're illegal in many states. And they're supposed to be done with two people, so someone can hold the child's ankles while the other one straddles the kid. Anyway, the aide who was driving later testified that he saw the boy was struggling, and he heard the other aide say, "I can be a good king or I can be a bad king." At some point, the boy became unable to breathe, and he died.

It became the title because it reminded me of how, when it comes to kids, the adults have all the power. And when the adult in question has no emotional connection to the child, and the child's welfare is turned over to that adult—as is the case in many institutions—terrible things can happen.

Durrow: This is a book about issues, but it's also a really good story—I read the book in almost one sitting. How much of the story is your story?

Nussbaum: My biggest worry is that people will shy away from reading such a book because it will be too sad. But it's not sad. The characters are juicy enough and funny enough, I think, to guide us through the dark places. I think it's important for the characters to be on the reader's side, if you know what I mean. Important in this book, at any rate.

The book is not my story, but the voice of Joanne is my voice. What the character does and what happens to her is not my story. I never worked in a nursing home. I never stayed holed up in my apartment for twelve days straight. I did use my own experience to flesh out Joanne. The details are me—why she hates manual wheelchairs, her fear of spiders, et cetera. The other characters' voices are either amalgams of people I know or once knew, or total inventions. But, again, that's the voice, not the story.

Durrow: I walked away from the book with the powerful message about the corruptibility of institutions for the disabled, but at the same time it wasn't just the institution that was failing the kids. It was almost as if the kids lived in different fiefdoms depending on who the good-king caregiver or bad-king caregiver was—even the well-intentioned caregivers get it wrong. I was really horrified by that. What does that say about solutions to these problems? This is not to say there is a single solution. But I am so glad your book is raising new questions. What do you hope the story will do for readers?

Nussbaum: Some of the characters struggle with their culpability, but that's because, I think, we all tend to blame ourselves for outrages that are really systemic. That's why I think all institutions are almost a medieval concept and need to be done away with, once and for all. A nursing home such as the one I describe is set up for failure. The aides are underpaid and overworked because it is good for the bottom line. It does no good to blame ourselves for so many of the dire problems that face us, because we look for the real culprit in the wrong place. *I should have known* or *If only I had done whatever* will never be a path to addressing real societal problems.

I don't aim to convince readers of anything in particular. Believe it or not, I hope readers will find the book entertaining and enlightening.

Durrow: What are your writing influences? Again, the voices are so clear, the dialogue really spot on. That's your playwriting background, I'm guessing. What inspires you to write? When did you know that writing was your calling?

Nussbaum: I love a lot of writers, but I can't say they've influenced me. Well, they've influenced me to love books. But I can't compare myself to other writers, because I wouldn't dare. I feel like I'm the kind of writer who uses what she has—for me that's a good ear and the fairly unique perspective in fiction of knowing the world of disability. And I have the desire, and the discipline.

When I get an idea, I'll start collecting things—articles, books, maps. That might go on for years before I decide to plant myself in front of my computer. It's a sense of being ready and really wanting to communicate. And, of course, having time.

Writing for me is an attempt to embrace readers, to reach out to them and tell them about something that's meaningful to me. I imagine a stranger's eyes on pages I've written. It's a weirdly intimate relationship. I hope I'm not reported to the Writers Special Victims Police for that.

Durrow: You write from the perspective of several characters of different races and ethnicities, and also from male perspectives. How did you approach writing those characters? Did you feel any obligation or discomfort in inhabiting their consciousness?

Nussbaum: I do feel an obligation to do right by the characters. I don't think I'd use different races and ethnicities if I didn't spend a good amount of time with people who are all over the map, so to speak. But it's a delicate thing. You have to be very specific, as you know. And when you overstep, even if it feels right to you, you need a good editor to save you from yourself. I hope readers feel each character has his or her own voice and not some generalized voice that sounds like what a white female would write. Excuse me, white female crip.

Durrow: I have to admit, your book made me cry—and I love that. Yes, I was heartbroken, but I also cried because I was heartened to see some of the characters find a measure of hope and agency. And when I was done with the book, I missed them. I mean, I have thought about them and wondered how they are doing. Do you think you'll revisit any of these characters or write more about their stories?

Nussbaum: I'm really not sure if I'll write about them again. I'd like to write about Yessenia again, but I've been thinking of a topic that probably doesn't have Yessenia in it. I don't know. Maybe I can sneak her in there somewhere.

This conversation first appeared, in different form, online at Powells.com. © 2013 Powells.com. Reprinted by permission.

Questions for Discussion

1. Discuss the title of the book, and the passage that it comes from (page 135). How does this title relate to various characters in the novel?

2. Discuss the relationship of Jimmie and Yessie. What does Jimmie derive from their relationship? What does Yessie get from Jimmie?

3. How do the disabled characters in this book compare with disabled characters in other books you've read?

4. Why do you think the author used a first-person narrator approach to telling the story?

5. Is it unusual to hear disabled characters tell their own stories? Why or why not? How might this impact the way you view disabled people in real life?

6. How does Joanne's perspective on things change over the course of the novel, and why? Does she think differently about love? About her disability? About her ability to change things?

7. The book makes the argument that institutionalization is cruel and inhuman. Why does our society continue to rely so heavily on institutionalization as a resource for disabled children?

8. The book makes the argument that abuse and neglect are a natural outcome of the institutional structure. Do you think institutions such as the Illinois Learning and Life Skills Center are still reasonable living alternatives for disabled people? What are some other possible alternatives to institutionalization?

9. What role does paternalism play in the lives of disabled people? Can you give some examples from the book?

10. The book talks a lot about jobs: job discrimination, jobs with low pay, overwork, relationships with coworkers, past jobs, and even possible future jobs. How important is your job in your life? Since more than 70 percent of disabled people experience chronic unemployment, how might this affect their adult lives?

11. If you could predict what some of the characters' lives would be like ten years from now, what might they be doing and where would they be? Yessenia? Jimmie? Louie? Pierre? Mia?

12. There is frequent debate concerning whether white writers can authentically represent characters of other races in their work. Disabled people often complain that books written by nondisabled writers can't authentically represent disabled characters. Considering this book and others, what's your opinion on this issue?

Susan Nussbaum's plays have been produced at many theaters. Her play *No One As Nasty* is included in the anthology *Beyond Victims and Villains: Contemporary Plays by Disabled Playwrights.* In 2008 she was cited by the *Utne Reader* as one of "50 Visionaries Who Are Changing Your World" for her work with girls with disabilities. This is her first novel.

Other Algonquin Readers Round Table Novels

Running the Rift, a novel by Naomi Benaron

A stunning award-winning novel that—through the eyes of one un-forgettable boy—explores a country's unraveling, its tentative new beginning, and the love that binds its people together. The story follows the life and progress of Jean Patrick Nkuba, a young runner who dreams of becoming Rwanda's first Olympic track medalist.

"Benaron writes like Jean Patrick runs, with the heart of a lion."
—*The Dallas Morning News*

"A culturally rich and unflinching story of resilience and resistance."
—*Chicago Tribune*, Editor's Choice

"Audacious and compelling . . . An authentic and richly textured portrait of African life." —*The Washington Post*

Winner of the Bellwether Prize for Socially Engaged Fiction

AN ALGONQUIN READERS ROUND TABLE EDITION WITH READING GROUP GUIDE AND OTHER SPECIAL FEATURES • FICTION • ISBN 978-1-61620-194-4

The Girl Who Fell from the Sky, a novel by Heidi W. Durrow

In the aftermath of a family tragedy, a biracial girl must cope with society's ideas of race and class in this acclaimed novel, winner of the Bellwether Prize for fiction addressing issues of social justice.

"Affecting, exquisite . . . Durrow's powerful novel is poised to find a place among classic stories of the American experience."
—*The Miami Herald*

"Durrow manages that remarkable achievement of telling a subtle, complex story that speaks in equal volumes to children and adults. Like *Catcher in the Rye* or *To Kill a Mockingbird*, Durrow's debut features voices that will ring in the ears long after the book is closed . . . It's a captivating and original tale that shouldn't be missed." —*The Denver Post*

Winner of the Bellwether Prize for Socially Engaged Fiction

AN ALGONQUIN READERS ROUND TABLE EDITION WITH READING GROUP GUIDE AND OTHER SPECIAL FEATURES • FICTION • ISBN 978-1-61620-015-2

Mudbound, a novel by Hillary Jordan

Mudbound is the saga of the McAllan family, who struggle to survive on a remote ramshackle farm, and the Jacksons, their black sharecroppers. When two men return from World War II to work the land, the unlikely friendship between these brothers-in-arms—one white, one black—arouses the passions of their neighbors. In this award-winning portrait of two families caught up in the blind hatred of a small Southern town, prejudice takes many forms, both subtle and ruthless.

"This is storytelling at the height of its powers . . . Hillary Jordan writes with the force of a Delta storm." —Barbara Kingsolver

Winner of the Bellwether Prize for Socially Engaged Fiction

AN ALGONQUIN READERS ROUND TABLE EDITION WITH READING GROUP GUIDE AND OTHER SPECIAL FEATURES • FICTION • ISBN 978-1-56512-677-0

A Friend of the Family, a novel by Lauren Grodstein

Pete Dizinoff has a thriving medical practice in suburban New Jersey, a devoted wife, a network of close friends, an impressive house, and a son, Alec, now nineteen, on whom he's pinned all his hopes. But Pete never counted on Laura, his best friend's daughter, setting her sights on his only son. Lauren Grodstein's riveting novel charts a father's fall from grace as he struggles to save his family, his reputation, and himself.

"Suspense worthy of Hitchcock . . . [Grodstein] is a terrific storyteller." —*The New York Times Book Review*

"A gripping portrayal of a suburban family in free-fall."
—*Minneapolis Star Tribune*

AN ALGONQUIN READERS ROUND TABLE EDITION WITH READING GROUP GUIDE AND OTHER SPECIAL FEATURES • FICTION • ISBN 978-1-61620-017-6

Pictures of You, a novel by Caroline Leavitt

Two women running away from their marriages collide on a foggy highway. The survivor of the fatal accident is left to pick up the pieces not only of her own life but of the lives of the devastated husband and fragile son that the other woman left behind. As these three lives intersect, the book asks, How well do we really know those we love, and how do we open our hearts to forgive the unforgivable?

"An expert storyteller . . . Leavitt teases suspense out of the greatest mystery of all—the workings of the human heart." —*Booklist*

"Magically written, heartbreakingly honest . . . Caroline Leavitt is one of those fabulous, incisive writers you read and then ask yourself, Where has she been all my life?" —Jodi Picoult

AN ALGONQUIN READERS ROUND TABLE EDITION WITH READING GROUP GUIDE AND OTHER SPECIAL FEATURES • FICTION • ISBN 978-1-56512-631-2

In the Time of the Butterflies, a novel by Julia Alvarez

In this extraordinary novel, the voices of Las Mariposas (The Butterflies), Minerva, Patria, María Teresa, and Dedé, speak across the decades to tell their stories about life in the Dominican Republic under General Rafael Leonidas Trujillo's dictatorship. Through the art and magic of Julia Alvarez's imagination, the martyred butterflies live again in this novel of valor, love, and the human cost of political oppression.

"A gorgeous and sensitive novel . . . A compelling story of courage, patriotism, and familial devotion." —*People*

"A magnificent treasure for all cultures and all time." —*St. Petersburg Times*

A National Endowment for the Arts Big Read Selection

AN ALGONQUIN READERS ROUND TABLE EDITION WITH READING GROUP GUIDE AND OTHER SPECIAL FEATURES • FICTION • ISBN 978-1-56512-976-4

A Reliable Wife, a novel by Robert Goolrick

Rural Wisconsin, 1907. In the bitter cold, Ralph Truitt stands alone on a train platform anxiously awaiting the arrival of the woman who answered his newspaper ad for "a reliable wife." The woman who arrives is not the one he expects in this *New York Times* #1 bestseller about love and madness, longing and murder.

"[A] chillingly engrossing plot . . . Good to the riveting end."
—*USA Today*

"Deliciously wicked and tense . . . Intoxicating." —*The Washington Post*

"A rousing historical potboiler." —*The Boston Globe*

AN ALGONQUIN READERS ROUND TABLE EDITION WITH READING GROUP GUIDE AND OTHER SPECIAL FEATURES • FICTION • ISBN 978-1-56512-977-1

West of Here, a novel by Jonathan Evison

Spanning more than hundred years—from the ragged mudflats of a belching and bawdy Western frontier in the 1890s to the rusting remains of a strip-mall cornucopia in 2006—*West of Here* chronicles the life of one small town. It's a saga of destiny and greed, adventure and passion, hope and hilarity, that turns America's history into myth and myth into a nation's shared experience.

"[A] booming, bighearted epic." —*Vanity Fair*

"[A] voracious story . . . Brisk, often comic, always deeply sympathetic." —*The Washington Post*

AN ALGONQUIN READERS ROUND TABLE EDITION WITH READING GROUP GUIDE AND OTHER SPECIAL FEATURES • FICTION • ISBN 978-1-61620-082-4